SONG OF A LOST CHILD

INVASIVE SPECIES: BOOK ONE

CRAIG WESLEY WALL

BROKEN NOSE BOOKS

Song of a Lost Child

Copyright © 2017 by Craig Wesley Wall

All rights reserved.

This book is a work of fiction. Names, characters, places, and incidents are products of the author's imagination or are used fictitiously. Any resemblance to actual events, locales, or persons living or dead, is entirely coincidental.

Book cover by The Cover Collection

❋ Created with Vellum

For my entire family,
your love and support means the world to me.

SONG OF A LOST CHILD

M *ay 26ᵗʰ, 1982*

JERRY HARRIS RAN FASTER than he'd ever run in his entire life, his fear of the twins much greater than his fear of succumbing to his asthma. Deeper and deeper into unknown territory he fled, taking hits from the inhaler on the fly, the sounds of his pursuers driving him forward. He focused on every stride, realizing one misstep could alter the course of his life.

"Get that spider-queer!" shouted Andy, forcing another bout of snickers from his twin brother.

Jerry missed out on this last bit of Andy Reed witticism. All he could hear now were the hissing breaths from his overtaxed lungs, performing the perfect impression of a torn bellows as they stoked the cold fire in his chest. His tired mind raced, searching for a way to elude the twins before his lungs gave up altogether.

The trail brought Jerry to a fork, splitting off in two directions. He stopped here to catch his breath and decide which way to take: right or left. The right-hand trail appeared worn and clear from use; Jerry could see a good distance down before it turned sharply. The left looked overgrown, almost non-existent, the entrance more of a suggestion than an actual opening, obviously not used often. Jerry inhaled more of the bitter medicine, wiped sweat from his forehead, and made a quick decision—take the left-hand path. The overgrowth would slow the bigger boys down and give him more coverage, more places to hide. The other trail would leave him too exposed until he made the turn; the twins would see him before he reached the bend. His mind made up, Jerry faced left, took one step toward his salvation, and stopped. He froze, unable to move, rigid as a statue.

Something was wrong. An invisible force glued Jerry's feet to the ground. Crippling dread overshadowed his fear of the twins. His torso prickled with goose bumps, his sweat-soaked shirt like ice on his skin. He wanted to move forward but his flesh quaked and his mind screamed for him to turn away, take the other trail, to go any way but this one. The tall trees loomed before Jerry, pushing against him.

An approaching shout from one of the brothers broke the spell, overruling any fears or doubts Jerry had about the trail. The Reed brothers scared Jerry more than the path less taken any day. Plunging into the overgrowth, he moved at a sluggish jog.

Pushing aside palm fronds and branches, Jerry ventured deeper down the menacing path, his misgivings fading the further he went, the terror seeping away. The trail seemed like any other part of the woods now—unfamiliar, but ordinary. Sawgrass sliced his flesh, drawing beads of blood across his hands and arms, but he refused to stop moving until the twins' shouts were weak in the distance. He slowed his pace, trying his best to creep through the dense brush without making a ruckus.

The brothers stopped at the vacated fork, catching their breath.

Between mouthfuls of air, Andy said, "You take the left and I'll go right."

"We should stick together," Jason said, his voice quavering.

"Don't be a pussy, that dork weighs half as much as you."

"I'm not afraid of him, you moron … it's just … ."

"What?" asked Andy, knowing exactly what his brother was talking about. They never took the left trail. It had been an unspoken rule as long as they could remember. The path just seemed … wrong. It always has.

"Okay," Andy said, nodding and jabbing his thumb to the right. "We stick together and check this way, he wouldn't go that way anyhow. And if we don't find him it ain't no big deal, we got all summer to kick his scrawny ass."

The brothers plodded down the familiar open trail, shouting their prey's name, taunting him with false conditions of surrender.

Tired, bleeding, his lungs being squeezed by unseen

hands, Jerry halted and sat down. Another slug from the inhaler that hung from a string around his thin neck calmed his wheezing and raw nerves. The forest surrounded him on all sides, actually comforting him, as if he were in the womb of the woods. He stayed that way for a while, tempted to lie back and fall asleep right where he sat, but the fear of waking in the dark—or worse, being awakened by the twins—proved enough to get him on his feet and moving once again.

Jerry stood and listened for several seconds. Birds chirped and insects buzzed. His pursuers were either being quiet or had moved further away, out of earshot. He decided to take a gamble and head back the way he'd came, back to the safety of the group. Jerry knew he could still find his way back, and that venturing any further would put him at risk of being dangerously lost. He crept forward, back toward the fork, careful not to make any unnecessary noises, eager to be out of the thick woods.

Jerry managed ten paces when a commotion in front of him stopped his legs mid-stride: the sound of movement through the brush. He eased his foot to the forest floor, and waited for the noise to repeat itself. The rustling of leaves and the sharp snap of a branch caused his heart to knock on his chest like a fist. Terrified, Jerry spun and continued his flight deeper into uncharted territory, convinced the brothers had found him. Unseen behind Jerry, a harmless Armadillo crossed the footpath and scooted through the vegetation on the other side, unaware of the events it had forced into motion.

Jerry moved faster now, turning to look to his rear every few seconds, certain he would see the Reed twins behind him, their sneering faces parting the greenery. He even mistook the clamor of his own struggle through the overgrowth, sure the twins were hot on his tail. His attention diverted, Jerry didn't see the wall of vines blocking the trail until he became trapped in it, snaring him like a fly in a web.

Panicking, Jerry cried out, thrashing his arms, his fear causing him to believe it actually was a giant web. He freed his limbs—dry vines and thin branches clinging to his hair and shirt—and took several shambling steps back, gasping for air. He took another hit of spray and looked up. What he saw caused his initial embarrassment over panicking like a fool turn to crushing self-defeat. The trail ended in a tangled wall of branches and vines standing twice his height, woven into the thick underbrush bordering the trail, blocking his way and any hopes of escape.

Trapped.

Studying the top of the wall, Jerry realized the dense trail had opened up to the afternoon sky at some point during his frantic run, revealing bruise-colored clouds galloping overhead—a storm closing in.

Great, he thought, his inner voice filled with sarcasm. *Maybe I'll get struck by lightning after I get beat up.*

He approached the wall and leaned his forehead on the barrier in defeat, too tired to go any further anyway, his asthma sapping the energy from his small body. Through the gaps of entwining branches and twirling vines, Jerry could discern something white on the other side

The other side?

Jerry's heart picked up speed again, this time with renewed hope instead of fear. He pried the branches and vines open. They parted easier than expected, as if someone had been through the wall already. In seconds, Jerry had an opening large enough for his small twelve-year-old frame to squeeze through.

Fending off dried creepers that clawed at his eyes, tugged at his clothes, and even tried to enter his ears, Jerry wiggled his way through into an opening.

A clearing of white sand.

A circular clearing. Too circular to be natural, Jerry thought. The white sand felt soft under his feet, unlike the hard forest floor just a few feet away on the other side of the strange wall of vines, giving him the impression of standing on the crest of an immense sand dune. More woven vines and branches made up the perimeter of the clearing, the surrounding wall keeping the impassable palmettos of the woods at bay.

The only way into the clearing was the way he had just entered.

Smiling, Jerry turned and mended the wall, enclosing himself in. *The twins will never find me in here. I'll just wait them out. Head home in a little bit.*

Jerry didn't notice the tree in the center of the clearing until he turned around again. How he hadn't noticed it straight away would remain a mystery. It wasn't an exceptionally tall tree—shorter than most of its neighbors in the surrounding woods—but it loomed over him like a giant nonetheless. The trunk stood roughly twenty feet away, but the thin, bare branches reached out to him, causing him to unconsciously step away until his back caressed the wall of vines. The trunk and branches of the tree, colored a uniform black—not burned (which had been his first thought) just an empty, lifeless black—stood out in stark contrast to the snow-white sand encircling it.

One thought echoed in Jerry's mind as he stared up at the black tree with the darkening clouds moving behind it like a polluted stream.

Get away from here. Now.

The twins were no longer a concern. He had to get out of this clearing and away from this tree even if it meant having to fight the evil brothers. Before he could turn to leave, dark bubbles formed and burst at the edge of his vision as a low squealing filled his head. Jerry rubbed his eyes and looked around for the source of the noise. He realized it was coming from him.

He couldn't breathe.

He instinctively reached for the inhaler around his neck, and for two everlasting seconds he stared at the broken length of string coiled in his palm.

The inhaler was gone.

Panic overcame his surprise. Frantic, Jerry searched around his feet, the white sand the same color as the plastic life-saving gadget. He fell to his knees and grasped fistfuls of sand, his vision now swimming with the popping orbs, his consciousness slipping.

Jerry's right hand grazed something hard. He fumbled with the object, dropping it twice. After an eternity, he lifted his hand to his face, his failing vision recognizing the familiar device gripped in his fist. Seconds from passing out, he willed the inhaler to his lips and pressed down, using his last ounce of strength.

The familiar *whoosh* filled his ears. And a gritty mist of sand filled Jerry's mouth and lungs as he struggled to inhale, choking the already dying boy.

Jerry collapsed onto his side, legs convulsing, kicking up sand. His back arched and his hands clawed at his throat as his sand-coated tongue protruded between blue lips, kissing the air like a beached fish. No matter how hard he tried, that precious air would not fill his feeble lungs. His eyes bulged, threatening to pop from their sockets. Jerry's spasms slowed to intermittent jerks. His hands relaxed, flopping to the sand like wounded birds, the expression on his purple face one of utter confusion. His eyelids dropped slowly as his life slipped away, the ominous black tree his last image of this world, its malformed limbs reaching to the leaden sky with an air of remorseless glee.

Jerry's frail, lifeless body rested in the white sand. The songs of birds and insects filled the surrounding woods, oblivious to the tragedy. Pregnant rainclouds marched overhead, their long shadows caressing the dead body. A rumble of thunder crawled above the clouds.

Seconds later, Jerry's eyes opened. A grin creased his pale face.

The dead boy sat up, and the woods fell silent.

I

THE SWAMP POTATO WAR

M *ay 24ᵗʰ, 1982*
Two days earlier.

THE OLD MAN gulped the humid morning air, one hand on his hip, the other clutching a double-barreled shotgun that rested on his right shoulder.

He studied the all too familiar scene before him through squinted eyes, twin fiery orbs glaring from the thick lenses of his glasses, the new day's sun already hot and bright as it crept up the pale sky behind the wretched tree.

Like a monument erected to all things corrupt and eternal, the lone tree stood in the center of the clearing, black and lifeless, just the way it has since the first time he had the misfortune of stumbling upon it, so many years ago. His eyes fell from the tree, examining the sand at its base for any sign of human disturbance—he found none.

Except for his scattered footprints, the white sand appeared as smooth as a deserted island's pristine beach. He then turned a full circle, scrutinizing his surroundings with paranoid mistrust. The lush woods encircling the clearing exuded the innocuous sounds of summer: birds singing, insects humming.

All was normal.

As normal as he could ever hope for in this poisoned glade in the woods.

Pushing his glasses up his sweaty nose with a forefinger, the old man released a grateful sigh of relief and bowed his head.

The tree was bare.

Not a single leaf sprouted from its dark branches. It had only been a dream. A nightmare.

Or a vision, he thought. *A portent. A warning.*

The dream returned to him: the image of the tree in full bloom, broad leaves sprouting from every branch, a crimson sky flowing behind it like a river of blood. He'd awoken in a cold sweat, a deep despair sinking into his chest, his skull throbbing from too many beers the night before. He'd dressed, grabbed his shotgun, and made the long hike to the clearing.

With his knuckles bone-white as he squeezed the worn wood of the old gun, eyes wide and alert, the old man chose the left hand trail without hesitation when he reached the fork in the path.

He never thought he'd actually be relieved to see the repulsive thing, its black branches outlined against the morning sky like the skeletal legs of some fossilized, extinct insect—its gratefully bare branches.

He filled his lungs with the heavy air again and turned to leave; but before exiting the clearing, the old man whirled, leering at the seemingly harmless tree for several seconds, shotgun at arms, as if turning his back on it would cause his nightmare to manifest.

The dreams were visiting him more than ever before, more realistic, with a sense of impending doom, setting the man's nerves on edge. The alcohol had been the only thing keeping the dreams at bay. Not anymore. Why now after all these years? After all the precautions he'd taken to keep the tree a secret? Nothing about its appearance had changed, and although weakened, he could still sense the warding spell surrounding the tree and trailhead.

Maybe I'm finally going crazy, he thought. *Or maybe I need to lighten up on the booze.* He barked a short laugh, and then clamped his mouth shut with a click of teeth. The innocent sound of his laughter seemed foreign in the clearing, in the presence of something so evil.

Like a fart in church. He cracked a thin smile at this thought, but held his laughter. He eyed the tree for several more seconds in complete silence, the wild sounds of the woods calming his buzzing nerves. Satisfied it was still dead—or at least dormant—he turned and left the clearing and the tree behind, saying a silent prayer that his nightmares would never become a reality.

Not on my watch, he thought, moving along the dense trail, but one word flashed in his mind like a neon bar sign as he began his journey home, buzzing in his tender, booze-addled skull.

Warning … Warning … Warning.

A distant train whistle pervades the tranquility of the sunlit woods, wailing the song of a lost child.

The lyrical piping of the train glides like mist around the oaks and pines, past the cabbage palms, winding through the woods, searching for an ear to fall upon.

Lewis kicks his heel back, engaging the coaster brakes, his bicycle fishtailing and sliding to a halt in the dirt and pine needles blanketing the trail. His thin chest heaves, struggling to catch a useful breath in the stifling humidity of the summer air. A buzzing cloud of hungry gnats and mosquitoes immediately home in on his new location, eager to feast. Lewis swats the air around his head to ward off the attack, and offers his ears to the train's imploring howl as it mingles with the persistent hum of the swarming insects.

Lewis has always loved the train's mournful cry. The sound makes him feel safe and secure, like things are still moving along on schedule—a daily affirmation of his existence in a world he often feels excluded from. However, some days the whistle called to him like the Pied Piper of Hamelin. Lewis would make the long journey to the tracks and watch the train rumble past, fantasizing of jumping onto one of the passing freight cars like a hobo from the movies, complete with a red bandana tied to the end of a stick, stuffed with all his meager belongings. Instead, Lewis would just watch until the last freight car and caboose traversed the small river bridge, vanishing around the bend, wishing it and his imaginary doppel-gänger a safe journey.

Sitting on his bike, Lewis closes his eyes; the rhythmic thumping of the train's wheels in the distance syncs to the racing thrum of his young heart. But this time, instead of his normal train-hopping daydream, the bemoaning whistle triggers unwelcome snippets of the previous night's dream—a warped reoccurring version of his vagabond fantasy. Like every time before, Lewis had awoken in terror, and as usual, he could only remember two things from the dream: something unseen in the deep shadows of a swaying boxcar, something whispering his name; and the overwhelming scents of burning wood and decay.

Lewis's eyes fly open, his reverie broken by the sound of tires skidding behind him.

Clinton, Lewis's best friend, slides sideways next to him, stopping his bike just short of a bone-crunching collision, spraying his daydreaming friend with a fine plume of dirt. Clinton's younger brother, Justin, repeats the well-practiced maneuver, easing to a stop a foot behind Clinton.

"What's up?" Clinton exhaled the question, gasping

for breath in the soupy summer air, coughing dirt from his lungs.

"Just waiting for you slowpokes," Lewis lied, too embarrassed to voice his confusing freight-hopping night-mare. Strange dreams have plagued his nights lately, causing him to wonder about his sanity.

"We were adding another block to the ramp," Justin said, somehow breathing normal even though sweat satu-rated his *STAR WARS* t-shirt.

It was a Monday, the first official day of summer vaca-tion. Lewis and Clinton were fresh out of sixth grade, Justin the fifth, and all three boys had spent most of the perfect summer day riding their bikes in the woods surrounding their neighborhood, racing along the familiar and well worn trails that meander through the slash pines and saw palmettos. They'd had the trail to themselves all afternoon, a rarity on most days, but especially rare on the first day of summer vacation, so the boys had taken advan-tage of this occasion and made a little addition to the trail.

One section of the trail—appropriately called 'the runway' by the trio—straightened out for a long stretch, allowing the boys to reach terminal velocity before the path twisted away once again. Upon entering the runway, the boys would stand on their pedals, legs pumping like pistons, whipping their bikes back and forth to the brink of disaster before hitting the first of many curves, their inside foot dragging the forest floor as they took the hairpin turns, pushing the pines needles into neat, compact mounds. It was on this stretch of straightaway that they decided to place the ramp.

The ramp had been Justin's idea of course; most of

their bad ideas seemed to originate from the youngest of the three. A few cinder blocks, a sturdy sheet of plywood, and the boys were instant daredevils. The scorching Florida heat and swampy humidity kept them saturated in sweat, and the lack of a breeze meant they had to create their own—the ramp provided this breeze. Building speed and soaring through the air felt wonderful on their drenched skin. Instant outdoor-air-conditioning.

Fear and self-preservation lessened with each launch from the rickety construction. When the initial fear of crashing melted away and the jump became boring, Justin would demand another block be added, increasing the stakes. The cinder blocks, as well as the wood, were supplied by a crumbling pile of assorted and potentially hazardous building materials left behind from the construction of their neighborhood, kindly dumped in the woods for adventurous boys to use however they pleased.

Soon enough, several more blocks had been added to the ramp. It was so high in fact, the boys were running short of precious landing room. Inevitably, the unwritten laws pertaining to young boys and bike stunts would be enforced, and somebody would have to get hurt—today's winner was little Justin.

The youngest of the three daredevils pumped his bike to maximum velocity, streaking down the straightaway, a fierce stare of determination and concentration tinged with a respectful dash of fear burning in his bulging eyes. Lewis and Clinton watched in rapt amazement as Justin hit the plywood ramp at incredible speed, and both onlookers cringed at the sound of the ancient board snapping in half, wrenching a surprised yelp from Justin as he hurtled over his handle-bars, through the air, sans bike.

Justin's feet continued to pedal his invisible steed, his arms wind milling, until he met solid ground again, performing the perfect imitation of Pete Rose sliding into home plate. Justin's face took the brunt of the impact, bouncing off the hard-packed dirt with a deep *thud*, his body sliding on the pine needles for several feet before grinding to a halt, motionless.

"Oh shit," Clinton blurted. "Mom's gonna kill me." He tossed his bike to the side, ran over to his brother's body, knelt down, and rolled the limp form over.

Dismounting his own bike, Lewis jogged over to stand behind Clinton. Resting his hands on shaking knees, he peered over Clinton's shoulder. Justin's face—spattered with blood and caked with dirt—showed no signs of life, his head wobbling on his neck as Clinton grasped his little brother's shoulders and shook him, shouting his name.

Justin's eyes fluttered open and he pushed his brother away. "Quit yelling, I'm fine," he said nasally, like he had a bad cold.

"You don't look fine, I thought you were dead," Clinton said, a hint of annoyance lacing the concern in his voice. "Are you okay?"

Justin stood and swayed like a sapling in a storm, nearly toppling, then regained his footing. Blood flowed from his swollen nose as he nodded to his older brother. He tilted his head back, pinching his nostrils shut.

"It looks broken," Lewis said, failing to mask the shaking in his voice, pointing to Justin's nose. He'd been a hundred percent sure he'd witnessed Justin's death.

Justin shrugged, staring at the treetops.

Satisfied his brother's condition wasn't terminal, Clinton walked over to the remnants of the ramp and righted Justin's bike. "At least your bike looks okay. Think you can walk it home?"

Justin displayed a bloody thumbs up.

His head tilted back, one hand still clamping his nostrils to stanch the flow of blood, Justin walked his bike along the trail toward home to get patched up, and to most definitely get chewed out for ruining yet another good shirt with bloodstains. A squadron of gnats swarmed the boy's face and hand, eager to roost on the congealing blood.

Lewis and Clinton, still on their bikes, escorted the injured boy. Like vultures they circled Justin as they talked about the crash, building the event into legendary-sized proportions, the height of Justin's failed jump already reaching upwards of twenty feet, and his body bouncing off the trail at least three times before stopping. In their retelling, the amount of blood that sprayed from Justin's nostrils went from cups to gallons in a matter of seconds.

Justin just listened and nodded as the older boys continued to rattle on about things twelve-year-old boys talk about: favorite baseball players, favorite television shows, comic books. They even worked their way up to talking about girls for a fleeting moment. They discussed which rides they would brave at the summer fair, horror films they planned to sneak into, and the latest games they wanted to play at the arcade; but the most important topic, the subject that always seemed to infiltrate their conversations lately, was this year's war—*The Second Annual Swamp Potato War.*

"I just hope I last longer this year," Lewis said.

Remembering the war, Justin smiled and nodded, still staring at the sky as he walked alongside his bike. His swollen nose had stopped flowing, but his face remained crusted with blood and drowned gnats. The dried blood cracked as he grinned.

Lewis had been the second man killed during that first war last summer, catching a small potato to the eye, the humbling bruise taking a week to dissipate, the embarrassment and disappointment of being the first on his side to die never fading.

"Yeah, you blew it, man," Clinton said, rubbing it in, following Lewis in a tight circle. He had battled to the very end, the last man standing for their side. The final barrage that killed Clinton made everyone watching wince, clutching spots on their own bodies, mirroring Clinton's pain.

The boys made their way out of the forest and onto the wide field of grass connecting the woods to the end of Lewis's street. They were only a few yards in, the tall grass whipping against their jeans, dragonflies taking flight from their approach, when Lewis heard his name shouted from the direction of his house, echoing throughout the streets.

Lewis was convinced his mother and father had the loudest voices on Earth. No matter where he happened to be in the neighborhood, he could hear them screaming his name, calling him home for dinner. Lewis's mother shouted solo today; his father had left yesterday for a weeklong business trip in California.

Lewis sighed. "Guess I gotta go."

"Yeah," Clinton said. "Man, your mom has quite a set … of lungs that is."

Justin laughed, spewing bloody snot through his fingers, the floodgates reopened.

"Shut up, Clint," Lewis said, knowing how much his friend hated the short version of his name.

"Whatever, see you tomorrow," Clinton said.

Laughing, the boys waved their good-byes as they parted and headed home for supper, all of them drained from the day's events, yet excited about things to come for the long summer ahead.

The crickets played their delicate instruments as the sun descended from the heavens, shrouding the quiet neighborhood of Poisonwood Estates with a cloak of scarlet fire, which would soon scorch the glowing sky into night.

3

Nestled in the central Florida woods near the east coast of the state rests the small, sleepy town of Hopkinsville, boasting a population of just over *4,000* citizens. A number that easily triples during a Space Shuttle launch from nearby Cape Canaveral, bringing temporary excitement to what many Florida residents consider to be the most boring town in the state.

Spectators from near and far gather on the banks of the Indian River, which separates the coast from the cape, vying for the best position to view the launch. While other towns closer to the spectacle absorb most of the crowd, latecomers find their gas, food, and lodging in Hopkinsville, boosting the small town's stagnating economy. One thing these visitors say upon returning to their respective homes is that the residents of Hopkinsville are some of the friendliest folks they've ever met. And also, that the town is indeed quite boring.

A thirty-minute drive east from the center of town will

send you splashing into the warm waters of the Atlantic Ocean. A fifteen-minute drive through the woods to the northwest of town will bring you to yet more woods, Lewis's woods, and the small community of homes known as Poisonwood Estates.

Constructed in 1965, these sturdy, single-story homes were meant for the growing space industry on Cape Canaveral, and the families of the men and women employed there. Unlike other small communities closer to the cape, the expected growth and expansion of Hopkinsville never quite reached expectations—never came close, in fact—and as a result, Poisonwood Estates was left isolated from the town. An island of homes in a sea of trees, with a two-lane road to town its only lifeline. Seventeen years later, the thick forest in between remained undeveloped except for a small one-runway airfield, and the new baseball park with its adjacent playground.

For Lewis and his friends, Poisonwood Estates comprised their whole world. School, the grocery store, gas stations, the movie theater, and every other convenience folks take for granted were all located in town. Which was fine if you had a car and were old enough to drive; however, the road to these amenities had long been deemed unsafe for bicycles, and most parents forbade their children to use it.

This isolation meant the boys spent a large portion of their free time in the surrounding woods. The sweltering months during summer vacation relegated even more time for them to explore the vast area of wilderness without the hindrance of school, teachers, and the most heinous, twisted invention of all time—homework.

Hopkinsville may have the unofficial moniker of the most boring town in the state, but growing up in Poisonwood Estates was fine for a child like Lewis: a child with a healthy—albeit morbid—imagination. Lewis found the stories and legends passed down about his woods fascinating. Stories of ghostly lights and eerie sounds warning children to keep clear of the woods at night, and yarns of strange creatures snatching the children who refused to heed these warnings.

For Lewis, the most intriguing and frightening tale had to be the local legend of the drowned boy, who met his end in one of the many storm drains of the neighborhood. The drains, built high up from the gutters, allowed ample space for a small child to fall through to the darkness below, lending some credence to the tale. For Lewis this evidence was plenty; he completely believed the story, even though the location of the unfortunate event seemed to change day to day.

Rumored to be on his way home from playing football with friends, the little boy found himself caught in a sudden torrential rainstorm, common for this part of Florida. His new football slipped from his fingers and washed away, swept down the rushing gutter. The boy gave chase and came within inches of his prized possession. In desperation, he dove for the ball, trying to rescue it before the looming mouth of the drain swallowed it—he was too late. Ball and boy were washed down the opening. The unfortunate child cracked his head on the concrete lip as he fell, dazing him. He drowned in the churning dark waters below.

The legend states that if you are brave enough to put

your ear close to a drain during a downpour, you can hear his ghost crying for help, echoing throughout the dark tunnels; but, if you get too close, his cold, dead hands will lash out and drag you down into his watery tomb. Lewis could easily envision those small hands, their flesh pale and slick as fish bellies, the fingernails caked with slimy green algae, latching on and ripping into flesh like bear traps.

Lewis loved the woods and his neighborhood; he wouldn't change a thing about where he lived. The weird tales fueled his imagination, instilling wonder and fascination, making the unexplored areas of the woods mystifying and forbidden, the perfect combination for fun in his twisted mind.

As long as Andy and Jason—the Reed twins—weren't involved that is.

Come to think of it, there *was* something Lewis would change about where he lived.

4

A s night seeped into the sky above his home, Lewis sat at the dinner table, finishing his meal. He paused with a forkful of mashed potatoes raised to his lips, recalling the day's events. He realized he hadn't seen the Reed twins while racing through the woods on that first day of summer. He also realized how lucky he'd been, the ramp and Justin's magnificent crash had occupied all of his attention, leaving him open to attack. Lewis knew from experience that you had to be vigilant, constantly glancing over your shoulder, ready to turn on the jets at any given moment, the twins lurking threat always present.

Big, mean, and ugly as sin, identical twins Andy and Jason Reed have bullied Lewis and any other kid within striking distance for as long as he could remember. The daily threat of being harassed by the boys has become routine, a simple fact of life for him and his friends. Over the years, Lewis's fear of the bullies has grown in accordance with their lumpy, misshaped bodies. They were now twice as big as Lewis, and twice as scary as they were just a year ago.

Lewis Frazier, on the other hand, was not big. Taller but much thinner than most of the other kids his age, Lewis has become accustomed to the twins' constant taunts about his physique, the list of hateful nicknames growing longer every year. There were the common garden-variety names: Beanpole, Twig, Birdchest, and Toothpick; and then there were the more creative ones such as Malnutrition-Boy (Justin's favorite), and the ever tasteless, Concentration-Camp-Boy.

It wasn't a question of appetite. Lewis ate like a ravenous cannibal, but never seemed to gain weight. When Clinton made an innocent comment about tape-worms, Lewis became obsessed with the image of a giant scaly worm living in his gut. A worm with a sucking mouth full of tiny sharp teeth (like the lamprey eel his science teacher had shown the class), plundering the food he shoved down his gullet. Every meal Lewis would think to himself, *time to feed the worm.* He even swore he could feel the slippery beast sliding around in his bowels, uttering low, hungry groans.

Three years older than Lewis, the Reed twins would soon be allowed behind the wheel of a car. The thought terrified Lewis. The thought terrified everyone. Lewis tried to assure himself that access to a vehicle would keep the deviant clones out of the neighborhood and out of his hair, but he couldn't help conjuring the image of the evil boys running him down while riding his bicycle, the car roaring off, the twins hooting and hollering like the *Dukes of Hazard* as Lewis's broken body bled out on the asphalt, twitching in their exhaust.

The twins despised Lewis, but they hated Clinton even more. Mainly because Clinton never let them push him around, even if it resulted in a beating, which it often did.

Lewis and Clinton have been friends since the day Clinton first encountered the duo, the same day Clinton saved Lewis from the twins, all the way back in third grade —at least that's how Lewis tells the story. Clinton always seems embarrassed, shrugging it off as no big deal whenever Lewis mentions it.

On that historic day, three years ago, daydreaming in his favorite perch high up in the nose of the rocket-slide, Lewis watched a baseball game unfold from the field next to the playground. Designed to resemble a vertical rocket ship landing on the planet, or perhaps gearing up for take-off back into deep space, the slide had been Lewis's prime spot to hide from the twins since its construction a year earlier.

Crewmembers accessed the rocket ship via a metal ladder ascending through the center of the structure, all the way to the top level. The first level—the largest but the most boring—never held any interest for Lewis. The slightly more exciting second level housed the slide allowing access to the planet's surface. The third level (smaller and as boring as the first) tapered inward toward the fourth and highest level—the nose cone of the rocket.

The nose had a comfortable capacity of one; just the way Lewis liked it. He considered himself a loner, not into the team sports like the one he currently watched from his favorite post.

Peering through the metal bars making up the exoskeleton of his ship, Lewis imagined the red clay of the baseball diamond to be the surface of Mars. The players—in their bright red and yellow uniforms, hats and batting helmets—were the Martians. With the ship's massive laser cannon, Lewis sighted a Martian in the on-deck circle swinging an aluminum bat—otherwise known as an alien death wand.

"Die, Martian scum," Lewis said, mimicking a laser blast and explosion followed by a rattling death scream.

The scene before him became an ordinary baseball game once again as a sudden violent shaking of the rocket slide snapped Lewis back to reality.

Like noxious fumes, devious laughter floated up to Lewis. His heart wiggled into his throat when he recognized the sinister laughs—the Reed twins. They had Lewis trapped like the proverbial cat up a tree.

The twins shook the rocket harder now. Sure the structure would topple, Lewis clutched the bars and prayed his ship would hold fast to the ground.

An unfamiliar voice shouted above the twins' laughter. "Hey!"

The rocket stopped swaying, but Lewis's white-knuckle grip on the bars remained.

"What do you want?" one of the twins asked. Lewis thought it must've been Andy, since he seemed to speak for the pair most of the time.

Lewis could see the source of the unknown voice now. A small kid stood on the sidewalk, waving his hand in greeting to the unseen twins below, a silly smirk stretched across his tan face. The kid made eye contact with Lewis and gave a single, quick nod. Lewis recognized him; the new kid in class. He'd started school last week. Lewis tried to remember his name, *Clayton? … No … Clinton? Yeah that was it, Clinton.*

"Just wanted to see if I could buy some potato chips from you guys," Clinton said.

A long pause followed as the moronic duo analyzed the odd request. Lewis could picture the twins exchanging confused looks, much like the one he felt scrunched on his own face.

"What?" Andy asked.

"Oh, I heard some old guys talkin', they said that your mom sells Lays on the corner," Clinton said in an innocent tone, then added, "for cheap."

Lewis gasped, held the breath, shut his eyes, and waited for the sounds of murder to ensue.

Another long pause came instead, as the idiot brothers absorbed the punch line. Then the slapping of several sneakers hitting pavement broke the silence. Lewis could see Clinton running, his face up and fists punching the air next to his ears, speeding down the sidewalk leading to the other baseball diamond; the brothers pursued, lumbering after the boy like crazed apes.

Lewis watched the chase from the safety of his nest until all three boys disappeared around a bend, obscured by the tall pine trees. Recognizing his deliverance, he descended the ladder, his unfailing imagination evoking a calm female voice in his head, *This rocket will self-destruct in T-minus twenty seconds and counting.*

Lewis reached the second level of the rocket and dove

face first down the slide, belly-flopping in the cool sand at the bottom.

Fourteen—

Thirteen—

Twelve—

He scrambled to his feet, stumbling in the sand as he tried to reach the escape pod—his bike.

He freed the escape pod from the bike rack and jumped on, pushing the sluggish pedals with all his weight.

Seven—

Six—

Five—

Lewis gained speed as his legs pumped faster, the tires buzzing on the fresh paved bike path, praying he was a safe distance from the ship.

Two—

One—

Zero.

Lewis kept his eyes forward as the rocket exploded behind him, sending flames and metal debris high into the air. He bent over his handlebars and pedaled home as fast as he could, feeling lucky to have escaped with his life.

The following day, Lewis sat in homeroom, glancing toward the open door every time a student entered the classroom, then back to the large clock on the wall, eager for Clinton to show. The tardy bell would blare out any second, and Clinton was still absent, causing Lewis to wonder if the boy had survived the incident. He'd never heard anyone talk to the twins like that before.

Clinton sauntered into the room, hung his backpack

on the back of his chair, and plopped down in his seat just as the shrill ringing of the tardy bell reverberated throughout the halls, as if he had planned the perfectly-timed entrance.

Not realizing he'd been holding his breath, Lewis exhaled, relieved to see the boy walking and breathing. Lewis wasn't surprised by the boy's appearance, but the rest of the class whispered and pointed, stealing glances. Clinton's right eye squinted through a bruised and swollen sunset—the classic shiner. His upper lip protruded, scabbed and puffy. A large band-aid clung like a leech to the bottom of his chin. He held his head high and focused on the teacher at the front of the classroom—nothing out of the ordinary.

Clinton made eye contact with Lewis and flashed him a half-grin, his hand reaching up to touch his crusty lip. Embarrassed, Lewis nodded, and offered the boy a timid wave.

After class, Lewis approached his battered savior. "Hey. Thanks for what you did yesterday. I'm Lewis."

Lewis held out his hand to shake. Clinton grabbed the hand and shook it like the older, cool kids shake. "Clinton. Not a prob."

Lewis felt the grating scabs on Clinton's knuckles and let go, pushing his hands into his jean pockets.

"They messed you up some, huh?" Lewis murmured.

"Nah, it's not that bad. I got some good shots in, kicked one of them in the balls and got away from 'em." Clinton laughed, touching his lip gingerly, his laugh switching to a low moan.

"Did you get in trouble?" Lewis asked.

Clinton shook his head. "Told my mom I fell off my bike."

Lewis giggled. He'd used that same lie before on his own mother.

"Who are those meat-heads anyways?" Clinton asked.

"Andy and Jason, the Reed twins. They're always looking to beat me up. I can't stand those jerks."

"You should call them the Twins from Hell," Clinton suggested, and the boys shared a laugh.

From that moment on, Lewis and Clinton had been best friends.

LITTLE DID LEWIS KNOW—SITTING at the table, enjoying his supper on the first night of summer—that in less than two days, something would awaken in his woods.

Something much worse than the annoying brothers.

Something that made Andy and Jason Reed, the dreaded Twins from Hell, seem like a couple of harmless choirboys.

5

After he finished supper, Lewis helped his mother with the dishes; he dried while she washed. Lewis treasured this ceremonial chore with his mom, talking to her about the day's events—omitting the bike ramp and Justin's crash, of course—feeling closer to her during the menial task than any other time.

Feeling something soft bump his leg, Lewis glanced down. Stretch, his sleek gray cat, stared up at him with his big green eyes. The cat stood on his hind legs, reaching up Lewis's leg as far as he could, performing his eponymous move with a soft meow.

"Can Stretch sleep in my room tonight?" Lewis asked his mother, knowing what the answer would be if his father was home.

"I guess so. Just don't tell your father, you know how he doesn't like him in the house."

Thanking his mother, Lewis trotted off to get ready for bed, the silken feline his meowing shadow.

After reading some comics, Lewis double-checked the list of potential warriors he and Clinton were planning to recruit tomorrow. The list was just a formality since all the kids on the roster already knew about and were ready for the war scheduled to take place Wednesday afternoon. Satisfied all names were present, Lewis filed the sheet of paper with the title, **THE GREAT SWAMP POTATO WAR of *1982*,** in his nightstand drawer, and decided to get some sleep. Stretch loosed a shrill meow and darted out the open door when Lewis turned off the bedroom light. He figured the cat must be too excited about being inside the house to go to bed just yet.

Before hopping into bed, Lewis flips on his *Creature from the Black Lagoon* nightlight, and walks across the darkened room to look out his bedroom window facing his street and the home of Old Man Boyd across the way. He stares out the window, focusing on three bushes dominating the lawn across the street, and then shuts his eyes, standing in silence for several seconds. This is a rite Lewis performs almost every night, a ceremony he secretly refers to as *The Ritual of the Shrubs.* Nobody, not even Clinton, knows of the bizarre nocturnal act.

Opening his eyes, Lewis once again focuses on the three tall, skinny shrubs on the old man's front lawn, silhouetted by the bright porch light behind them. He quickly ducks down out of sight. His cheek to the cool wood panel wall, Lewis senses the sentinel bushes changing shape in the shadows, their forms morphing into something horrific, their leaves and branches swishing and snapping as they alter their benign state, their daytime façade crumbling away to show their disguised hideousness—their nocturnal identities.

Tonight, Lewis imagines the three bushes are rotting zombies in search of human flesh. He can hear the hungry moans from the trio of undead as they search the empty street with maggot-filled eyes. He can hear the shuffling of their burial shoes across grass, asphalt, and the grass of his own front lawn as they lumber across the street en route to his open window, smelling the fresh young meat hiding there.

With a look of mock terror, Lewis stares up at the dark square of his window, waiting for their pale, decomposing faces to come into view, pressing against the screen, their black teeth gnashing at the flimsy barrier.

Lewis rises to face the monsters, his right hand becoming a pistol, and giggles at the sight of the three harmless shrubs standing guard on the lawn across the dark street. He calmly shoots all three bushes in the head, closing one eye for perfect aim. Smiling, Lewis dives into the safety of the bottom bunk—he had a fear of falling off the top bunk—and falls asleep in a matter of minutes.

The following morning, Lewis had just finished his breakfast when the familiar *'shave and a haircut'* knock rapped at the front door. He jumped out of his chair, ran to the door, tapped out his *'two bits'* from his side, and flung it open to Clinton's smiling face. Together, the boys rode off to recruit the cannon fodder needed for their private war.

LAST YEAR, in the fifth grade, while painting portraits of dead presidents and other historic figures, Lewis and Clinton concocted The Swamp Potato War. Like most great ideas, it fell into their laps, a gift from the ether.

On that day, Lewis met Clinton and Justin at their house before school. He met them at their house every school day (he had to pass it anyway on his route to the only bus stop in the neighborhood). As always, the brothers were waiting for Lewis on the front porch. When he marched up that particular morning, cradling a bundle of bright wildflowers, Clinton and Justin exploded into mocking laughter.

Clinton's falsetto voice rang out from the porch above Justin's high-pitched giggles, "Oh Lewis, you shouldn't have."

Lewis shook his head. "Shut up. Where's yours?"

"Where's my what?" Clinton asked, his smile straightening into a tight line.

"Your plant? For the science report?"

Clinton slapped his hands to his head. "Oh shit. I totally forgot."

The assignment had been to bring an indigenous plant or flower, write a short report about it, and read the report to the class.

Now it was Lewis's turn to laugh. "You're screwed, man. Mr. Jackson is so gonna call your folks."

As if shaking off a giant spider, Clinton shed his backpack. He took off running, vaulting the fence to his backyard, disappearing behind his house. Rustling noises and disembodied curses filled the air, followed by a triumphant hoot of joy. He appeared on the opposite side of the house, dirt smeared across his blue t-shirt, clutching something in his fist, the grin pasted on his face again.

"Who's screwed now?" Clinton said, holding the vines high in the air, sprinkling dirt into his blonde hair. Pale, bumpy spheres hung from the vines like giant spider egg sacs.

Lewis recognized the creepers and their clinging lumps straight away. "Swamp potatoes? You serious? What about the report?"

Shrugging, Clinton boasted, "No prob. I'll do it on the bus."

Later, in front of the class, Clinton concluded his brief report on the amazing swamp potato and its many uses, bowed to his fellow students, and turned, beaming at the teacher sitting behind the gargantuan wooden desk.

Mr. Jackson removed his glasses and rubbed his eyes, releasing a mournful sigh. He returned the thick black frames to his nose and leaned back; the spring on the old chair popped and groaned as he spun to face Clinton. "Not bad, Clinton. Not bad for a report you obviously wrote on the bus ride to school. However, what you hold in your hand, what you refer to as *swamp potatoes*, are actually called *air potatoes*."

Clinton's smile once again dropped from his face. "Air potatoes?"

"Yes," the teacher continued, pointing to the vines in Clinton's grip, a scowl of disdain warping his features. "That is the scourge of the Florida wilderness. A foreign vine introduced from overseas. Non-indigenous, in other words. It has obliterated the native plants and trees of our state's ecosystem, invading and killing anything in its path.

Every time you throw one—which, by the way, cannot be classified as a use—you are helping to spread this invasion. Please do everyone a favor, young man, and throw those in the trash on the way back to your seat."

Clinton dropped the potatoes into the trashcan with a resounding hollow *thunk,* and plopped down into his chair, huffing a sigh of failure.

"Smooth move, Ex-Lax," Lewis whispered from the seat next to Clinton.

"Shut up," Clinton hissed.

Lewis, still giggling and badgering Clinton about the failed impromptu report, took his assigned seat for their next class, Social Studies.

Mrs. Headley—Lewis's favorite teacher and secret crush—scribbled on the blackboard, the chalk tapping and sliding across the dark surface with speed and grace, small flecks of white falling like snowflakes from the words, drifting down to the ancient carpet. She finished writing and underlined two words with bold strokes of chalk, turned, and spoke the words out loud, "Warfield Woods … Who here has ever heard of Warfield Woods?"

Not a soul raised a hand. Students glanced around the room to see if anyone knew the answer. No one did.

Mrs. Headley nodded, a look of shame on her face. "That was once the local name of the woods that surround Hopkinsville, especially the area around Poisonwood Estates where a few of you live." Her eyes met Lewis's as she said this, causing his cheeks to burn; he thought she easily beat out any of *Charlie's Angels* in the looks department. "Now," she continued, "everyone just refers to them simply as 'The Woods'. But they were called Warfield

Woods for good reason. Because there were actual wars fought there just a little over a century ago. Men, possibly your ancestors, killed and died in these woods, on this very soil, to have what you and your families have today."

Lewis paid more attention than ever before, even going as far as to take notes, something he seldom did. He clung to the teacher's every word as she taught the class about the Seminole Indians and their wars with the United States Army for the control of Florida. How they fought three wars in total, against all odds, and were never truly defeated. She explained the broken promises given to the Seminole leaders, and the eventual forced exodus of the tribes from their native homes. Lewis couldn't believe all this had happened right here in his own backyard—in his woods.

The large clock on the wall above the teacher went unnoticed for a change, and when the dismissal bell rang out, Lewis jumped in his seat. He blinked several times, focusing on the round clock, thinking the bell must have malfunctioned, but the hands didn't lie. Everyone remained in his or her seats, waiting for the teacher to finish. "Remember class, just because a name of a place is forgotten does not mean the events that took place there need to be forgotten as well. Dismissed."

"Clinton Marsh, please stay after," Mrs. Headley announced above the murmur of students filing toward the door.

A chorus of *oohs* filled the classroom as Clinton trudged his way to the teacher's desk. Lewis waited by the exit, curious as to what his friend had done this time.

Mrs. Headley must have sensed Clinton's tension.

"You're not in any trouble, Clinton. I just wondered if you were still interested in re-painting the columns."

Relieved, Clinton remembered her request from last week and answered quickly, "Yeah … Yes ma'am."

Well known for his artistic abilities, Clinton often found himself in trouble for drawing during class, but the teachers couldn't help admiring his creativity and talent. Lewis always looked forward to reading the short comics Clinton created, and marveled at how well his friend could draw.

"Good. I'll tell your Phys Ed coach where you'll be."

Clinton spied Lewis by the door and had an idea. "Mrs. Headley? Can Lewis help? It'll get done a lot faster if he does."

She looked at Lewis and flashed him a conspiratorial smile. His burning cheeks were now upgraded to a four-alarm blaze. "Sure. I'll tell the coach."

The columns were in the middle of the school, in the central hub, where the hallways converged like the spokes of a wagon wheel under the large bubble of an opaque white skylight. Each square column had a life-size painting of an historical figure on each side. Abraham Lincoln, George Washington, Benjamin Franklin, Martin Luther King Jr., and several others the boys didn't even recognize graced the uprights. There were four columns total, giving the boys sixteen different paintings to touch up. The elements and the passing of small hands had worn away the details over the years.

The boys came up with the idea of the war while they painted.

The notion of waging a mock war on an actual battlefield was too tempting to pass up. Lewis took a break from painting, his excitement over the plan etching a grin on his face that would not subside. "Warfield Woods," he uttered with great pride. "What if there's like an actual sacred burial ground or something out there? Or maybe skeletons of bodies that were never found."

"That would be pretty cool," Clinton said, concentrating on his touch-up of Honest Abe.

"Or maybe arrowheads. Or guns."

"Speaking of," Clinton said. "What should we use as weapons?"

Lewis's first idea involved rocks from slingshots, but they both agreed that would probably cause too much damage. They wanted it to be fun, not deadly.

"Why don't we just throw swamp potatoes," Clinton suggested.

"Don't you mean air potatoes," Lewis said, correcting him with a giggle.

Clinton shook his head, his expression serious, his bright blue eyes intense. "Screw that. I'm calling them swamp potatoes."

"We could," agreed Lewis, "the woods are covered in them and they're perfect for throwing. We just need to get enough people to make it an actual war, though. Otherwise it'll just be the same old story—me and you throwing them at your little brother."

"Don't worry about that. I know plenty of guys in the neighborhood that'll want to be in on it."

Clinton came around the column to check on his friend's progress and pointed to the painting with the end of his brush. "Who the heck is that supposed to be?"

Lewis stopped painting. "What do ya mean? It's Benjamin Franklin, isn't it?"

"It was. Why did you give him sunglasses?"

Lewis shrugged. "It's Florida? And … well … I kind of messed up the eyes."

Clinton laughed. "You turned him into a balding hippie."

In the time it took the boys to finish the columns, clean the brushes, and return the paint to Mrs. Headley, they had a basic outline of rules for the war.

These rules were simple: two equal-numbered teams would face-off from opposite sides of Horse Crap River—the name given to the wide drainage ditch that fed rainwater into Horse Crap Lake. The boys hadn't a clue who'd named the lake, but it fit perfectly; a foul stench rose from its boggy bottom that had the appearance and consistency of its namesake.

Three whistles would be blown. The first signaled the combatants to gather as much ammo as possible before the second whistle blew five minutes later, warning them to get into position and prepare themselves for the final whistle heralding the start of the war.

Only swamp potatoes were allowed. Anyone caught using anything else would be ejected. If you're hit with a potato, anywhere on the body, you're considered dead and out of the contest. However, if you catch a potato—baseball mitts were permitted—then you're still in the game and can use the captured projectile on your foe.

The war ended when one side was massacred, giving the survivor(s) and winning side bragging rights for the rest of the summer.

LEWIS AND CLINTON, with Justin tagging along, biked to every house on the list, successful in recruiting the required sixteen warriors to even the sides. Everybody agreed to show up the following day at high noon, prepared to do battle. This gave them a total of nineteen soldiers—counting Lewis, Clinton, and Justin—and when Jerry "Muttley" Harris showed up, it would give them the even twenty they needed.

6

L ewis felt sorry for Jerry. The poor kid's asthma and overprotective parents kept him from participating in any sports and activities; basically, they kept him from having fun in general.

Well, Lewis felt sorry for Jerry *some* of the time. If Jerry hadn't been such a tattletale maybe the other kids wouldn't be so mean to him, and maybe Lewis wouldn't exclude him from so many everyday adventures. The only reason Lewis let Jerry participate in the war was to keep the boy from spilling the beans to his parents; Jerry had promised to keep quiet if allowed to fight.

Lewis liked Jerry enough, and had tried to be better friends with the frail asthmatic over the years, but every time he let Jerry hang out with him and his gang, some slanderous information always found its way into the hands of the enemy—their parents. Not to mention, the boy's wheezing and the constant whoosh of his inhaler would become so annoying, Lewis had to rack his brain to invent a reason to be somewhere else, quick (his excuses were becoming more outlandish as the years passed and Lewis was sure Jerry was wise to the lies). Then the guilt would set in. Lewis would tell himself Jerry couldn't help his condition, and he would let him back into the circle, and the vicious cycle would start over again.

Unlike other kids in the neighborhood, Lewis and Clinton never called him "Muttley"—at least not to his face—even though Jerry didn't seem to mind the moniker, and even though Clinton had created the nickname.

On the day of the war, Jerry showed up as expected, and once again he showed up wearing his homemade *Spider-Man* mask. The mask, fashioned from red panty-hose, had been hand-painted by Jerry himself—a fact he stated with great pride whenever he got the chance. The eyes were a little lop-sided, but the webbing wasn't too bad. However, the boy's greasy hair stuck out in patches where the pantyhose had run, making him look like a bizarre *Marvel Chia Pet*.

"Hi, Lewis," Jerry shouted, his voice muffled by the mask but the excitement behind it audible enough.

Lewis waved him over. "Hey, Jerry. You can be on my team again." A fact both boys knew had already been decided, but made Lewis feel good to say it, and Jerry feel good to hear it.

"Killer," Jerry said, using one of Lewis and Clinton's favorite words from last year.

"Maybe you should take the mask off so you can see better," suggested Lewis, knowing all too well he wouldn't take his advice, but trying to save Jerry some dignity.

"The mask gives me better reflexes, kind of like a Spidey-sense," Jerry insisted, crouching into a ready-for-action *Spider-Man* pose, laughing his wheezy laugh, a perfect impersonation of the cartoon dog he's named after: Dick Dastardly's canine sidekick, Muttley. As customary, he followed the laugh with a hit from the inhaler dangling on a string around his neck. Everyone—Jerry included—knew he had the reflexes of a dead cat.

Refraining from comment and checking his list, Lewis clamped his mouth tight to stifle the giggle begging to be released. He mentally penciled-in and checked-off Jerry's name. All warriors present, so far so good.

Clinton turned away from a group of kids perched on the edge of the ditch and strutted toward Lewis, an excited grin on his face. "There's no need to pick teams this time, everyone's already taken a side."

"Is it even?" asked Lewis.

"Yep. Ten on ten."

"Let's do it," they chorused in unison.

They couldn't have chosen a better day to start a war. A brilliant blue sky pocked with lumbering white cumulus clouds shined down. A cool breeze rustled the trees, hinting at the approach of a summer storm. Lewis wasn't concerned; the war should be over long before the rain blew in.

Lewis, Clinton, Justin, and Jerry all crouched in silence next to one another behind an old fallen elm tree, awaiting the sharp trill of the third whistle—the honor of whistle-blower given to one of the younger kids sitting on the retaining wall separating the homes from the woods, eagerly awaiting the battle.

So much for keeping it a secret, Lewis thought.

The boys' cache of potatoes sat next to each of them, ready to be thrown; all except Jerry's, who cradled his ammo in his t-shirt, his right fist already loaded and cocked for action.

Lewis broke the tense silence. "Okay, when the whistle blows, peek over the tree to see where the enemy are before you stand up to throw. Hopefully they'll give away their positions."

Clinton nodded. "Good idea."

"Gotcha," spat Justin, wide-eyed and antsy.

Before Lewis could get a confirmation from Jerry, the final whistle blew long and loud like the call of a maniacal jungle bird. Lewis, Clinton, and Justin, their eyes bugging out, glanced over the tree to sight the enemy, when next to them roared a fierce cry, "DIE! DIE! DIE!" The boys' heads whipped around in harmony toward the scream. They froze, flabbergasted, as Jerry "Muttley" Harris hurdled the fallen tree, firing projectiles in rapid succession from the stash in his deflating shirt, screaming like a berserker through his home-made mask.

Lewis peeked over the tree again, following the possessed asthmatic, gawking in amazement as one of Jerry's potatoes hit Billy Keener smack in the middle of his ginger covered forehead with a dull *thud*.

The remaining enemy could only watch, also mesmerized, as Jerry careened pell-mell down the steep incline of the ditch without falling, and continued launching potatoes into enemy ranks, hitting one more stupefied opponent in the chest.

Lewis could not believe his eyes: Jerry "Muttley" Harris kicking some major ass.

Then the unavoidable happened—Jerry's ammo ran dry. Stranded in the open, he spun and crawled as fast as he could back up the sloping wall of the ditch. The dirt wall crumbled in his grasp, hampering his ascent. For the first time ever, Jerry resembled the character his mask portrayed him to be, as potatoes thumped into the dirt next to him, the opposition fully recovered from their brief astonishment. Lewis's soldiers launched a barrage of their own, trying to protect their brother in arms, but to no avail.

The first potato hit Jerry in the back, halting his frenzied climb. He punched the dirt once, calmly stood, and began his slump-shouldered walk of shame to the wall, where the dead soldiers could watch the rest of the war unfold.

That's when the second potato hit Jerry.

The baseball-sized potato caromed off the boy's skull, whipping his head back and sending him on his ass, the rocks at the base of the ditch crunching beneath his jeans.

Wincing, Lewis sucked in a breath as if he could feel Jerry's pain. The action paused as everyone focused on Jerry sitting at the rocky bottom of the ditch, one hand to his masked head. Lewis knew Jerry would run home crying for sure this time, bringing his paranoid, overprotective mother down here to end their fun. He realized he had to stop the boy, to somehow keep him from spoiling the war. Before he could call out to Jerry—tell him to walk it off, everything would be fine—the boy stood, muffled sobs leaking through his mask. Then, just as predicted,

Jerry did run; however, to the surprise of everyone, he fled up the opposite side of the ditch and vanished into the woods, his sobs consumed by the dense foliage. This unforeseen act shocked both sides so much it took several seconds for the violence to resume.

7

Jerry had planned all along to go out in a blaze of glory, to shock everyone watching. He'd known he wouldn't last very long, that he would be an easy target right away, but he didn't give a damn about winning; he only wanted some respect from the neighborhood kids for once. He chided himself for crying, but pride flowed through him for not running home to his mother.

Walking now, his anger fading, Jerry smiled beneath the mask, remembering the stunned faces of the boys he'd pegged. He had killed not just one, but two of the enemy, much better than he had expected. He tugged the mask above his mouth and inhaled the bitter spray, calming his agitated lungs. Jerry gasped as he touched the tender lump on his head. The pain energized him.

He exhaled his signature smoker's laugh, and thought, *I won. I finally got the better of them.*

Jerry stared at the perfect summer sky, the sun warm

and diffused through the pantyhose. He felt good for a change. His adrenaline had leveled out, and the pain in his head had subsided to a dim throb. Believe it or not, he felt amazing.

He peered down the trail he'd been following; he didn't recognize this part of the woods. This didn't come as a shock—his mother forbade him to go too deep into the woods. In fact, she didn't let him stray far from the house at all. In his anger, he must have ventured further than he ever had before. He stopped and turned, deciding to head back before he got himself lost, and to watch the rest of the battle unfold, show them they couldn't beat him. But an all too familiar voice stopped him short, freezing his muscles.

"Hey, Muttley. Oops, sorry … Hey, Spidey."

Looking up, Jerry's eyes widened beneath the mask when he saw Andy Reed blocking the path, his fat arms crossed, a huge grin on his cruel face. Behind Andy stood his twin brother, Jason, with the exact expression. Jerry's good mood deflated and he wondered how long the twins had been following him, sending a chill up his scalp.

"Where ya headin', dipshit?" asked Andy.

"Just going home," lied Jerry.

"Bullshit, you're goin' back to hang out with your faggot friends," Andy said, his grin turning to a sneer. "They stopped playing their gay little game when you took off. Guess they knew you'd rat them out to your faggot dad." Obviously proud of his inventive use of the English language, Andy's smug, shit-eating grin returned.

Jerry's mind raced. The twins must have heard the whistles and been watching them all along. He made a mental note to tell the gang when he saw them again, and stiffened, realizing his predicament: he was deep in the woods with the evil Reed brothers blocking his way back.

Trying to mask the shaking of his voice, Jerry asked, "What are you guys doing way out here in the woods?"

"Huntin'," they both said, as if they shared the same insidious brain as well as the same hideous face.

Neither boy carried a gun, but Jerry spied the large hunting knives strapped to their belts. "Hunting what?" he ventured, his mental gears winding, calculating his options: attempt to dash past the big goons? Or run deeper into the unknown forest and hope they tire before they catch him. Jerry removed his mask, stuffing it in the back pocket of his jeans, opting for the latter course of action.

"Huntin' spider-chicken," Andy responded, forcing a cackle from his stupid brother, which in turn made Andy laugh. Snorting like pigs and slapping high-fives, the brothers failed to notice their quarry taking flight deeper into Warfield Woods.

En route to his meeting with the tree.

❧

JUSTIN SAT on the cinder block retaining wall, watching the battle. Several of the other "dead" boys sat next to him, cheering on their respective sides. Justin's death had come just moments after Jerry's heroic kamikaze attack and subsequent flight into the wilds, but not before he had killed one of the enemy himself. Unfortunately, that one enemy happened to be Katy Lee, the lone girl in the battle, and Justin knew he'd just earned a lifetime of smart-ass remarks from his older brother. He glimpsed over at her, sitting on the wall. She turned and met Justin's gaze, offering him a sweet smile. He quickly turned his face away, grinning uncontrollably. Maybe it was worth a lifetime of heckling after all.

Soon, several "ghosts"—as he liked to call them— joined Justin on the wall as the fight whittled its way down to a stalemate. Two combatants were left for each team: Brian and Paul on the enemy side, Lewis and Clinton on his side. As it turned out, Jerry's surprise attack had taken care of the opposition's best warrior with a beautiful head shot, giving Lewis's side the advantage from the outset; Billy Keener sat on the wall, separate from the group, still fuming, a blooming bruise on his freckled forehead.

From his position on the wall, Justin could see his brother and Lewis as they hunkered down against the protective rim of the ditch, their lips moving, discussing a war-winning strategy. Justin could only imagine the tactics they were dreaming up.

"We're screwed, dude," Clinton whined.

"No we're not," Lewis whispered. He lobbed a potato across the ditch like a grenade to keep the enemy distracted while he thought of something. "But we can't sit here throwing blindly all day, we're gonna run out of ammo real soon. We have to do something."

"Like what?" Clinton asked, catching an enemy grenade and adding it to their dwindling pile.

Lewis took a deep breath. "I'll draw their fire and you sneak around and surprise them from behind."

Clinton nodded. "Good plan, but you're much faster and smaller than me."

"Not that much smaller," Lewis argued. "What's your point?"

"*You* should sneak around, and *I'll* take the hits."

Lewis stared at the ground, pondering the plan, when Clinton pushed him and blurted, "GO!"

Lewis grabbed some ammo and moved to his left as fast as he could go without being seen by the enemy, bent over, hidden by the weeds choking the lip of the ditch. He halted at the flattest and widest section of the trench—the part he had to somehow sprint across unnoticed. Behind him, he could hear Clinton shouting as if possessed, and took that as his cue to brave the daunting stretch of exposed battlefield.

Taking a deep breath, Lewis scurried across, focusing on a clump of bushes on the far side. No shouts or potatoes came his way, indicating that Clinton's distractions were a success. Still hunched, Lewis crept up the enemy side, careful to stay out of eyesight of the spectators on the wall. A warning from them would spell his demise.

The exposed backs of his enemies came into view just as the "dead" boys on the wall gave away his position. Lewis let loose with a ferocious flurry from the stash in his shirt—a nod to the fallen Jerry—all the while thinking a new rule should be implemented to keep the "dead" warriors silent. Lewis pegged Brian in the back with a small potato as the boy pumped his fist and yelled, "Gotcha"—making it clear Clinton had met his end.

I'm the last man standing. Our last hope. He thought all of this with an air of melodrama, as time did something strange—it slowed to a crawl. Lewis watched himself—as if through the eyes of a stranger—throw a potato at the final obstacle to his victory: Paul.

After seeing Brian's shocked expression, Paul spun just in time to dodge the potato. The lone enemy crouched, Lewis's shot sailing harmlessly past, and launched a potato of his own, larger than his fist.

Lewis felt the breeze and heard the deadly projectile sizzle past his right ear. Pissed off and desperate, he let fly his last potato, and last hope of winning the war. Still crouched, Paul saw it coming and sprung erect to avoid being struck, only to take the impact straight to the testicles. Grabbing his crotch, Paul released a high-pitched squeal and collapsed to the ground in a fetal position.

Cheers erupted from the wall of spectators as Lewis raised his fists in victory.

The raucous and unsportsmanlike celebration lasted until the adrenalin wore off and the pain from the stinging projectiles set in. Lewis and Clinton's team were all smiles despite the aches they felt.

Lewis clapped Clinton on the shoulder. "Thanks for taking those hits for me. I owe you one"

Clinton shook his head. "If you hadn't nailed them *then* you would've owed me. But you did, so we're even. Nice shot by the way, Paul's balls must be killing him."

Lewis and Justin laughed as Clinton mimed Paul's moment of testicular agony, the other members of the winning side pumping their fists in the air, chanting, "PAUL'S BALLS … PAUL'S BALLS … PAUL'S BALLS."

Lewis interrupted the routine. "Anyone seen Jerry? We need to tell him we won."

"He probably took the trail back to the field," Clinton said. "I'm sure he's home right now with an icepack on his head."

Lewis glanced to the sky as a shadow consumed them. Ashen, gunmetal clouds tromped overhead. Thunder grumbled in their wake. "Yeah, I guess so. I hope he didn't get hurt too bad."

8

Inhaling the humid air, slumped over with their hands on their knees, the twins stared at the ominous mouth of the overgrown path.

The boys had walked the other trail for at least half an hour, trying to coax Jerry out of hiding to no avail. They finally worked their way back to the fork to rest, catching their breath under the darkening sky.

Andy glanced at his brother, frowned, and shook his head as if he could read his twin's thoughts. "That little pussy wouldn't go that way. He probably hid and made his way back to the neighborhood. We should get back too, before the rain starts."

"Besides," Jason said, trying too hard to sound brave. "He's expecting us. I want to surprise that little shit when he least—"

"Shh. Did you hear that?" Andy interrupted, raising his hand to silence his brother.

Jason shrugged, and whispered, "What?"

"I heard someone laugh. I bet it's Asthma Boy … there it is again."

They both heard it then, from somewhere in front of them, in the thick bushes lining the path—a child giggling.

"Is that you, spider-fag?" Andy hollered, hoping his brother couldn't see the gooseflesh the laugh had raised on his sweaty arms.

Another evil titter answered him, a taunting giggle. The brush to Andy's left shook with a soft rustling, the palm fronds swaying in a benign come-hither gesture. Andy crept to the stirring bushes, his steps slow and unsure. He stopped within arms reach as the thickets froze.

"Come on out, man. We're not gonna hurt ya, I promise," Andy announced to the still woods.

Infuriating silence greeted his command. Andy parted the thick tangle of palmetto leaves before him, bent over, and stuck his moon face in the shadowed opening. "Get your ass out here you little shit or I'm coming in after ya."

Jason, lurking behind Andy, tried to see past his brother's broad back. "You see him, Andy? You see the little asshole?"

Instead of an answer, Jason heard his brother's quick intake of breath, followed immediately by a soft thump like a baseball hitting a catcher's mitt. Andy snapped upright, hands chopping down to his thighs as if standing attention to an invisible drill sergeant. He staggered backward, hands convulsing, his back stopping inches from Jason's face. A thick gargle filled the air around Andy's head, like a child blowing bubbles in a glass of milk.

"You okay, Andy?" Jason asked, resting a hand on his brother's twitching shoulder. Andy dropped to his knees, his teeth clicking together with a hollow pop, and then fell forward onto his face, sending up a plume of dirt.

Initially unseen by Jason, the jagged branch skewering Andy's throat erupted from the back of his neck as his face met the forest floor. The collar of Andy's t-shirt tented for a second, then tore, revealing the lethal point jutting from the left of his spine.

Jason gawked as syrupy blood jetted from the gaping wound, strangely reminding him of the cherry Slush Puppie machine at the Minute Mart. Strands of deep red and yellow-white flesh swung from the tip of the long spike as Andy convulsed on the forest floor. An overwhelming coppery scent filled the damp air.

"You okay, Andy?" Jason repeated, staring in wide-eyed shock and disbelief, his courage leaking away along with his brother's blood.

Jason heard the wicked laughter again and lifted his head in slow motion, his neck muscles disobeying his mind's command to *not* look. A face leered at him from the bushes with an evil rictus grin stretched ear to ear—a grimace of sadistic satisfaction. A face that reminded Jason of Jerry Harris, the puny kid from the neighborhood, but instead conjured every horrible nightmare his fractured mind could recall.

Locked into Jerry's gaze, Jason felt his strength drain away; he fell to his knees behind his prone brother. Seeing his brother die had been bad enough, like watching a film of himself being murdered. Those eyes, however, were even worse.

The sclera of Jerry's eyes blazed blood red; the iris—once hazel—now shone a vivid yellow, the diseased yellow of infection. Matching black pits of absolute despair made up the center where the boy's innocuous pupils once resided.

Jerry parted the foliage and stepped out into the fading light, the storm clouds now shading the sun, hiding the horrific scene from its innocent, comforting glow. He reached down and pulled the stick from Andy's neck with all the emotion of a fisherman removing a hook from a fresh catch; it slid out with a wet sucking sound like a sneaker being freed from mud. The body lifted slightly, then slumped back to the dirt, twitching twice before falling still again.

Jerry admired the gore-soaked stick, and once again bore his fiendish stare into the terrified eyes of the supplicating twin. He savored Jason's fear, as the bully-turned-coward released the contents of his bladder, darkening the front of his jeans.

"You okay, Andy?" Jason mumbled under his breath, shaking, the dark stain spreading down his legs.

The large hunting knife on Andy's belt drew Jerry's attention. The blade whispered with mischievous gratitude as it slid from its sheath. Jerry held the weapon up to his face like a discerning shopper checking the quality of the merchandise. The waning light reflected from the blade's smooth surface as he turned it in his small hand. He held the bloody stick next to the blade, comparing the two. Jerry licked the sharpened stake, slurping up the large morsel of flesh at its end, and tossed the inferior weapon into the woods.

Chewing the meat with a complacent grin, the thing that is now Jerry stepped in front of the quivering Jason, placed a cold left hand on the boy's shoulder as if to comfort him for the loss of his brother, and slammed the knife into the bully's soft belly. Jason whimpered, his expression one of surprise, as Jerry twisted the knife and sliced upwards, unzipping the boy's substantial abdomen, the tearing of cloth and ripping of flesh indistinguishable. Jerry's grin broadened and his eyes widened as hot blood showered his jeans, and slick intestines splashed onto his navy blue Vans.

Still grinning, Jerry slid the knife free, enjoying the sound the blade made as it exited—like a wet kiss between lovers. Jason's eyes rolled back into his skull, showing nothing but white. Jerry backed away and beamed with delight as Jason fell forward next to his twin brother with a grotesque *squish*.

The thing that had once been little Jerry Harris admired the pathetic bodies as if they were priceless works of art. The blood and gore fanned out onto the trail, wrenching a chuckle from the horrible thing residing in the reanimated body of the puny asthmatic.

9

Lewis and Clinton were still at the battlefield enjoying the victory when the first fat raindrops began to fall. They both looked to the sky, then each other, and began their short trek back to the neighborhood without saying a word. The other kids, Justin among them, moaned their disapproval and scattered to seek shelter from the approaching storm, fleeing in different directions to their respective homes.

They heard Jerry's name riding the swift breeze, meeting them as they stepped onto the swaying grass of the connecting field. A woman—Jerry's mother, they presumed—shouted the name, drawing out each syllable into a melancholy dirge.

Lewis looked at Clinton and saw his own feelings of confusion and alarm reflected in the boy's features. It was the first time either one of them had heard Jerry's name called before. It felt strange and disheartening.

"Jerry isn't home yet," Lewis said, the tone of dread

apparent in his voice. "We should go talk to his mom and let her know what happened."

"No way," Clinton protested, shaking his head. "She'll be pissed off as hell. Remember the last time he got hurt on his bike? She yelled at *me* for that. What's she gonna do this time?"

"Yeah, but what if something bad happened to him?"

Still shaking his head, Clinton agreed, "Okay. Let's go."

❧

JACKIE HARRIS STOOD on her front porch as the first rumble of thunder rolled across the sky like a giant bowling ball, never quite reaching the pins at the end of the lane. She called her son's name again.

Jerry had been so excited this morning, telling her he was going to meet Lewis and some other friends to play softball. This seemed a little odd at the time since Jerry hated sports and didn't have any friends—besides Lewis—that she was aware of, but she sent him off to play anyway, making sure he had a full inhaler.

She'd been working in the garden when the first drop of rain hit her on the back of her gloved hand. She stared at the wet spot where the drop had soaked in, and felt a sudden surge of panic.

Where is my son?

Now, standing on the porch, she spied Lewis and Clinton jogging toward her. She started shouting questions, wringing her hands together as if trying to wash something filthy away.

Clinton kept quiet as Lewis recounted the story to her, expecting her to lash out and blame him for her son's absence.

"Which way did he run?" she asked.

"He went into the woods but he should've been home by now," Clinton said.

"I'm sure he's fine," Lewis reassured her. "Don't worry, we'll go look for him before it starts coming down hard."

Lewis grabbed Clinton by the shirt, dragging him off the porch, leaving Jerry's panic-stricken mother there, calling for her son.

As they jogged back to the woods, Clinton asked, "What do you think happened, dude? I mean he didn't seem like he got hurt that bad. Do you think he had an asthma attack or something?"

"I don't know. But I've been thinking. You know who we didn't see all day?"

"Who?" Then, as it struck Clinton, his steps quickened. "Oh shit. The Twins from Hell."

10

Twins. A good omen.

It seems a hundred and fifty years of imprisonment has not weakened her much. She dispatched the oafish twins with surprising ease considering the pathetic, scrawny vessel she found herself in. It felt wonderful to kill again. To once again see, smell, and taste the blood of her favorite game: humans. The minuscule taste of flesh left her yearning for more, but she knew from experience she must be careful; she must control her bloodlust if she wanted to stay in this realm. She must protect the body of the child she resided in, and to do that, she needed slaves.

First, she needed to move these bodies. She must carry them back to the clearing and her tree so she can make use of them. The brains of the boys were not damaged in her brutal attack, this she had made sure; she needed them intact if she wanted the boys to help in her quest for vengeance—her quest for blood. The mess she'd made of the boy's abdomen shouldn't be a problem, but she must remember to control her enthusiasm in future converts. It would be a bit messy, but he would serve his purpose.

She knelt down, grabbed Andy by the armpits and picked him up, slinging his corpse over her shoulder like a sack of flour. The unbelievable sight of the puny boy hefting the stocky teen went unseen, the quiet woods void of any living human eyes. Andy's cooling, congealing blood rolled down her back. Her vessel's thin legs quaked beneath the weight but managed well enough as she marched off down the forbidden trail toward the tree, the source of her power. She reached the wall of vines—a new renovation to her home, constructed by whom she did not know, or care—and dumped Andy's body to the dirt, leaving it there while she fetched his brother.

The rain started to drop and thunder rolled across the sky just as she reached the disemboweled corpse of Jason Reed. She grabbed an ankle and dragged the body down the trail to reunite him with his brother. His intestines—a knotted tangle of muddy rope—followed along like an obscene wedding train.

Reaching the wall of vines, she carried each boy through the gap separately, lying them face up in the white sand. The brothers could have looked like they were sleeping if not for the mortal wounds they each displayed —Jason's much worse than his brother's.

She looked at the tree through Jerry's eyes. A single leaf stood out against the black wood, growing from the tip of a thin branch. The large leaf's contrast was gorgeous, bright green with crimson striations coursing through its rubbery flesh. She marveled at its beauty, anxious to add more of the stunning leaves to the many branches of her tree.

Kneeling next to the bodies, she hauled in Jason's gritty intestines and shoved them back into the jagged cavity of the boy's belly like stuffing a Thanksgiving turkey. She then opened his mouth wide, a silent scream frozen on his pale face. She repeated this with Andy's mouth and scooped up a large heaping of sand, the fine granules slipping through the small fingers of her vessel. She raised her cupped hands above Andy's yawning mouth and spread them apart, letting the sand fall down the dead throat. She repeated the ritual with Jason. She used her fingers to push the sand down their mouths before forcing them shut. She stood and backed away, waiting, the rain pattering on the foliage around her the only sound, like the ticking of an enormous clock.

She didn't have to wait long.

First, Andy's eyes opened and he sat up like a catapult. Then, his brother's eyelids rolled up and he too sprang into a sitting position, spilling his muddy guts into his lap. The dead brothers turned their heads in unison to look at their creator with eyes glinting yellow like hers.

Jerry—or the thing now piloting his corpse—smiled with delight as two more gorgeous leaves bloomed on the tree. She looked at her dead boys, the first of many to do her bidding, beaming with joy. A proud mother.

The things that were once Andy and Jason Reed smiled back at her as the sky opened its veins, baptizing the newborn evil.

11

L ewis and Clinton—with help from a curious Justin —searched the woods, shouting their friend's name, the notion that something terribly wrong had befallen Jerry seeping into each of the boys' minds. Thunder and looming clouds covered the sky above the searchers, fueling their morbid thoughts, their calls becoming louder and more anxious as the rain fell harder.

They searched the area close to the battlefield, knowing Jerry wouldn't venture too deep into the woods. After a quick circuit of the main trail, Lewis emerged from the brush, his shoulders hunched against the annoying raindrops as he walked to the edge of the potato-littered ditch. He hoped Jerry was just hiding, maybe embarrassed about crying in front of everybody. The dark maw of the drainpipe caught his eye, but he shook the idea from his head—Jerry would never go in there. The twins were the only kids Lewis knew of that braved the tunnel; he'd seen them exiting the drainpipe on several occasions. They would hide in there to smoke weed or drink booze and do whatever felonious things they do.

Lewis could feel and smell the charge in the air as he surveyed the area. The heart of the storm was almost here, and it promised to be a good one, of that he was sure. Clinton and Justin appeared on the opposite side of the ditch, both shrugging to Lewis, their frowns telling him all he needed to know. He motioned for them to join him, the increasing thunder and wind making it impossible to communicate across the wide ditch.

The brothers trudged up to Lewis, their hair plastered to their scalps.

"Nothing?" Lewis shouted to the pair.

Clinton shook his head. "Nothing. We didn't go that deep, though."

Lightning flashed, the boys cringed, and an earth-shaking clap of thunder followed a second later.

"We need to get outta here," Clinton yelled.

Lewis nodded. "Yeah, you guys go home. I'll stop by Jerry's house to see if he came back. Call you later."

The boys ran to the field and split in different directions: Clinton and Justin toward their home, and Lewis toward Jerry's. The rain pelted Lewis harder now as he hurried his way to the house, hoping Jerry had snuck home during their failed search.

Lewis knocked, waiting for Jerry to open the door with a grin on his face like nothing had happened. The door flung open and Jerry's mother stood in the doorway, her tight look of concern melting into tears when she saw the disappointment on Lewis's face. From two streets over, above the clamor of the quickening storm, Lewis could hear his own mother shouting for him to come home. He backed off the porch into the rain as more tears flowed from the eyes of the sad woman standing before him.

"I gotta go, Mrs. Harris," Lewis said. "I'm sure he's fine. We'll find him," he added, feeling the familiar pang of guilt he suffered whenever he deceived an adult.

The giant bowling ball rolled across the sky once more, this time slamming into the pins with a deafening crack, tearing the fabric of the sky. Lewis and Jerry's mother looked upward with frightened anticipation, as if they expected the heavens to come crashing down.

Lewis spun and ran for home just as Jerry's father turned his sleek sedan onto the street, home from work. Lewis glanced at the car, turned away, and ran faster, his guilt increasing as he fled the scene.

Lewis recounted the day's events to his mother as he stripped out of his wet clothes in the laundry room, peeling off the clinging material like a shedding snake, dropping them to the floor with a clammy smack. She was on the phone with Jerry's mother before he had finished putting on dry replacements, offering reassurance in a soft tone Lewis only heard when she spoke on the telephone. She talked to Jackie Harris in a way that surprised Lewis, in a voice of familiar camaraderie; he had no idea the two women even knew one another.

Lewis checked in every few minutes in the hopes of receiving some good news, peeking his head around the corner into the kitchen where his mother paced, the long spiral cord of the telephone twisted around her thighs. Each time he made eye contact, she covered the phone with her hand and shook her head, a worried look in her eyes.

Lewis tried his best to stay busy as the rain upgraded to a full force deluge, making it impossible to go outside. He wanted to call Clinton to see if he had heard anything different, but his mother still cooed reassurances into the phone. The lack of contact drove him insane with worry. After what seemed like an hour, his mother hung up, made Lewis a quick meal in silence, and was back on the phone, alerting other parents in the neighborhood. Lewis didn't have an appetite. He shared the meal with Stretch, who purred at his feet, patiently waiting for another helping of mac-n-cheese.

After dinner, Lewis sat nodding off in front of the television, chin bouncing off his chest, when his mother tussled his hair and signaled him to go to bed. She told him not to worry, the adults were taking care of it, and Jerry would be just fine. He didn't argue; the events of the day had drained him physically and mentally. He went through the rigmarole of preparing for bed in a dazed state, moving like a lethargic robot, the battery running low.

Before lying in bed, he approached the window to perform his nightly ritual, but could only stare at the three hedges across the street, his imagination incapable of mustering any horrifying scenarios. The rain still poured down in sheets. He thought of poor little Jerry out there in the storm, injured—or worse. He shook his head to dislodge the picture that flashed in his mind like a photograph: the image of Jerry's body laying in the dark woods, his open eyes and mouth filling with rain.

He'll turn up, he assured himself. *He'll show up with a big grin on his face, I just know it.*

With a sigh, Lewis backed away from the window and crawled into the dry safety of his bed. He lay awake, staring at the window, until his exhausted brain forced sleep upon him.

Lewis was in the woods shouting for Jerry. The sky was clear, the sun bright and hot. He ran down an unfamiliar trail, shouting the boy's name, fleeing something on the path behind him. He ran as hard as he could but moved at half-speed, like running underwater, his feet sinking into the deep sand of the trail. The train whistle blared behind him, the bleating sound devouring his shouts. Lewis turned to see his pursuer, but saw nothing through the thick growth of the strange trail. The familiar chugging of the locomotive bore down on him, the ground quaking beneath his feet. The train's whistle changed. It became a human scream, a wail of pain rising into a deafening shriek of hatred. The thumping wheels morphed into the blustering roar and crackle of fire. Lewis turned and ran again as the screaming blaze pursued. The thing behind him closed in, a lioness stalking her prey, close enough for Lewis to smell the rotting meat stench of its hot breath as it blew across the back of his exposed neck.

Lewis snapped awake, face down in bed, the dream dissipating like mist. A strange scream echoed in his head. He touched the back of his neck, the skin warm and slick with sweat. The morning sun beat down on him through the window. He now recognized the scream. It came from the kettle. His mom must be making her morning tea.

When the incessant sound persisted, Lewis arose to

investigate. He found the kitchen empty, removed the kettle from the burner, and called out, "Mom?"

No answer; she must be outside.

Lewis dressed and stepped onto his front porch and into a scene from a movie. His street bustled with activity despite the early morning heat and humidity. Several police cars and a fire engine were parked at the end of the road, in the grass field leading into the woods. Lewis felt shame over his excitement, but cops and firemen were seldom seen in Poisonwood Estates, and never this many at once. But he realized what this meant—Jerry had never come home. The events from the day before came pouring back in.

Children and their parents milled around to see what all the commotion was about. Most of them had to know already, making Lewis a little nervous; he couldn't help but feel slightly responsible for Jerry's disappearance.

He heard his name called and searched the crowd for the familiar voice. Clinton pushed some younger kids out of the way, ignored their sour looks, and jogged over to the porch, a mingling of concern and fascination gleaming on his face.

"Dude, have you heard?" Clinton asked.

"What?"

"Jerry never came home and they haven't found him yet. They're searching the woods for them right now."

"Them?"

"Yeah. Andy and Jason never came home last night either."

"Shit," Lewis blurted. "I knew those jerks had something to do with this."

"Probably," Clinton said, nodding.

"Have they found anything?"

"Not that I've heard."

For Lewis, Clinton, and several neighborhood kids, most of the day was spent answering the same questions over and over from police and parents alike: *Do you know the boys? Are you friends with the boys? Enemies? What kind of relationship does Jerry have with the twins? Do you know if they do drugs? Do* you *do drugs?*

By the end of the questioning, Lewis could sense their suspicions mirrored his own: the Reed twins more than likely had something to do with Jerry's disappearance.

Lewis thanked the stars the focus stayed on finding the boys, and not on why Jerry had gone into the woods in the first place. But he caught glances from Jerry's parents as they spoke with the authorities, subtle glances that held a glimmer of blame in them. Or maybe he was just being paranoid. Lewis didn't see Mr. or Mrs. Reed anywhere, but the twins' older sister stood about, chain-smoking cigarettes and answering questions.

By the end of the day rumors were spreading like wildfire among his friends. Lewis heard some boys say Andy and Jason killed Jerry, chopped his body into small pieces, and buried them throughout the woods, and then ran away, probably stealing a car. Others claimed a child molester kidnapped all three boys and killed them, or had them tied up in a basement somewhere, torturing them. Lewis and his peers apparently shared the same morbid fascination with the macabre.

The most ridiculous rumor by far, claimed that Crappy—the legendary giant alligator living in Horse

Crap Lake—had all the boys for supper, storing the remains of their carcasses in the sewers for later consumption. Crappy the Alligator was just a fun story the neighborhood kids told each other, and a child molester didn't seem feasible—Andy and Jason could defend themselves. However, the first rumor wasn't all that farfetched to Lewis. He knew Andy and Jason Reed well enough, and it didn't take a stretch of the imagination to envision them as sadistic murderers.

As Lewis watched the concerned faces of the crowd, the photo image of Jerry returned—the dead eyes and gaping mouth filled with rainwater. Only this time, Andy and Jason were standing over the still body.

They were laughing.

II

A FEAST OF VENGEANCE

T he rigorous search for the missing boys lasted until nighttime crept over the woods. Not a single clue had been found, the heavy rain from the previous night hampering the searchers' progress, the soggy ground slowing them down. Lewis figured the rain would have washed away any evidence anyhow.

Once again the events of the day left Lewis drained, not to mention a little frightened. He had watched enough horror movies to know this type of situation always ended poorly. *This is real life not a movie,* Lewis repeated to himself several times, but his twisted imagination kept showing him snippets of a horror film starring Jerry and the evil twins, directed by Lewis Frazier.

With access to the woods denied, Lewis, Clinton and Justin had ridden their bikes around the neighborhood, trying their best to occupy their minds with mundane thoughts, pushing their worries for Jerry to the side for a while. For a change, Lewis was thankful when he heard his mother calling him home. He decided to stay indoors after supper, and noticed his mother's look of relief. He wondered what his mother had been imagining all day while she too tried occupying her time with meaningless tasks.

Later, Lewis turned off the television he wasn't watching anyway, kissed his mother, and marched off toward his room. He read for a while—*The Three Investigators* solving yet another mystery for Alfred Hitchcock— before finally throwing in the towel.

Lewis brushed his teeth, his tired face staring back at him like a stranger from the bathroom mirror, an older version of himself. The image of Jerry fleeing into the woods looped in his mind. Lewis hoped it wasn't the last memory he would have of the sickly boy. He returned to his room and turned off the light, the faintly glowing square of his window challenging him to create a new horror scene. He flopped into bed instead, skipping the ritual of the hedges altogether this time, fearful of the images his warped and worried mind might conjure.

Sleep came faster for Lewis this night, the accumulative affects of two days of stress wearing him down. He slept solid for several hours until something awoke him from deep sleep, his eyes springing open like miniature jack-in-the-box lids. He glanced at the glowing digits of the alarm clock; they read *2:03*. Confused as to what had jolted him from his slumber, Lewis propped himself on his elbows, searching the shadows of the dark room with sleep-fogged eyes. He'd forgotten to turn on the nightlight. The streetlight shining through the window was his only source of light, bringing the faint shadows of his room into focus as his eyes adjusted to the gloom.

The eyes from the *Dawn of the Dead* poster on his wall stared back in the dark, sending a shiver through him. He unlocked his gaze from the zombie on the poster, and searched his room some more. Except for his breathing—which was faster than normal—and the gentle click of the loose ceiling fan as it swayed back and forth, he heard nothing out of the ordinary.

Nothing. Must have been dreaming, he decided.

Satisfied he was alone in the room, Lewis shut his weighted lids and let his head fall back onto the soft pillow. He yawned heavily and his breathing slowed. Soon, Lewis teetered on the cliff of sleep. He was about to fall from the precipice into the land of dreams, when the sound of laughter forced his eyes open again. Stiff as a board, Lewis lay in bed. His skin shuddered from the wave of ice water rolling through his veins from toes to scalp. He waited for the sound to repeat itself.

The room remained silent. Lewis once again assured himself he'd been dreaming.

The faint laughter reached him again, mocking his conviction. It came from outside, through the open window. From somewhere close.

It's just someone laughing, he thought.

Then why am I scared shitless?

Peeling the thin sheet away, Lewis crept from his bed, wincing at the creak of the bed springs, terrified to break the silence left in the wake of the laugh. He stood, reached for the light, and stopped with his finger touching the switch; something inside Lewis pleaded with him to leave the light off, to stay hidden in the shadows. He obeyed the inner warning, and in the dark, shuffled across the carpet to the open window, forcing his legs against their will, his ears straining to pick up any sounds. The night exuded an uncharacteristic hush. The buzz of crickets and cicadas— normally active on a sweltering night like tonight—were nonexistent.

Lewis looked out the window at the quiet and empty street. Nothing moved under the pale glow of the street-lights. The houses he could see from his window were dark except for their porch lights. Despite the unusual quiet, all seemed normal. He glanced across the street toward the home of Old Man Boyd. Everything was as it should be, the silhouettes of the four skinny bushes stood out on the old man's front lawn.

Lewis did a double take.

Four bushes?

Lewis froze as one of the bushes peeled away from the other three and sprouted arms, then legs, taking the form of a person. The dark shape walked from the shadows, across the old man's yard toward Lewis, and stopped. Lewis could feel the uncontrollable tremor spread throughout his body like an electric current as he recognized the figure. Standing on the edge of his street, bathed in the puddle of light from the streetlamp, stood Jerry Harris.

Lewis crouched as instinct took over, his wide eyes peeking over the sill, locked onto the lurking figure across the street. Jerry swiveled his head from side to side like any normal kid would do, checking both ways before crossing the street, a huge grin on his face. Only, this kid didn't look normal, the smile too big, like the skeleton in science class. Lewis couldn't pinpoint it, but something definitely seemed out of sorts with Jerry. His clothes were stained dark and shimmered with wetness, the whiteness of his teeth glowed in contrast to his grimy face.

Resisting the urge to call out his friend's name, Lewis clamped his mouth shut, covering it with his hand. Jerry walked into the middle of the street, stopped, and walked out of view, headed in the direction of the woods, his stride confident and almost cheerful.

Lewis turned and sat down hard under the window, his back sliding down the wall as his heart bounced up his chest, threatening to jump out of his open mouth onto his lap. He gasped for air, realizing he had held his breath during the entire incident.

That was Jerry!

That was not *Jerry!*

Waiting until his heart dropped from his throat back to its normal position, Lewis turned and grabbed hold of the windowsill, and like a rock climber clinging for life, pulled himself up by his fingertips and peered over the sill.

The street appeared empty.

He stood up and pressed his face against the rough screen, trying his best to see further down the street, not sure if he *wanted* to see anything. Nothing there. He looked across at the three innocent bushes standing guard. No Jerry.

The insects started their nightly performance as if nothing had happened.

What did just happen? Did I really see what I think I

saw? Did I dream that? Was that another one of my weird nightmares?

Lewis pinched his arm to confirm he wasn't dreaming —the pain seemed real enough. He left his room, crept down the hallway, slithering across the thick carpet of the living room toward his mother's bedroom, stopping in front of her closed door. He lifted his fist to knock, then dropped his hand back to his side. He was already starting to doubt what he'd seen, the image of his missing friend seeming less corporeal with every passing second, fading like a dream upon awakening. He could picture his mother stroking his head, telling him in a soothing voice that it was just that, a dream, not to worry and go back to bed.

He listened to her soft snores on the other side of the door and decided against waking her. What exactly would he tell her anyway? He wanted to be sure. He had to be sure. The only way to do that would be to look for himself. Until he did, he wouldn't be sleeping tonight.

Back in his room, Lewis put on jeans and sneakers, crept down the hallway again, this time heading for the front door. The thick shag carpet masked his movements as he passed his mother's room, her slow breathing still audible.

He unlocked the front door, the metallic click deafening in the silent house, and turned the handle. He had to see for himself, to make sure he wasn't dreaming, or crazy. He opened the door, thankful for the freshly oiled hinges, and looked down the street before stepping onto the front porch, closing the door behind him, taking care not to lock himself out.

Standing on the stoop, Lewis felt exposed under the glow of the porch light, like being on stage for a school play, the whole world watching. His street remained quiet, the houses still dark except for their own porch lights that always burned through the night. He hoped everyone was asleep at this hour. The sight of a twelve-year-old boy wandering around would definitely raise suspicion, especially with today's chaos.

He stood there on the porch, unsure of what to do next. Lewis shrugged to nobody and walked to the spot in the street where he had seen Jerry. *Thought* he had seen Jerry. He turned to his bedroom window to get a fix on the proper position. Lewis stared at the dark square of his window and imagined himself crouched below the opening, hiding from Jerry. He wondered again why he had stayed hidden, what instinct had kept him from turning on the light and shouting Jerry's name?

I was afraid, he thought. *Something about Jerry scared the crap out of me.*

He shook the thought away. Cursing himself for forgetting a flashlight, Lewis bent down to look for evidence of the boy's existence. It only took a second to find something. The dark stain, illuminated by the streetlamp, stood out on the road at his feet, in the exact spot Jerry had been standing.

Blood, was the first thought to enter his mind. Lewis shook his head.

It's just water, or motor oil, that's all.

Lewis stood still, studying the stain, convincing himself of its innocent nature, when he heard it again— the same sinister laugh that had yanked him from deep sleep. It sounded far away, barely audible, but unmistakable against the hum of insects and quiet of the night.

Rooted to the spot, Lewis felt as if his skin had suddenly constricted over his entire body at once, like wearing a suit three sizes too small. His sneakers adhered to the macadam, his leg muscles like cold stone. Lewis wanted to run, the distance of the laugh not far enough for comfort, unwillingly stuck in a crouch in the middle of the road. He took a deep breath and turned his gaze in the direction of the sound. Without a doubt, the laugh had come from the dark woods at the end of his street.

As control of his body crept back in, Lewis stood. He stared down his street, toward the wall of impenetrable blackness at the end of the grass field. He turned to look at the front door of his home, then back to the dark woods. Lewis rifled through his options until he came to a decision.

I'm going into those woods. I need to know.

But first, he had to make one stop.

"Clinton, wake up."

Clinton rolled over, grunted, and fell back to sleep.

"Hey, wake up," Lewis hissed, tapping on the screen, causing it to rattle in its frame. Lewis heard another grunt, some shuffling, and Clinton's sleepy face appeared at the window.

"What?" moaned Clinton, scratching his head through a mop of crazed blonde hair.

"Quiet," whispered Lewis. "Meet me out back."

"Lewis?"

"Yeah. Wake up and meet me out back."

"I'm sleeping," whined Clinton.

"Just do it. It's important."

"All right. Stop making so much noise." Clinton's face disappeared so Lewis made his way to the back door like a thief in the night.

The journey to Clinton's house had been quiet and

uneventful, but terrifying nonetheless. Lewis had wanted to ride his bike to his friend's house, but there'd been no way to retrieve it from the garage without waking his mother; the inside door to the garage was in his parents' bedroom, and the big metal door on the outside made too much of a racket when slid open. So, he'd made the trip on foot.

Lewis kept expecting to hear the laugh from every yard he passed, turning his head around every few feet, sure there would be somebody following him. More than once, he almost lost his nerve, thinking himself crazy for even considering going into the woods, the safety of his room beckoning for his return. He doggedly plodded on, if there was one person that would believe him, it was his best friend.

Clinton, wearing only cut-off sweatpants, rubbing his eyes and shuffling like the undead, stepped through the back door into the shadowed back yard. Chewy—his brown, scraggly-haired mutt—followed him, moving off to the bushes, uninterested in Lewis.

Lewis raised his hands and pleaded, "I know it's late but this is super important."

"What?" Clinton asked, still whining. "Do you know what time it is? If my folks wake up I'm dead."

Lewis sucked in a deep breath before saying, "I saw Jerry, dude."

"What?" Clinton repeated. "Where? When?"

"In the street, outside my window, like, fifteen minutes ago."

Clinton rested his hands on his hips and offered Lewis a half-grin. "What was he doing?" Clinton's tone suggested he was prepared for a practical joke, or he questioned his friend's sanity.

Lewis paused, his brow furrowing. "He was … smiling."

Clinton waited for Lewis to say more, realized his friend was serious, then said, "So he's okay then. That's awesome."

"No," Lewis said, staring at the ground, "that's the thing. I have a feeling he's not okay. It wasn't … a good smile." He lifted his head and met Clinton's sleepy eyes. "You know what I mean?"

"Not really," admitted Clinton, shrugging, and shaking his head.

Lewis sighed. "It looked like Jerry. It was Jerry, but … I felt like I was looking at a total stranger. Something was weird about his eyes and the way he was smiling. It just felt … wrong.

"Does that make *any* sense?" Lewis asked.

"Nope. Not really."

"You think I'm crazy," Lewis said.

Clinton smiled. "I know you're crazy. Where is he now?"

"I'm pretty sure he went into the woods. I wanna go find him."

Clinton stood there with his hands on his hips, nodding at Lewis, then his eyes popped open as he realized what his friend meant. "What, now? At night? In the woods? You *are* crazy."

"Shhh. We won't go in that far, okay. I just want to check it out. Who knows, maybe I was only dreaming, but I really don't think I was."

Clinton sighed and watched as Chewy trotted through the dog door, done with his business. He turned back to Lewis and stared at his friend for several seconds. "Okay," Clinton said, caving in, the pleading look in Lewis's eyes not giving him much choice. "I'll go get dressed and grab a flashlight. Be right back."

Clinton turned and walked back into his house. As he passed under the outdoor light, a dark bruise stood out on his back, just below his left shoulder blade. Lewis assumed it was from the war, and shook his head at the events that have unfolded since that fun-filled afternoon just over a day ago; the victory he had so desired, now trivial.

Upon Clinton's return, the boys agreed it would be much faster to climb Clinton's back fence and cut through the Nelson's yard to the next street over instead of walking all the way around—the Nelsons were in their eighties, half deaf, and slept like the dead. This route would also keep them off the street, unseen by anyone that happened to still be awake. The boys had used this path with great success many times, just never this late at night. In fact, they've never done anything this late at night.

The first hiccup in the boys' quest came before they even left Clinton's side of the fence. They were in the process of scaling the rickety chain-link—Lewis straddling the only stretch of fence clear of bushes, his toes hooked in for purchase as the fence wobbled to and fro, and Clinton waiting to hand over the bulky flashlight—when a fierce hiss froze the blood in their veins.

"What the hell is that?" Lewis asked in a shaking whisper, his grip tightening on the cross bar of the fence as he nearly lost his balance.

Clinton jumped back. "Snake … don't move."

"Use the flashlight, jackass," Lewis whispered over the malicious hissing. "Shine it in front of me."

Clinton thumbed the switch, directing the powerful beam at the top of the fence just in front of Lewis. Six inches from his friend's crotch, partially obscured by the bushes, perched a massive demon with glistening black eyes, bared yellow fangs, and coarse, matted gray fur. The creature's muscles fluttered, its sharp talons clasped to the top bar of the fence, ready to lunge and tear a chunk from Lewis's privates.

With a clicking of claws, the beast lurched forward, its tapered snout full of needle-like fangs coming in for a taste. Both boys released a high-pitched scream, instantly covering their mouths. Lewis tumbled off the fence, crashing hard into Clinton, sending them both to the ground in a tangle of limbs. Lewis groped for the fallen light, retrieved it, and illuminated the creature.

"Holy shit," Clinton exhaled. "It's just a 'possum."

"An opossum," Lewis corrected, gasping.

"Whatever you call it, I think I just shit my pants. Maybe we should go the long way before we wake up the entire street," Clinton said, glancing back at his house, expecting to see lights flick on at any second.

"Sounds good to me," Lewis agreed, staring at the frightened, innocent marsupial in the glare of the light.

Clinton stood and dusted himself off. "This is starting out crappy, Lewis. I hope you know what you're doing. Are you sure you saw him?"

Lewis stood and passed the light back to Clinton. "I wasn't dreaming if that's what you mean. There was a kid outside my house. And that kid looked just like Jerry. And if I told my mom everything I told you, she would think I'm bat shit crazy. I'm going into the woods to find him. You with me or not?"

After a short pause, Clinton said, "Yeah, I'm with you. Let's go."

Together they headed off toward the woods—the long way—to search for Jerry, ignoring the omen crouched on the fence, warning them to go back home.

Back to the safety of their beds.

While the boys were having their encounter with the demon on the fence, Maggie Burton lounged on her sofa watching television a few streets over, just a few doors down from Lewis's house. At thirty-eight years old, Maggie was divorced and living alone, which suited her just fine after a troubled marriage like the one she had endured for a decade. Sometimes she would get lonely, but it was a small price to pay for her freedom. She'd been enjoying that freedom—watching whatever she wanted, whenever she wanted, without having to worry about being verbally and physically abused by a drunk husband—when a knock at the front door sent her good spirits spiraling away, dropping a shroud of dread upon her like a damp blanket.

Knowing it must be her ex-husband, and knowing he would be drunk and possibly belligerent, Maggie took her time answering the knock. She sighed hard, slapped her knees, stood, and moped to the front door.

Gazing through the peephole, she was surprised to see an empty porch instead of the familiar drunk face swaying under the glare of the outdoor light.

She opened the door, poked her head out, and looked around. "Dave?" she asked the quiet night. "I'm going to call the cops if you don't leave me alone. Remember that little thing called a restraining order?"

No response. Not even the crickets answered her.

Her porch, and the entire street for that matter, remained silent as a tomb. She searched the driveway and street for Dave's truck. Her Datsun sat alone in the drive, the street empty. She quickly shut and locked the door (the absolute silence unnerved her more than actually having to deal with the drunken jerk) and returned to the den where the couch and the soothing, faithful glow of her television awaited her. She turned up the volume with the remote, preparing to plop back down onto the sofa, when another knock boomed out, much louder this time, shaking the door on its hinges.

She threw the remote onto the couch and stomped to the door, her anger increasing with every step. Furious, she skipped the peephole, unlocked the door, and flung it wide open.

"Listen you son of a …"

She recognized Andy and Jason Reed at once. The young punks had come by the house on a few occasions to buy joints from her ex-husband; she hated the way they leered at her, especially the one time they stopped by after she had kicked Dave out.

Her eyes moved from one boy to the other. Their heads were down as if studying the socks on her feet, their filthy hair glistening under the light. Then she noticed Jason's grimy hand holding a dirty bundle of what appeared to be some sort of wet rope against his belly.

"Are you guys okay?" she asked. "Everyone's been looking for—"

She stopped when the smell hit her, causing her to retch—the rotten stench of dead animal.

The boys raised their pale faces into the light and smiled. A puckering hole in Andy's throat dribbled dark fluid onto his stained shirt. When she saw this, and looked into the boys' yellow eyes, she knew something was most definitely wrong. They were already reaching through the doorway, pushing her back, before she could even consider shutting the door.

Jason's guts smacked the front step as he reached out and seized Maggie's throat, stopping her scream dead in her lungs. He waded in, entering the woman's home, his feet punting his unfurling intestines, lassoing Maggie's retreating ankles as he squeezed her delicate neck. She tipped backward toward the floor, both hands grabbing Jason's wrists, unable to free her throat from the vice-like grip, her breath and voice shut off like a bent garden hose. White flashes like bursting light bulbs filled her vision, and a low hum invaded her head as she felt her body tilting backward.

… *She's in the shallows of the river, just a child, being baptized under the summer sun, the preacher's prayer muffled as she's submerged into the cool water, the sun's glare sifting through the dancing leaves of the trees at the river's edge, sparkling across her tightly sealed eyes like gemstones.*

Jason knelt with Maggie as she fell, slamming her head

onto the tile floor, the back of her skull cracking like a gunshot.

… *She hears a muffled pop, like the sound of a firecracker tossed into a well, the report reverberating in her head. She opens her eyes to blackness; she's in the dark well, the minor explosion hammering her skull, her body sinking into the frigid water at the bottom, the circle of light above shrinking to a pinhole.*

Her arms flailed, punching the air twice before slapping back down to the floor, her hands flopping weakly like dying fish in the bottom of a boat.

… *She floats from the cold water, the glowing circle of sun above growing larger until it fills her fully with its soothing warm light.*

Andy followed his brother into Maggie's home, eased the door shut, and unsheathed the hunting knife from his brother's belt, savoring the sight of the dark puddle expanding from the woman's ruined skull like a blooming rose. Beaming with excitement, Andy knelt on the opposite side of the woman's prone figure, raised the blade above his head with both hands, and brought it down on Maggie Burton's mid-section with such force the tip snapped off when it met the tile floor beneath her. With the broken knife, Andy perforated the dead woman's belly over and over again like a sewing machine; her blood and viscera filled the air, coating the furniture and walls.

Using his hands, Andy pried the mutilated abdomen wide, dipped his entire head into the intestinal soup, and slurped, breathing in the woman's fluids like a drowning victim gasping for precious air. Jason made similar noises while gorging on the dead woman's throat, his front teeth shattering to pieces as he chomped into her spine.

From the other room, canned laughter spewed from the television, accompanying the ill-mannered feeding frenzy.

❧

SHE COULD FEEL the energy coursing through her as the boys devoured the woman. The beautiful salty taste of the woman's blood and flesh filled her mouth, as if she were there, partaking in the much-needed meal herself. She felt alive when she fed. She felt unstoppable, the life-giving nectar affecting her like a narcotic.

The weak inhabitants of this place would be hers, just like so many times before. Her long absence has turned out to be a blessing; she could not sense any fear or knowledge of her in the minds of the boys.

She has been forgotten over the years.

She lounged in her new hiding place—the labyrinth of underground tunnels she saw in the boys' minds, the sewers and drains beneath the streets. She relaxed, safe, as her others fed, feeding her, making her stronger.

Her time has come again. This time she had plenty of flesh to choose from, conveniently located in her woods.

Her own personal larder.

15

E scaping detection despite Clinton's nervous chatter throughout the entire journey, the boys stood at the entrance to the woods, the wall of vegetation looming before them like an oily black tidal wave against the night sky. The only sounds present were the hissing of their tense breathing and the constant drone of frogs and insects.

Staring into the black, dense tangle of vine-choked forest, Lewis wished he had never looked out his bedroom window earlier. The incident with the opossum had shaken his nerves, but not his determination to find out if Jerry had been standing outside his window, on his street, or if he had imagined the entire ordeal.

"Maybe he didn't go into the woods, dude," Clinton whispered for the third time. "I mean you didn't actually *see* him go in did you?"

"No ... I heard laughter coming from this way."

"That could have been anyone," Clinton said. "It was

probably someone watching a *Saturday Night Live* rerun too loud or something."

Lewis snorted. "In the woods? No. It was Jerry. And something was wrong with him."

"Did the laugh sound like Jerry's? That wheezing Muttley laugh he has?"

The question surprised Lewis. He hadn't thought about it at the time, but the laugh had definitely not sounded like Jerry's. It had been clear, as if the boy's asthma had been miraculously cured.

"Yeah," Lewis lied, unsure of why he felt the need to do so. "It was Muttley."

Clinton clicked the flashlight and directed the bright beam into the woods; the blackness swallowed the light. Lewis felt as if he could reach out and touch the dark—a physical barrier—believing his finger would disappear as if dipped in ink. He tilted his face to the sky; the moon was nowhere to be seen, hidden somewhere behind a blanket of clouds.

"It's so dark," whispered Clinton, as if reading Lewis's thoughts.

Lewis held out his hand. "Give me the light, I'll go in first."

Clinton passed it over and asked, "You notice something weird?"

"What, you?" Lewis said, a lame attempt to lift the tension.

Ignoring the quip, Clinton whispered, "The bugs stopped, dude."

Clinton was right. Their heavy breathing was the only sound. No bugs or frogs sang, no breeze rustled the trees, nothing scurried from their approach. Lewis had the feeling the woods were listening to them, eavesdropping on their conversation.

"Maybe we should go home," suggested Clinton. "Come back tomorrow morning when it's light out."

"Clinton, I'm going in. With, or without you."

"All right … jeez, which way?"

Lewis thought for a moment before saying, "We can take the main trail straight out. Then we can head back on the trail that comes out near the wall behind Old Man Boyd's house. If we don't find anything, we can cut through his yard and we're back at my house. How's that sound?"

"Sounds great," Clinton said with a sarcastic grin, then muttered, "I hope we don't find anything."

Lewis breached the veil of darkness and entered the woods, Clinton following on his heels. The flashlight's beam made the surrounding shadows even darker, the gloom an actual weight on their bodies, a living entity crowding in from all sides. Several yards in, Lewis paused to listen to the silence. Clinton tapped him on the shoulder, causing him to jump. "Go," he urged. "Let's get this over with so I can go back to bed."

They followed the trail for several minutes, the sound of their progress painfully loud in the silent woods, stopping often to listen, all the while searching the ground for any sign of Jerry's presence. They sloshed through lingering puddles on the trail where the day's sun had not been able to reach.

Lewis scanned the forest floor with the light, his eyes following the bright circle like a hypnotist's medallion.

The woods seemed dead to Lewis, undisturbed, and he had a sense they'd chosen the wrong path, that Jerry hadn't come this way. Regardless, he continued forward, compelled to move deeper as if pulled by the beam of light.

They came to the mouth of the connecting trail leading back to the neighborhood. Lewis walked past it without a glance, concentrating on the ground at his feet.

"Hey," Clinton hissed. "We're going this way, remember?"

Lewis illuminated the mouth of the trail. Clinton stood there, vehemently stabbing his index finger toward the opening. Lewis sighed, nodded, and started down this new path. The trail looped out, cutting deep into the woods before swinging back toward the homes. They passed the location of their secret fort, hidden under piles of leafy camouflage. Lewis, Clinton, and Justin were the only ones who knew of its existence.

Clinton stopped to admire their handiwork. "We should work on the hideout tomorrow, make it even more invisible."

"Yeah, sure," Lewis grunted in agreement, scanning the ground with the light.

The boys trudged along, the woods offering no clues or sounds to validate Lewis's claims. They finally reached the retaining wall separating the woods from Old Man Boyd's back yard.

Most folks with homes bordering the woods dumped their grass clippings and yard trimmings over the wall— Mr. Boyd was no exception. Mountains of the dead grass reached to the lip of the wall in several spots. The boys sank into the saturated mounds as they hiked up, filthy water welling up around their feet, filling their sneakers. Their skin instantly itched from the disturbed top layer of sun-dried clippings.

Lewis's wavering light flashed across something red, half buried in the prickly grass. He trained the beam on it. "Clinton. What's that?"

Clinton waded over and picked it up. "Holy shit. It's Jerry's mask," he said, his chin dropping. "You were right, he was here."

Clinton held the damp *Spider-Man* mask in front of him with the tips of two fingers as Lewis tromped over to inspect the find, the slashing beam of his flashlight swimming with disturbed grass particles. That's when the boys heard the distant laugh, seemingly turning the steamy night air cold in an instant. They hunkered down, shoulders touching, backpedaling to the wall, pressing their backs against the rough cinder blocks, eyes focused on the dark woods from which they believed the sound had originated.

With their attention focused on the woods in front of them, neither boy noticed the scowling face scrutinizing them from above, looming over the wall. Or its wild eyes burning twin holes in the tops of their heads.

Until it spoke.

"What are you kids doin' out here this late?"

Lewis gasped, dropping the light. Clinton cried out, "Don't kill me!"

"Is that you, Lewis?" the voice asked.

"Mr. Boyd?" Lewis croaked, his mouth bone dry.

"Yes. Now get your butts over here," commanded Mr. Boyd.

Lewis retrieved the flashlight. The boys climbed the wall, eager to be out of the woods, their hearts still pounding in their chest as they stood in front of the man, the whites of his eyes glaring in the darkness.

"Turn that thing off," Mr. Boyd said, gesturing toward the light, slurring the words together. He swayed back and forth, and Lewis could now make out the sour tang of booze wafting from the old man. "That one of you mule-heads out there cacklin' like the devil?"

"No, sir," Lewis said. Lowering his head, he added, "You wouldn't believe me if I told you who I think it is."

"You think it's one of them missing boys, don'tcha?" the old man said with indifference. He raised a can of beer to his lips and slurped.

Both boys gazed at the man, slack-jawed, unable to speak.

Mr. Boyd scratched the gray stubble on his cheek and nodded. "You boys go on home now. I won't tell your folks I seen ya out so late. But don't go messin' around them woods no more. They've gone bad." He turned his head and spat on the ground like a man who'd just discovered a worm in his apple.

Lewis regained his ability to speak. "Mr. Boyd, why would you say—"

"Go home," he snapped, waving the beer in the air.

Clinton grabbed Lewis by the arm. "Yessir, we're going, sorry we bothered you."

Clinton pulled the stammering Lewis across the back

yard, through the old man's front gate, across the street and onto Lewis's front lawn.

"What are you doing?" whispered Lewis, yanking his arm free.

"Getting us away from that crazy old man, that's what."

"He knows something," Lewis hissed, pointing at the home of Mr. Boyd.

"Yeah, no shit," Clinton agreed, raising the wet mask still clutched in his fist. "He obviously had something to do with whatever happened to Jerry, and probably the twins. We need to show this to someone."

"They searched those woods all day," Lewis said. He grabbed the mask and shook it at Clinton. "How did they miss this when we found it in the dark?"

"Maybe he just tossed it over. I mean, what is he doing up at this time of night?"

"The same thing we are, stupid," Lewis said, lowering his voice to a whisper again. "That weird laugh woke him up. Look, I've lived across from him my whole life, he's a little weird, but I know he wouldn't hurt anybody. Besides, it doesn't explain what I saw, or what we heard, or what he said. I'm sure Jerry dropped this recently."

"You're crazy. That old guy probably killed all three of them."

"Then who did I see earlier?"

Clinton shrugged. "Probably Jerry's ghost."

Lewis smiled. "And you call me crazy?"

"What are we supposed to do then?"

Lewis pointed across the street again. "I'm going over

to his house tomorrow to find out what he knows, and you're coming with me."

"Why would I do that?"

"Would you rather explain to your parents what you were doing out here at three in the morning?"

"Blackmail? That's messed up, Lewis," Clinton said, then pointed to his friend. "Wait, you won't say anything because you'll get in trouble too."

"Don't care," Lewis said, shaking his head and crossing his arms.

Clinton stared at the determined look on his friend's face. "Okay," he sighed, giving in once again. "But if that maniac kills us and buries our bodies in his back yard, it's your fault."

"Awesome. Come over in the morning and we'll see what he knows. If he won't talk to us, then we show someone the mask. Okay?"

"Okay … see you tomorrow. That is if I can make it back into my house without getting caught," Clinton said, then added under his breath, "you're gonna get us killed." He turned and sauntered off in the direction of his house. "Dumbass," he whispered to himself.

❧

AFTER THE TWINS finished feasting on the carcass of Maggie Burton, the thing inside Jerry's corpse instructed them to put the shredded remains into garbage bags from the woman's kitchen, and dump the bundles into the stinking lake she had gleaned from their minds; it was a waste, but she was sated for now, and she preferred to feast on fresh meat. The boys—each looking like an evil Santa —shouldered the bags and made their way through the woods, passing the trail Lewis and Clinton had journeyed down just moments earlier. They tossed the gore-filled sacks into the deepest part of the lake, watching them sink. Thick, black bubbles popped on the lake's surface as the bags filled with the foul water.

There wasn't much she could do about the mess made of the woman's dwelling, her fervent lust for warm flesh and blood had taken over, the frenzied attack beyond her control for a brief moment. Harvesting memories from the boys' minds, she knew the woman lived alone and hoped nobody would discover the macabre redecoration of the home until her siege was in full force.

Having the twin boys as her first victims and servants proved very fortunate indeed. They were big, strong, and seemed to have an intense dislike for everyone. Even though the boys were quite dead, their brains still had a trickle of life; she could sense their memories and strongest emotions—which in their case, turned out to be hate. Their deviant minds and malevolent hatred toward everyone and everything gave her valuable insight on many of the inhabitants of her new domain. She adored the human mind: so weak and pliant, easily usurped after death, basic carnal instincts the strongest emotions leftover in a resurrected corpse. Conversely, the memories of her current vessel did not offer much information on the area and its people. She sensed mostly fear and loneliness in its mind.

After disposing of the remains, she called the boys back to her new lair, the place she had foraged from their heads—the system of drainage tunnels underneath the streets and homes. The perfect refuge. She could hide during the day and hunt at night, using the storm drains and manholes to come and go as she pleased, snatching her meals from the bounty of human cattle. She no longer concerned herself with guarding the tree; as far as she knew, there was no way to destroy the dismal cell. It had been meant to imprison her forever, but she had discovered a way to break free—albeit until her vessel expired. She had no clue as to what would happen if the tree somehow did fall once she was liberated from its grip.

Thoughts of her tree brought with it snippets of memories. *Her* memories. However, as usual, she viewed these slideshow of images as if they belonged to another being, from another time.

She closed her eyes and let the scenes with their accompanying emotions play out: a woman's burnt corpse, the scent of cooked flesh filling the air; sorrow for the dead woman, replaced instantly with murderous rage; joy, as she spread disease amongst the people responsible for the woman's death; anger at the men who'd finally captured her, ending her orgy of pestilence, strapping her to the tree; torturous pain, as the flames engulfed her own body.

Then, her true life had started, with her first vessel, and the uncontrollable urge for revenge.

And her all-consuming newfound lust for blood.

Her second death had come after many more reprisals. Then nothing for a long, long time. She slept. She dreamed. She plotted, her need for retribution germinating, flourishing. Finally, she'd awakened in a new vessel, in this strange land.

Her land.

She opened her new eyes and the visions faded. Distant memories of a distant past. She focused on the present, on her quest for flesh and blood—on her vengeance.

As she rested in the musty tunnels beneath the inhabitants of Poisonwood Estates—sated, her belly full—she rifled through the twins simple, devious memories like thumbing through the pages of a mindlessly boring book, searching for pertinent information. One word kept peeking through the clutter of their minds more than any other—a name. An image of a scrawny, pale youth accompanied the offensive word. The name of a boy not well liked by the pair. A name also known by her vessel.

Lewis.

16

Lewis was finishing his bowl of cereal, slurping the sweetened milk leftover, when the familiar knock came at the front door. He placed the bowl in the kitchen sink, jogged to the door, and returned the shave and a haircut with his two bits. He opened the door to a frowning Clinton, shoulders slumped, the antithesis of Lewis's exited mood.

Lewis clapped his hands together with a loud pop. "Let's go see what the old guy has to say, shall we?"

Despite having trouble sleeping after last night's excitement, Lewis felt energized. His first thought upon rising from bed that morning was to tell his mother everything, but reconsidered when he visualized the look on Jerry's face, and recalled the flippant, then aggressive reaction of Mr. Boyd. Something strange was going on, and Lewis meant to find out what it was.

Clinton raised a finger, but Lewis closed the door, pushing past his friend before he could make a better suggestion. Dejected, Clinton followed Lewis as he marched across the street to the home of Mr. Boyd. Glancing to the right, the boys could see a squad car and a few people milling about the grass field, the search for the missing boys resuming. This sight fueled Lewis's need for an explanation from the old man. He passed the three bushes on the front lawn without notice; during the light of day they were just bushes.

Lewis mounted the porch and stepped to the front door. He hesitated, fist raised, poised to knock, his bravery suddenly seeping away as he stood on the old man's porch. Before he could muster the courage to either bring his fist down, or turn back toward home, the door swung open with an eerie creak. Mr. Boyd—sporting a wife-beater tank top that bulged at the belly, Bermuda shorts, and blacks socks—blocked the doorway, a frown of disgust greeting the paralyzed boys on his doorstep.

When the boys remained silent, Mr. Boyd asked, "What do you mule-heads want?"

Lewis stammered, the slippery muscle in his mouth ignoring his mental commands, " … Uh … we want to talk … about last night. About what you said you thought … we thought … the laughing in the woods was."

"Huh?" Mr. Boyd said with a smirk, one eyebrow raised like a comma.

Lewis wrangled his tongue into submission and said, "What you said about the laugh belonging to one of the missing kids."

Mr. Boyd stared at Lewis with blood-shot eyes. "Trust me, boy. You don't wanna know."

"Know what?" Lewis asked.

"Go on. Go home." Mr. Boyd waved them away and moved to shut the door.

"So I guess I should go talk to the cops then," Clinton blurted, surprising himself and Lewis.

The old man glanced at the police cruiser, looked each boy in the eyes for several tense seconds, then stepped back, his threatening scowl melting into a look of sorrow and regret. "Come in."

Lewis entered the home of his longtime neighbor for the first time. The old man was rumored to be crazy, and never talked much with his neighbors, but Lewis had always considered the old guy to be pretty nice. He would always smile, raise his hand, or nod his head in return whenever Lewis waved. However, upon entering the man's house, Lewis felt as if the rumor might have a hint of truth to it.

Like most of the homes in the neighborhood, Mr. Boyd's house presented the same layout as Lewis's, but seemed much smaller—cramped and unwelcome. He realized why as he followed Mr. Boyd down the short hallway and into the living room. Books were stacked everywhere.

Shelves packed full of ancient and new tomes overflowed onto the dingy carpet where they started new stacks like stalagmites, leaning against the walls, some pillars reaching as high as Lewis's waist. Against one wall sat a table, covered and overflowing as well, sheltering even more volumes underneath. Old newspapers littered the few spaces not claimed by books. The house smelled musty and damp, like the school library, only concentrated into this tiny room, the thick, dusty air making Lewis lightheaded. Lewis blinked several times, forcing his eyes to adjust to the gloomy morning light fighting to penetrate the soiled curtains covering the shut windows. At least the house was nice and cool, the air-conditioner humming away.

Mr. Boyd closed what appeared to be a journal or diary resting on the table, stabbed some loose pages with handwritten notes into a nearby book, closing it too, and motioned toward a grimy vinyl sofa. "Sit down, I'll getcha boys somethin' ta drink. Sweet tea? Lemonade? Soda Pop?"

The boys sat down, instantly feeling dirty as the couch sent dust motes scurrying to find a new nest.

"Sweet tea, sir," Lewis said behind a sneeze.

"Nothing for me, thanks," added Clinton.

Mr. Boyd turned and strolled toward the kitchen. Before he disappeared around the corner, Lewis noticed a thick, raised scar on the old man's right shoulder, curling under the thin fabric of his tank top. It looked as if something had tried to tear his arm from his body. The ringing of ice on glass and the sloshing of liquid reached the boys on the sofa. Lewis felt a tap on his leg and looked over to see Clinton shaking his head, genuine fear in his eyes, his brow furrowed with unease.

He waved Clinton off as Mr. Boyd returned from the kitchen and handed Lewis a murky glass of cold brown liquid, several white half-moon shaped ice cubes floating on the surface. The old man opened the beer in his other hand, ignoring the clock on the wall reading *9:30* am. Lewis had the impression the old man hadn't slept for quite a while, and didn't follow a normal schedule.

"Cheers," he said, tipping the beer back, taking an enormous swallow.

"Cheers," Lewis echoed, taking a miniscule sip of his tea.

It was delicious.

Clinton studied his friend, searching Lewis's face for the classic signs of poisoning, ready to bolt for the front door if he started convulsing.

"That's good," Lewis said to his host. He turned to Clinton. "It's good."

Mr. Boyd slammed his beer onto the bar—the one surface free of books—white suds spuming over his hand, and shouted, "NO! It's NOT good!"

"No really, it's good," Lewis pleaded, chugging the tea to prove his point.

"Not the tea, dummy. I'm talkin' about the situation. The situation is not good."

Lewis and Clinton both asked, "The situation?"

Mr. Boyd took another chug of beer, wiped froth from his lips with his hairy forearm, and gazed at Lewis through thick glasses, his eyes magnified behind the lenses like two green fish in a fishbowl, a sad expression on his stubbly face.

"You're gonna have to kill your friend," Mr. Boyd said, addressing Lewis.

Lewis stared at Clinton, who looked back at Lewis with panic.

"Not him, dummy. Your friend out there." Mr. Boyd gestured toward his back yard—toward the woods. His face sagged. "When I heard about them missin' kids I hoped maybe it weren't happening. Then I heard that damn cackling, and I knew." He placed the foaming beer on the bar, disappeared into the kitchen again, and came back with a fresh replacement. The boys' faces still showed terrified concern and confusion. Sucking in a deep breath and exhaling long and loud, the old man fell into the recliner across from the boys.

Reaching up, Mr. Boyd grabbed the old beer from the bar, and sucked out the remaining foam. He crushed the empty can, launched it through the air into a trash bin in dire need of being emptied, and gazed at the stunned pair on the couch.

He opened the fresh beer with a liquid *pop* and *hiss.* "Sit back and listen, boys. I'm gonna tell you a little story. This is very important, and whether you believe me or not, this is the honest truth."

17

The year was *1836,* and the battle against the Seminoles in Florida was at its bloodiest.

Titus Boyd was just eighteen when he volunteered to fight for the Army, following in the footsteps of his older brother, George. "Pride for his country" was what Titus claimed to be his reason for joining, but the folks close to Titus knew he was seeking revenge for his brother's death; the fact that his brother had succumbed to malaria didn't seem to matter to the young man.

Under the command of General Jesup, the Army was making progress in driving the Indians west toward surrender, or into the swamps of the extreme south of the territory; however, a few small bands of rogue Seminoles had managed to escape their lines, refusing surrender, wreaking havoc on forts and settlement outposts.

Titus, chosen for his marksmanship and superior tracking skills, had been assigned to a small unit of twenty battle-hardened soldiers to hunt down these renegade fighters. Despite being the youngest and least experienced of the band of soldiers, Titus became an integral part of the tight-knit group quick enough, his mastery with a rifle and inane sense of humor the catalysts for his fast acceptance.

For several days the unit tracked a particularly bothersome group of Indians deep into the Florida wilderness (not far from where Lewis sat on the sofa, absorbed in the tale rolling off the tongue of his beer-swilling neighbor—the great-great-grandson of Titus Boyd), the trail of destruction left in their wake making them easy to follow. When the team caught up with the marauding force of Seminoles just as the sun peeked above the horizon, they discovered an unexpected, grisly scene: a massacre of unparalleled depravity.

The bodies were mutilated beyond recognition. If not for the clothing and weapons, the soldiers would've found it difficult to identify the corpses as Indian. Torn limbs were strewn among the carnage; flies swarmed, feeding on the drying blood covering the campsite. They counted roughly ten bodies, though it was hard to tell exactly; most of the disfigured dead were half-eaten and stacked on one another like refuse. The band of Seminoles they'd been tracking numbered approximately thirty men. The whereabouts of the remaining Indians was a mystery.

Shocked by the hideous scene before them, the soldiers milled around the massacre, pondering what could have done something so horrendous. The Florida Black Bear and the Red Wolf both prowled these woods, but were not known to attack humans, and the unit agreed it couldn't be the work of any sane men. They could think of nothing that could slaughter and devour this many well-armed warriors. They simply stared at the desecrated flesh in puzzled horror.

With their attention diverted, and the cacophonous hum of feeding insects filling their ears, the unit was caught off guard by the Seminole ambush. The mystery of the remaining Seminoles' whereabouts had been solved.

The expressions on the Indians' faces as they attacked the unit were like nothing Titus had seen on a human before. He'd witnessed courage, fear, anger, and even hatred etched on the countenance of many men, but never this look of hunger, malice, and lust melded into one terrifying grin of pure evil, mirrored on the features of every attacking Seminole. The eyes of their assailants were the worst part: inhuman, diseased and bloody, gleaming with delight, a hideous yellow glow emanating from their core.

The Indians attacked without weapons, slashing hands and crushing teeth their only offense. It proved to be enough. The brutality and surprise of the onslaught dispatched half of Titus's team in a matter of seconds—dead, in shock, or too injured to fight. The men still able to engage in combat quickly learned that bullets and blades had little effect on the rampaging savages.

Titus, however, managed to stop one of the ravenous men with his rifle, shooting the snarling maniac in the forehead. The crazed man slumped to the ground after his brains chased the bullet through the ragged opening in his skull. With no time to reload the rifle, Titus drew his pistol and shot another attacker in the temple at close range with similar gruesome results.

Searching for another loaded weapon, Titus snatched

a nearby pistol from the ground, only to find it already discharged. He holstered his pistol, stuffed the other in his boot, grabbed his rifle, and did what instinct instructed him to do—he ran. Titus fought his way through the violent chaos of the frenzied horde, using the butt of his rifle as a club, smashing the teeth from one smiling face. Somehow he managed to battle his way through the blinding smoke of discharged weapons and mist of spraying blood. He found the path that had led them to the ambush, incurring several gashes and scrapes from ripping fingers and teeth. His face and clothes spattered with the blood of his brothers, Titus darted down the trail.

Bleeding from his wounds, his adrenaline running low, Titus tired quickly. He stopped and turned. None of his fellow soldiers followed; none of the enemy pursued. Titus could hear screams in the distance. Screams of excruciating pain. Screams of terrifying pleasure.

Titus Cotton Boyd had not been raised a coward. With shaking hands sticky with blood, he managed to open the breach of his rifle and load the weapon. He took a deep breath and started back toward the screams when a voice called out from behind.

"NO!"

Titus stopped and spun to face the voice, rifle aimed and ready to fire. A young Seminole stood twenty feet away, his hands up, a rifle hanging off one shoulder.

"Don't go. You will die," the Indian said. His wide, pleading eyes stood out against the dark paint on his face.

Titus—seeing that this man was not insane like the others, and could have shot him in the back if he had wanted to—lowered his rifle. "You speak English," was all his shocked mind could muster.

The screams in the distance stopped, unsettling silence taking their place. Titus could see fear creep into the Indian's eyes as the chilling hush fell.

"Come. Please," the man urged, gesturing for Titus to follow.

Not having much choice, alone and confused, Titus followed the stranger, struggling to keep up with the man's quick strides. His eyes never left the Indian's back as he led Titus through the thick brush, the sun brightening as it burned off the morning clouds, revealing patches of beautiful blue sky. The stunning blue was transposed against the images replaying in Titus's mind: visions of his friends being butchered.

They traveled this way for what seemed at least a mile, when the man stopped, held up his hands again, and gestured to a small dark opening in the dense brush.

Titus, still not trusting the stranger, mimicked the gesture and said, "After you."

The Indian nodded once, pried the entrance wider, and walked through the opening in a low crouch, disappearing from sight. Now Titus wished he'd gone first, the image of his head being lopped off with a tomahawk as he entered, bent over, flashed in his mind. Titus looked around him at the quiet woods, and with reluctance, followed the Seminole.

Once inside, Titus stood. He glanced around the small covered shelter, happy to still have a head to turn. The Indian motioned for him to sit, then rearranged the vines, sealing the opening.

They were hidden under the thick branches of a large fallen oak, covered with full, luscious vines, concealed and camouflaged from outside view. Some branches had been removed, making the hollow larger. Small bones littered the area next to a smoldering fire pit.

"You've been here awhile?" Titus asked.

"Yes," was all the man offered.

Titus looked into the Indian's dark eyes, remembering the strange glow projecting from the eyes of the attackers, and relaxed a bit; this man was obviously scared, not a threat. The man was coated with blood and grime, marring the large blue shirt hanging from his shoulders. A red cloth wrap, torn and filthy, covered his head. Long, coal-black hair cascaded from underneath the headgear. Despite the man's soiled appearance, he seemed healthy— wiry and strong. Titus decided his best tactic was to try to be amicable.

"I'm Titus. What's your name?" he asked, his voice calm but his hands still shaking.

"Chitto," the man said, drinking from a small gourd, offering it to Titus.

"Chitto," Titus repeated, accepting the gourd and drinking from it. Warm, but refreshing water filled his mouth. He swallowed, sighed, and handed the gourd back to Chitto. "What the hell happened back there? What was wrong with those men? Are they the ones who slaughtered the other Indians?"

The man stared at Titus, eyes wide with fear, and something else Titus could only perceive as shame. "We set her free," Chitto said, and a single tear rolled down his face, cleaning a path through the grime caked to his cheeks.

Titus waited for the man to continue, but his patience was gone. "Who? Who did you set free?"

Chitto shook his head for what seemed like forever to Titus, before offering, "Her name is lost. No one has spoken it in a thousand years. She is the witch of these woods. She is the reason no man lives here. This place is evil. *She* is evil."

Confused, thinking this lone Indian must be in shock or suffering from an early stage of the mental illness infecting his fellow warriors, Titus scanned the area for a weapon just in case he had to defend himself, his rifle too cumbersome in the tight quarters.

"What happened to your men?" Titus asked, spying a large rock within arm's length, just large enough to do damage. "Why are they acting so … deranged?"

Chitto's eyes were threatening to spill more tears as anger replaced the fear and sadness. "Those are not my men. My men are all dead. They belong to *her* now. She controls their bodies and minds. She is angry. And she is hungry."

Titus stood to leave, inching closer to the rock. "You're crazy too. I think I'll be going now."

Chitto raised his hands, motioning for him to stop. "No. Please. I will show you. Come."

The Indian stood, cleared the entrance, and stepped outside. Once again, Titus followed.

The day was bright and warm now, the sky an expanse of perfect azure. Titus stared up at the sky, the dried blood on his face pulling his flesh taut. His wounds had stopped bleeding, and the meager drink of water seemed to have returned his strength. *Maybe that was more than just water,* he thought, stretching his limbs, recalling tales of the Seminoles' miracle herbs and potions.

Chitto started off down the trail.

"Where are we going?" Titus asked, his fragile trust in this man wavering with every moment.

"Back," Chitto said, pointing down the trail. "I will show you so you will understand. She will have some of your men now."

Chitto led Titus back toward the sight of the massacre, stopping several times to listen to the woods. Titus was unsettled by the strange silence, and for the first time noticed the absence of the turkey buzzards that were always present whenever something dead was close by. It was as if the woods were emptied of all living things except them—trespassers in the land of the dead.

Titus followed the Indian like a shadow, keeping as quiet as possible, the slightest noise deafening in the silence. The trek back seemed longer than he remembered, and Titus was just beginning to think the Seminole was lost when Chitto dropped to a crouch and slowed to a crawl. Titus did the same. That's when the sounds came to him, faint but persistent, becoming clearer with every small step: grunts, growls, moans of rapturous bliss, and the unmistakable smacking and chewing sounds that accompany a grand feast. Chitto stopped behind a thick clump of palmettos. He turned and signaled for Titus to be silent, then pointed ahead through the dense brush.

Following the man's finger, Titus couldn't believe what he saw. Some of his company still lived.

Bewildered, Titus watched the bloodied soldiers milling amongst the equally blood-covered Seminoles. The sworn enemies wandered about like strangers at a party. They squatted on their haunches, retrieving objects from the ground, stuffing their mouths with the finds, tearing into them, chewing and growling. A group of men Titus knew well were on their hands and knees, bent over a slaughtered soldier. At first, Titus thought the men must be praying over their lost brother, then the truth registered like a slap to the face: the men were feasting on the body, dipping their red faces into the torn carcass like a pride of lions feeding on a downed wildebeest.

Titus spied a soldier holding a dismembered hand, gnawing on the fingers, moaning with delight. Others consumed glistening organs like children at a birthday party devouring delicious wedges of cake. Titus started to stand, to ask his brothers why they were eating the dead bodies of his friends, his powers of reasoning replaced with complete shock. Chitto grabbed Titus by the shirt, forcing him down, jarring the stunned man back to Earth.

Unable to protest, rendered mute from the sight of the macabre feast, Titus allowed Chitto to lead him back to the safe distance of his lair. The journey passed him in blurs of greens and browns, his mind unable to focus on anything, pulled the entire way by the wrist like a lost child.

Titus regained the use of his voice when both men were secure beneath the cover of the fallen tree.

"Oh my God," Titus whispered, staring at the ground, sitting with legs akimbo. He raised his head and looked at Chitto standing above him, his sworn enemy, now his only companion in the forbidden woods. "What are we going to do?"

"You believe what I have told you?"

Titus held the Indian's gaze for a brief moment, then slowly nodded. As if snapping from a daze, Titus forced the slow nod into a furious shake. "No. You haven't told me anything. I don't know what's happening. Or what to do."

"We need to find the first and kill him," Chitto stated in a calm voice. "Then, she will return to her world."

"Kill who? Return to where?" Titus asked, his confusion and frustration sending his voice up an octave.

"The first man she claimed must be killed. Then the evil will be locked away again. I was not at the ritual. I did not want to have a part in it. I do not know who was the first."

Titus threw his hands up. "What. The hell. Are you talking about?"

"They released her—the evil—to kill the white man. She will posses or slaughter anyone who dares to live here. They wanted to corrupt this land the white man has stolen."

"Stolen?" Titus said, standing. "This land was bought."

"Yes," agreed Chitto. "Bought from those that did not have the right to sell."

Titus took a deep breath, calming himself, and sat back down. "Right. I get it. So, your men released her, this … evil, to ruin the land. If you can't have it, no one can. That about right?"

"That was their thinking, yes."

Titus shook his head and grunted an exhausted laugh

before saying, "Okay. Maybe you should just start at the beginning. I want to know what I'm up against here. I want to know what could possess my men to eat one another. What is this *evil,* and how do we stop it?

Chitto nodded and sat down in front of Titus.

This is the story he told him.

THE TREE IS HER STRENGTH. Through the years men have tried to destroy it, but nothing worked. Neither fire nor ax could harm it. Men have tried to dig the tree from the Earth; the soil is harder than granite.

Thick vines covered the ground around the tree, growing through the stony soil from its protected roots. The tendrils extended in a wide circle surrounding the base of the trunk, adorned with beautiful, plump red berries. These tempting berries are as deadly as they are lovely; anyone unfortunate enough to eat them would die an agonizing death.

But death is not the end.

The body of the poisoned soul would come back to life with an insatiable hunger—the hunger for blood, the temptress that resides in the tree now living in the body of the resurrected.

Once set free in her new body, she would kill. On some victims she would feed, fulfilling her desire for flesh and blood. With others she would spare their bodies, force the poison fruit of her tree down the dead throat, and that one would rise as well—hungry. She would repeat this, gathering an army of undead bloodthirsty killers that she controlled.

She is them. They are her.

A local tribe that came under attack from these dead soldiers prevented a further outbreak of evil, killing every last demon, sending the witch back to her tree. But once again the tree could not be destroyed. Axes shattered on its dark skin, fire was absorbed, cast back upon them, encircling them in a ring of flames. They then burned only the vines and their deadly berries, merely to find them back the following morning, healthy and succulent.

The tribe's medicine man implemented a spell to create a barrier around the tree, a spell often used to protect the village from outsiders—from enemies. Fear would fill the heart of anyone who entered this ring of magic, sending them the opposite direction, keeping them from the harmful berries. Next, the medicine man once again had the vines burned, salted the scorched ground, and covered the blackened ring with the white sand from his ancestors sacred burial ground. He prayed for the spirits of his people residing in this consecrated sand to keep the poisonous fruit at bay.

For days the old medicine man visited the circle of white sand alone, chanting his incantations at the edge of the clearing, beseeching the spirits for their help. The vines did not return. The berries did not grow. It seemed his prayers had been answered.

Or so he believed.

The shaman enlisted the aid of an elder tribesman, a great tracker and hunter, to find the clearing and tree. This man had been to the tree before, assisting in the torching of the vines, and spreading of the sacred sand. The great hunter returned defeated, ashamed, failing the old man's request.

The medicine man was elated. His spell had worked. Only he knew the location of the witch's tree. He visited the clearing often to insure his spells were working and to strengthen them as much as possible.

On what would turn out to be his last visit, the old man decided to bring his apprentice. The young man was learning the ways of the shaman quickly and would make an excellent replacement when it came time for the medicine man to join his ancestors guarding the tree. Today would be the understudy's final and most important lesson: strengthening the cloaking spell protecting the tree from unwary travelers.

Standing on the edge of the clearing, the medicine man began his incantations, his hands raised to the sky, eyes closed. The apprentice stood behind his mentor, watching every move. The young man was tuned to every syllable, recalling his lessons that led up to this important moment, when his teacher groaned in pain, clasped his hands to his bony chest and toppled like an ancient oak in a storm, face first onto the sacred white sand.

Stunned, the student watched helpless as his teacher gasped for air, inhaled the sand, coughed once, and was still.

Dead from a failing heart.

The young man rolled his teacher onto his back; white sand coated the shaman's face and lips. The old man stared through him, the once wise and kind eyes now lifeless.

The student closed the sightless eyes and sat down at

his teacher's feet. He cradled his sorrow-laden head in his hands, and wept for his teacher. He stayed this way, tears leaking through his fingers, his quiet sobs the only sound in the woods, until a rustling caught his attention. The student lifted his head, wiped the tears blurring his vision, and cried out in fright at what he saw.

The old man was sitting up.

The kind eyes were replaced with the wild, frenzied eyes of a demon, the once gentle, wise face, now a snarling grin of pure malevolence.

Time seemed to slow for the young man as he locked eyes with the creature, once his mentor and friend. The beast released a feral growl and lunged forward, hands formed into claws. The student scooted away, the creature's raking fingernails peeling skin from his cheeks.

His face stinging, the student crawled backward, the blood hot as it flowed down his face and neck. The old man pitched forward to his belly and crawled toward his apprentice on all fours like a hungry panther.

The student's right hand fell on something large and solid. He instinctively latched onto the object, stood, and raised the large rock above his head with both hands as the teacher-turned-creature reached his scurrying feet. The young man smashed the heavy rock down onto his teacher's head with all his might. The rock shattered into several pieces as the old man flattened to the ground.

Gasping for air, the tears flowing once again, the young man looked to the sky and closed his eyes, begging forgiveness from the Great Spirit. After a few seconds, his breathing slowed to normal.

The student yelped when a hand grabbed his ankle

with brutal force. He fell to the forest floor again, kicking his legs as the man he once loved tried to rise, still gripping his ankle, somehow alive. The apprentice flailed blindly for another weapon, his hand falling on a shard of the broken stone. He clutched the fragment, turned, and swung it in a sideways arc, connecting with the old man's soft temple. The crunching grip released his leg, as the old man dropped to the ground again.

The young man stood, rock in hand, and watched in horror as the old man/creature tried to rise again; the student cried out in anger and sorrow as he brought the rock down on the shaman's skull once more. Blood and brains splashed across the young man's screaming face as he hammered the stone down, a staccato beat, slowing like a dying heart, until finally stopping.

The old man lie still, his skull shattered like a dropped egg.

The pupil stood above the dead man and dropped the hair and gore-caked rock to the dirt next to the ruined head.

The young man understood, knowing the witch's power, and turned to curse the evil tree, the source of the calamity. He froze when he saw the leaf. A single bright green leaf had grown on the bare tree. While he watched, the leaf fell from the branch without a sound, floated like a feather to the white sand, and withered away before his eyes.

Upon his return to the village, the young man told his terrible story. He asked for help to bring the body of his mentor back to the village for proper burial. He and his aids searched for the tree, but the spell proved too strong, not even he could find it again, and after days of searching he gave up and did the only thing he could think of to keep his people safe.

❧

"THE TRIBE MOVED, abandoning these woods that hold so much evil, praying their ancestors would rest and protect others from the tree," Chitto said, finishing his tale.

Chitto stared at Titus, shame obvious on his dark face. "My leader believed the barrier spell has weakened over the years. He was correct. We found the tree. I knew as soon as I saw it, that what we planned was wrong."

Chitto's face hardened, so Titus asked, "What did you do?"

"I tried to stop them. To tell them the evil could not be controlled. I was beaten, knocked unconscious. When I awoke, my brothers were killing each other. It was too late. Many of my men were dead. The others ran, carried me with them. Days later the witch and her puppets found us. Only I escaped."

"That was the massacre my men found?" Titus asked.

"Yes. Now her army has grown even larger. We must stop her."

Titus wasn't sure if he remained in shock from everything that had transpired during this nightmare of a day, but he believed the Indian's story with all his soul. How could he not? With his own eyes he had witnessed his brothers feasting on fresh corpses, men eating the flesh of other men. That was all he needed to see. Titus stood and paced the small space for several moments without saying a word, digesting the Indian's tale, trying his best to find a reason *not* to believe the unbelievable story.

Finally, Titus stopped pacing and faced Chitto. "So. We need to kill the first man that was … turned?"

Chitto nodded, a brief look of gratitude washing over his stern face. "Yes. She is them, they are her. But it is hard to kill that which is already dead."

Titus shrugged. "Not exactly. I stopped two back there with headshots. Kill the head and they die. Just like the old shaman."

"Yes," Chitto said. "This is why I need your help. With my stealth and speed, and your guns, I think we can defeat her."

Titus nodded and released a heavy sigh. "What's the plan?"

18

To Titus, the plan seemed simple, but insane. He stood outside in the fresh air, the day waning, Chitto standing next to him. "You're going to use yourself as bait, lure them down this trail right here, and I'm going to shoot him … her … in the head."

"Yes," Chitto said, pointing up a nearby tree. "Climb this tree. Use your rifle. It should allow you the best shot."

"And how will I know which one to shoot?" Titus asked, looking up, scoping the perfect niche for his rifle.

"We only know the first is one of my men, a Seminole," Chitto said. "She should stay at the back of the group, letting her others fight for her. She must protect her vessel."

"Should?" Titus didn't like the uncertainty of the word. "Great. What if I miss?"

Chitto offered a smile. "Do not."

With a single nod of his head, Chitto turned and fled down the trail.

Here we go, thought Titus as he slung his Hall Rifle over his shoulder. He loaded his martial pistol, as well as the other he had retrieved during the ambush, storing them securely—one in his holster, the other in his right boot. If he missed with the rifle, the pistols would give him two more chances, but only at close range. He doubted if he would have time to reload.

He climbed the dead elm tree bordering the trail, straight to the perfect spot he had spied from the ground; it stood higher than he realized, roughly twenty feet from the forest floor, but the view of the trail was perfect. He set the rifle in the crook of the branch and waited.

He didn't have to wait as long as planned—Chitto was quite fast on his feet—which was good. Time was not something they had much of. The sun dipped toward the horizon; night would be here soon.

In the distance, Titus could hear faint screams and growls swelling in volume with every passing second. A thought came to him, *what if all of the creatures chase Chitto back here and she's not with them? Then what? We'll be overrun.*

Titus forced the negative thought from his mind. If that happened, then they would deal with it. He took a deep breath and sighted the mouth of the trail, at the point where it turned onto the straight path leading underneath his sniper's nest. He had a clear view for a perfect shot. He readied himself as the animal sounds drew closer.

First, Chitto came into view, sweat shining on his determined face as he negotiated the turn, nearly stumbling, running straight toward Titus.

Then they came.

Filthy, covered in dried gore, smelling of the grave and rancid meat even from this distance, they chased his new friend like a swarm of escapees from a sanatorium. Some ran normal; others lurched and stumbled from their injuries. Some were missing arms, or dragging entrails. They ran unorganized, bumping into one another, allowing Chitto a safe distance in front.

Titus stopped counting after ten. The group was too jumbled to get an accurate count. He had to assume they were all following and that his target would be with them. Indian and white man filled the ranks of the reanimated, men Titus recognized, good men that were once his friends, now crazed and murderous fiends.

When no more of the snarling predators entered the trail in pursuit, Titus sighted the forehead of rearmost one —an Indian, uninjured, grinning with demonic pleasure.

That's her, that's the one … I hope.

Titus inhaled, held the breath, steadied the rifle, and squeezed the trigger as he exhaled.

Smoke billowed as the long rifle boomed, exposing his perch. The intended target stumbled to the dirt, half of his head flying away in large chunks and a fine mist.

Chitto sprinted past the tree.

The crazed men still followed.

You shot the wrong one, Titus chided himself.

Most of the madmen followed Chitto, but the last four creatures broke off from the group and clambered up the tree, clawing at the crumbling bark, and each other, to reach their next meal. Titus climbed as high as he could, the brittle branches threatening to crack under his weight.

When he could go no higher, he looked down just as the lead beast—a fellow white soldier—grabbed his boot. Titus smashed the butt of the rifle on the creature's skull repeatedly until it released his foot and fell to the ground in a useless heap thirty feet below.

The dead soldier was immediately replaced with another one from Titus's unit. He dropped the rifle, freed his pistol from its holster and fired down at the lead demon. The shot bored a hole in the man's forehead, just above the left eye; the contents of the man's head showered the two remaining creatures beneath him. Titus watched in sadness as the demonic gleam faded from the young man's eyes, turning him into a normal human once again, a human he'd known well. The dead soldier released the tree and fell, taking one of the two rabid climbers with him as he did.

Smoke filled the air around Titus. The dead tree shook, threatening to dislodge him as the fourth and last climber came within reach, an excited sneer spread across his dark features. Titus launched the spent pistol at the Seminole and watched the heavy weapon career off the man's face, fracturing several teeth; the smile never wavered.

Titus reached down, off balance, to retrieve the other pistol from his boot. He was too slow. The Seminole latched onto his wrist and pulled with surprising strength, dislodging Titus from the tree with ease.

It felt to Titus as if he hit every branch of the tree on his long journey to the ground. Painful as this was, it slowed his descent enough so the fall didn't kill him or render him unconscious. He hit the forest floor with a resounding thud, landing on his back, every ounce of air knocked from his lungs in one giant, painful cough.

Dazed, the copper taste of blood on his tongue, Titus reached out with sluggish muscles for the pistol, sliding his boot up to meet his hand. The ground had knocked the energy from his body along with his breath. He could feel the sting of grating bones in his side. From above him, high in the tree, came a fierce growl, and Titus remembered why he was trying to retrieve the gun. Looking up toward the sound, he saw the Seminole leap from the tree. Titus felt the firm wood of the weapon caress his palm. He slid the pistol free, raised it, and squeezed the trigger in one fluid motion.

The face of the falling man vanished in mid-air, replaced with an exploding spray of crimson. Brains, hair, and bone ejected from the back of the falling man's skull. A split-second later the body crash-landed onto Titus, followed by bits of the Indian's destroyed head, dropping like viscous, fetid rain around him.

Titus heaved the limp body of the Seminole from his chest, flipping the leaking corpse to the side. Covered in gore and the overwhelming stench of blood, Titus remained on his back, listening to the now quiet woods, too tired and in too much pain to fight any longer.

After several seconds, the silence of the woods was broken. Someone approached, laughing softly as they shuffled closer. Titus recalled the beast that had been knocked from the tree. He mustered the strength to lift his head. He wanted to look into the eyes of his enemy even if he lacked the energy to fight him.

Chitto appeared, alone, pushing his way through the

brush, stumbling toward Titus, a huge grin on his shining face.

A nice, normal, friendly smile.

Wide-eyed, Titus turned his head, and stared at the faceless Seminole sprawled on the ground next to him. "Got you," he whispered, then let his head drop back to the ground. Grinning, he gazed at the blazing red sky as the sun sank past the horizon. Chitto flopped to the ground beside him and exhaled a tired chuckle, admiring the fiery glow as well.

Surrounded by malodorous carnage and the scent of spent gunpowder, Titus closed his eyes and laughed along with his new friend.

❧

MR. BOYD PAUSED, pulled himself up from the recliner with a deep groan, and disappeared into the kitchen. *Pop. Hiss.* He returned with another open beer, plopped back down in the chair with another groan and gulped half the can down, the liquid sloshing down his pulsating throat. He belched, released a contented sigh, and looked at the boys perched on the edge of the sofa.

"Story-tellin' sure does make a man thirsty," Mr. Boyd said, sipping some more of the cold beverage and leaning back in his chair.

When the silence became unbearable, Clinton asked, "Well? What happened next?"

"Oh. Well, the next day they burned the bodies of their friends and parted ways. Sadly, Titus never saw Chitto again. Another unit scouting the area investigated the smoke and found Titus. He had two broken ribs and was covered in blood and bruises. He tried to explain what happened to his men, but they assumed he was suffering from heat stroke or shock. Or was just plain out of his gourd. Once rested, Titus decided the best thing to do was to keep it all to himself, and concocted a story of your garden-variety Indian ambush. He realized everyone would either think him nuts, or if they did believe him— which was a slim chance—they may want to use her the same way the Indians had."

"Native Americans," Lewis murmured.

"Huh?" Clinton and the old man chorused, staring at Lewis as if he'd just spoke in tongues.

"Native Americans. Indians are from India," Lewis said.

"Well." Mr. Boyd leaned forward. "Whatever you call 'em, they stayed away from them woods. *These* woods. Titus searched for the tree for years, he had it in his head that he could destroy the thing, but he never did find it."

The old man stood and stretched, his bones popping like brittle twigs. "No matter. You can't destroy the damn thing. Trust me, I've tried."

"You've tried?" Lewis asked. "So you know where it is?"

"Of course. That's the only reason I moved out here to the damn sticks. Sold my folks' place in town to buy this dump. Been keeping an eye on things since those idiots built this neighborhood smack dab in the middle of the evil bitch's backyard."

"Why didn't you tell anyone?" Clinton asked.

"Same reasons Titus had for clammin' up. They

would've called the men in white coats. I didn't want anyone to think I was crazy," he said, twirling his index finger around his ear.

Lewis and Clinton exchanged glances, the irony of the comment not lost on either.

"Found the damn thing in my late teens on a huntin' trip," he continued. "Had been looking for it for years, was starting to think the story was just that—a story. Stumbled on it by complete accident while chasing quail through the brush. Was concentrating so hard on that bird I guess I went right through the protective spell without even noticing."

Mr. Boyd stared at the dirty carpet, his eyes lost, glazing over with the memory. "I knew right away that it was *the* tree my dad had told me about. The one from Titus's story. It scared the pants off me. Got so scared I dropped my shotgun and ran."

"How did you try to destroy it?" Lewis asked.

"Didn't at first. Told my folks about it. My mom said not to believe the crazy story and my dad made me promise to never go there again. But I had to get my shotgun. I waited a few days and finally mustered up the guts to get my gun. Decided, what the hell? I'll bring an ax, some matches, see what happens."

He finished off the beer, let loose a tremendous belch and crushed the can. "The second time I definitely felt the spell. Almost turned back home, but I loved that gun. They don't make 'em like that anymore. Anyways, the stupid ax flattened like a pancake on that tree, and every time I put matches to it, the damned thing would suck the flame up and fire would sprout up some place at the edge of the clearing, like it was trying to trap me inside the circle, just like the story I told ya. One little match touched to the bark would cause a fire ten, twenty times bigger. Nearly burned down the whole stinkin' woods. Tossed sand on the flames until it went out, then stopped when I realized what I'd been touching. That sand … the sand that turns you. Trust me, I haven't touched that stuff with my hands since."

Mr. Boyd dropped back into his recliner, wiping his hand on his shorts, a sour frown on his face. "Tried poison, chainsaw, and been looking in all these books for something." He pointed to the books on the table. Lewis could read the spine of one—*History of Celtic Druids.* "All I've found is some old Viking folk tale that sounds similar, but offered no dang solutions. No, there's no way to kill that damned thing. Not even sure if we should," he finished, tossing the crushed beer can over the bar and into the kitchen sink.

"Then what can *we* do?" Lewis asked, pointing to himself then Clinton.

"*We,*" Mr. Boyd replied, pointing to himself, then the boys in turn, "have to kill the first one infected. Just like Titus did. That's the only way to stop her."

"Yeah, but we don't know if Jerry was the first or if one of the twins were," Lewis stated calmly, wrenching a startled glance from Clinton.

Mr. Boyd looked at Lewis and then Clinton, his eyes full of sincere regret. "We may have to kill all three of 'em."

Clinton raised his hands in surrender and catapulted

to his feet. "Okay, I'm outta here. You've both lost your minds."

Mr. Boyd jumped up as well and shouted, "If we don't do something she will destroy this entire neighborhood: your families, your friends, and most likely me and you too, so I don't give a rat's ass if you believe me or not. You came to ask me what I know, well I told you what I know."

"Clinton, sit down," Lewis urged in a soothing tone, then turned to his neighbor. "I believe you, Mr. Boyd. Clinton didn't see Jerry. I did. I felt like something was wrong with him. But after hearing your story I know for sure now."

"Okay. Even if all this is true," Clinton said, sitting back down next to Lewis, "what the heck are we gonna do? Chop off their heads? Blow their brains out? I don't know about y'all, but I don't think I can do that."

"Well, I'm afraid that's all the advice I got for ya, son," Mr. Boyd said, flopping back down into his chair. "Nobody's gonna help us with this problem. Not the police, not your parents—nobody. This is somethin' we gotta do ourselves, unless you wanna be sent off to the funny farm."

Neither boy responded to this, so Mr. Boyd continued, "You boys remember a year back or so, that backhoe operator uncovered all them ancient human remains?"

"Yeah," Lewis answered. He remembered watching the story on the news and what a huge deal it had been at the time, especially since it happened so close to home. One of the most significant archeological finds in recent history, the newscaster had said. Over one hundred skeletons had been unearthed from the mass grave. The one tidbit that had excited Lewis the most had been the fact that several of the skulls still had brain tissue preserved inside them, leading him to conjure up images of revived mummies and oozing skeletons crawling from the muck. "That was only five miles or so away. He was digging to build a house or something. The Windover Bog People, right?"

"Right," Mr. Boyd said, pointing at Lewis, then lowered his voice. "That was because of her … the witch. Those people buried their dead deep in the bog of the swamp, using stakes to keep the bodies down, because they feared the witch would bring them back. They buried 'em so deep the peat in the swamp preserved them bones."

"Wait. How do you know that?" demanded Clinton.

"I had a dream about it," the old man said, tapping his skull, a toothy grin on his face.

Clinton raised his hands in mock surrender once again and looked at Lewis. "Oh, okay. He had a dream about it."

Mr. Boyd glared at Clinton, leaning forward, pointing to the boy's chest. "Don't ignore your dreams, boy. They have a funny way of coming true. Especially for those of us living here in Poisonwood, so close to that evil thing in the woods. It's like it leaks something. Some kind of … toxin, that worms its way into your dreams." Mr. Boyd's glare dropped to his feet, his eyes clouding over, as if remembering something he'd rather forget.

"They say those bones are over a thousand years old," Lewis said, saying anything to get the image of *his* recent dreams from his mind, and also trying to diffuse the tension between Clinton and Mr. Boyd.

Mr. Boyd shook his head. "They carbon-dated those suckers. They're more like seven or eight thousand years, son. That's my point. How the hell do you kill somethin' that's been around for that long? I'll tell you how. You don't. You just do whatever you have to do to keep it from winning."

Mr. Boyd leaned back in the recliner. "You're gonna have to kill your friends. I'm sorry, boys, but that's just the way it is. They're already dead anyways."

Lewis and Clinton looked at each other for a moment. Without saying a word they both stood.

Lewis spoke first. "Okay, Mr. Boyd. Where do we start?"

A proud grin flashed across the old man's wrinkled features as he nodded and stood as well. "You can start by calling me Clyde. Mr. Boyd was my old man's name. I've got to get a few things ready, so come by tomorrow morning and we'll pay a visit to her little tree. That's where they're most likely hiding out."

Lewis and Clinton agreed and were moving toward the front door when he added, "Oh, and boys? If you see any of those missing three … just come get me.

"And one more thing … stay out of those woods for the rest of the day."

❧

NEITHER BOY HAD a clue they were being watched.

Lewis and Clinton exited the home of Mr. Boyd under her vigilant yellow eyes. From the deep shadows of the storm drain she watched the pair leave the house and cross the street.

The hated boy … *Lewis.*

She watched her prey like a hungry lioness as they entered the home across the street.

Tonight, she thought, and turned to face her minions, *tonight we add to our little group.*

She then proceeded to probe the vapid minds of the twins, gathering the intelligence needed for the night's hunt.

19

When the boys stepped into the welcome normalcy of Lewis's bedroom, Clinton asked, "So, what are we gonna do for the rest of the day?"

"I don't know. I definitely think we should stay out of the woods, like he said."

"This sucks," Clinton said, lifting the lower bunk mattress, fishing out a hidden copy of *Fangoria*. He thumbed through the issue, barely glancing at the photos he'd looked at a dozen times already, needing something to replace the horrific images engraved in his mind from Mr. Boyd's story. Huffing, Clinton closed the magazine and tossed it on the bed. "Maybe we *should* tell our parents, or maybe the cops."

"Yeah, right. I can just picture their faces as we tell them that story. We'd end up in a padded room wearing straightjackets. Mr. Boyd would probably be thrown in jail. Then who'd stop her? And if we just tell the cops I saw Jerry, they'd send even more people back into the woods to look for him, and they might end up just like him. "

"So you totally believe Old Man Boyd's story?" Clinton asked.

Lewis sighed. "I do. I mean it makes sense, ya know? If you'd seen Jerry last night you'd believe it too."

Clinton shook his head. "But why would Jerry, or even the dumb twins, eat sand? I mean I know the dude from Old Man Boyd's story accidentally breathed it in, but what are the chances of that happening again?"

Lewis tugged on his bottom lip, thinking. He released his lip and snapped his fingers. "Maybe Jerry didn't have a choice. Remember when the twins made me eat mud?"

Clinton's eyes widened. "Oh shit," he whispered.

"Yeah."

Both boys were silent for several seconds as they pondered the enormity of the situation, and their roles within it.

Clinton broke the quiet. "Maybe I should come back later and stay here tonight."

"Yeah. Good idea. That way we can go over to Mr. Boyd's house first thing tomorrow morning, see what kind of plan he's come up with. I'll okay it with my mom."

Clinton started toward the door. "I'll do the same. See you later."

Clinton left his best friend's house with his head hung low. *This is starting out to be one crappy summer,* he thought, hopping on his bike. He pedaled toward home, his mind fighting against the notion of an evil zombie-making witch living somewhere in his woods. If she *was* out there, and if Jerry *is* dead, she was going to pay, that was for sure.

He rolled within inches of a storm drain, crinkling his nose at the foul stench wafting up to him, and continued on his way home, unaware of the peril lurking only inches away.

From the darkness of the drain, a small boy's wicked glare followed the homeward bound youth until he vanished around a corner.

Clinton.

His name is Clinton.

LEWIS KEPT himself busy while he waited for Clinton's return. He tried watching television but couldn't keep his mind off tomorrow and what it might bring. He also did some chores—shocking his mother—to eat up time and subdue his overactive imagination, but nothing worked. He could not shake the dread he felt, the feeling tomorrow was going to change his life forever—for the worse.

Lewis had the urge to confide in his mother every time she walked past, but caught himself each time, knowing she wouldn't believe him, possibly jeopardizing any chance of halting the events Mr. Boyd had warned him about. His mother assumed her son's odd behavior stemmed from his worries over his missing friend, and left him alone with his thoughts, offering a reassuring smile every time their eyes met.

The prospect of seeing the tree terrified Lewis. If Mr. Boyd's story spoke the truth, then what could a couple of twelve-year-old boys and a sixty-five-year-old man do against something so ancient and powerful? He also asked himself the most important question of all: could he kill Jerry? Even if it wasn't actually Jerry? Lewis wasn't sure if he could. On the other hand, when it came to the question of killing the twins, Lewis smiled and nodded ... *Yeah, I think I could do that.*

Lewis was in his room pondering these questions when Clinton's signature knock tapped out its familiar melody at the front door, pushing the morbid thoughts from his head.

THE BOYS never left the safety of Lewis's backyard except to go inside for more refreshments. When Justin joined them around midday, the three played several games of pickle and wiffle-ball before Clinton sent the younger boy home for supper, acting as if everything was copacetic.

Actually, everything did seem right with the world; birds sang and butterflies danced under a picturesque sky filled with the sweet scent of jasmine and honeysuckle, as if the threat of impending death didn't exist. The boys played and laughed, the thoughts of witches, evil trees, and the living dead momentarily forgotten. However, as the sun dipped below the horizon, the onset of darkness chased away the joyous mood, once again sending their spirits spiraling down like a crashing plane.

After supper, the boys huddled in Lewis's bedroom. No matter how hard they tried, the subject of the tree and the witch worked its way into their conversations.

"What do you think we'll find tomorrow?" Lewis asked.

Clinton busied himself sketching a scene for a new comic, the pencil scratching across the paper, the tip of his tongue protruding through his lips. "Hopefully nothing. Let's talk about something else."

"Okay. Sorry, dude. Actually, it's getting late. We should probably just go to bed so we can start early," Lewis said, glancing at the detailed drawing in front of Clinton: an enormous dark tree with an evil face and giant maw of dripping fangs towered over a terrified boy, a shotgun falling from his shaking hands.

Clinton placed the sketchpad on the dresser and announced, "I get top bunk." He said this every time he slept over, even though he knew Lewis never slept on top. Clinton launched off the bottom bed, flew through the air, bouncing onto the high mattress. Stretch, who had been asleep on Lewis's bed, jumped up and hissed, fleeing the room. Lewis switched the light off—remembering the nightlight this time—and settled in.

The boys stayed awake for a while, chatting in the dark, the conversation a comforting reminder to each other that they weren't alone. This time they managed to stay off the subject of tomorrow's daunting task. They discussed their favorite *X-Men* and how they would fair against other superheroes. They even rehashed the events and victory of the war, somehow omitting Jerry's fatal run into the woods as if it had never happened, trying their best to make the memory a happy one.

Soon enough, the sounds of slow, heavy breathing floated down to Lewis, bringing a smile to his face. He always lasted longer than his friend. He often wondered how much of his conversations were wasted on a sleeping Clinton. Like always, the familiar sound of his friend's light snores hypnotized Lewis, lulling him toward slumber as well. He stretched out on his side, drifting in and out of sleep. A cool breeze seeped through the open window, mingling with the flow from the wobbling ceiling fan, evaporating the moisture from his scalp. Finally, Lewis dropped off into the realm of deep sleep. The reoccurring nightmare wasted little time in disturbing his slumber.

… He's hopping onto the moving train, hauling himself into the warm, dusty air of an open freight car with surprising ease, sitting on the edge with his shoes dangling above the passing rails. Rust flakes onto his palms as he clasps his hands to the metal edge of the car. The scent of burning wood assaults his nostrils, but there are no flames in sight. The sun-drenched woods slide past, a blur of greens under a perfect blue sky. He's at the mercy of the train as it carries him away from his small town on its journey to alien cities, propelling him toward adventures only the mind of a twelve-year-old can fathom. From the deep, dark recesses of the boxcar— between the blaring of the whistle—odd noises reach his ears: wet lapping sounds, and a low animal grunt, followed by a muffled tearing like pages being torn from a sodden book. Lewis squints into the darkness, his limbs frozen in place, his muscles like hardened clay as a thin stream of dark liquid creeps from the shadows, angling across the dirty floor of the rocking car, threading its way toward his precarious perch. The noises cease; the wheels thump beneath him. A single word floats out of the blackness. The strange voice is familiar, full of malice, turning the warmth of the car frigid. The word

slithers through the chill, just above a whisper, as the tepid trail of blood reaches his cold, paralyzed hand ... "Leeewiiissss".

Lewis snapped awake, his name echoing in is head. His wide eyes stared at the springs of the mattress above, the bottom of Clinton's bed, barely visible in the weak green glare of the nightlight. The memory of the previous night and the rude awakening from Jerry's laughter forced its way into the forefront of his thoughts.

Rumbling snores filled the room, drifting down from the bed above. Lewis sighed with relief and relaxed the taut muscles in his neck.

The snoring woke me up, that's all, he assured himself.

He closed his eyes, but sleep eluded him this time. He could not recall Clinton ever snoring so ferociously before; the grating sound kept him awake.

Lewis was about to wake Clinton when he heard it— sinister laughter, the same as the night before. Lewis sprang to a sitting position, the hairs on his arms trying their best to jump from flesh that had turned rigid as stone.

Not again oh shit please not again.

He clutched the blanket in a death-grip and forced himself to look at the window, relieved to find the frame void of any faces. He strained his ears but heard nothing; even the snores above had ceased.

"Clinton," Lewis whispered. "Did you hear that?"

Silence from above.

"Clinton," he whispered louder this time, and heard the laugh again.

Lewis crawled from his bed, his hands shaking, and

walked in a crouch to the window. He peered over the sill, nobody there, the dark street outside quiet and empty. He stood there staring out his window, focusing on the pools of light cast down from the streetlamps, searching the shadowy spaces in between for any signs of movement, sure he would see someone. He knew Jerry or the twins were out there somewhere.

The laugh came again.

From behind Lewis.

Lewis spun, his heart pounding against his sternum. The nightlight shined bright enough to burn away all but the deepest shadows. The room appeared to be empty, just himself and Clinton, sleeping on his side, his back facing Lewis.

"Clinton, wake up," Lewis spat, his mouth as dry as paper.

Lewis stifled a scream as the laugh came once more, from the bed where his friend slept. He could see Clinton's shoulders bouncing with each sadistic giggle.

"That's not funny, man," Lewis gasped, holding a hand to his thumping chest. "You jerk, you scared the crap out of me."

Clinton shuddered, the bed shaking, as the laughter swelled in volume.

"Hey! Stop it," demanded Lewis. "That's not funny."

The laugh stopped. Clinton and the bed ceased moving, as if a switch had been thrown. The room was so silent Lewis thought he'd gone deaf.

"Clinton?" he whispered, thankful to be able to hear his own voice, but once again received no response. Lewis approached his friend on legs that had turned to boneless tubes of quivering jelly, and reached out a trembling hand to Clinton's shoulder. His fingers were inches away when Clinton's head swiveled around to face Lewis—bones cracking, tendons and ligaments in his neck squeaking and snapping—until his head turned completely backward.

Lewis stared into his friend's glimmering yellow eyes. A hungry smile split Clinton's face, his teeth glowing a pale green in the half-light. Clinton's ashen face lashed out like a cobra, his teeth biting into Lewis's still lingering fingers.

Lewis screamed and pulled his hand free, leaving two dripping fingers behind in the jaws of his best friend. Clinton flipped the digits into his mouth like sticks of gum and chewed, crunching on the thin bones. He swallowed them down with a loud click in his throat, his alien eyes emotionless to his friend's scream of agony.

Oh god oh god they got him they got him oh god, Lewis's mind ranted as he squeezed his wrist, a fountain of blood pumping from the ragged stumps of his missing fingers, the dark fluid hot against his cold flesh. His breath puffed out in short coughs, the pain flaring white-hot down his arm. He backed away from the bed, from the grinning nightmare that had replaced his best friend in the world, when something grabbed his legs. Lewis looked down to see small, filthy arms protruding from the darkness under his bed—the arms of a child, latched onto his bare ankles with crushing force.

Lewis crashed onto his back as his feet were pulled out from under him, the back of his head thumping into the carpet and the unforgiving slab floor beneath. He screamed again, the thick carpet burning the flesh on his back as the arms pulled him under the bed where several pairs of yellow eyes and the foul stench of rotting flesh awaited him.

Lewis awoke in his bed. Somebody gripped him by the ankle, shaking him. He looked up to see Clinton standing at the foot of his bed, a worried look on his face. The overhead light glared, burning his eyes.

"Are you okay?" Clinton whispered, still clutching Lewis's leg.

"Yeah … bad … dream," Lewis managed between quick breaths. He lifted his hand in front of his face, wiggling his fingers—all five of them. A strange echo of pain persisted, a tingling in his hand and wrist. *I must have been sleeping on my hand,* he thought.

Clinton released his grip. "I guess so. You were shaking the whole bed. Sure you're all right?"

"Yeah," he repeated, relieved to see his friend's normal blue eyes. "Sorry. Just bad dreams."

Clinton nodded as he released an enormous yawn, turned off the light, and jumped back in bed, resuming his slumber with ease.

Lewis, on the other hand, stayed awake for the rest of the night.

20

As night descended on the secluded neighborhood, three figures crept from the street's depths to begin the hunt. She followed the twins as Jason—still cradling his guts with one arm—pushed the heavy manhole cover to the side with a low rasping scrape, and emerged from the hole. Andy came next, holding a glass jar filled with a white substance in one hand, and turned to help the small boy once known as Jerry Harris from the dark bowels of the streets. The missing boys stood in the night air, gleaming with dank wetness, surveying the quiet street.

She searched the memories of the twins for her next easy prey—someone to add to their little group, or perhaps someone to feast upon after they recruited the hated, scrawny child called Lewis—when a car turned the corner and headed their way. The hive-mind engaged, and in unison, the trio ducked behind a row of nearby trash-cans an instant before the car's headlights washed over them.

The car slowed and turned into the driveway just a few yards from the boys' hiding spot. When the fancy sports car squealed to a stop and the headlights were extinguished, a man and woman exited the vehicle, laughing hysterically. The pair met at the front of the car and embraced, kissing and groping each other, moans of pleasure leaking through joined lips. Panting, the couple separated and stumbled up the drive to the front entrance of the house, laughing even louder as the man dropped his keys while fumbling with the lock. He retrieved the keys and succeeded in unlocking the deadbolt, the woman cheering her valiant savior as they entered the house and slammed the door, shutting out their drunken laughter.

The thing residing in Jerry's corpse stood and walked toward the front door, the twins following with smiles matching her own. She walked alongside the vacated car, the gleaming metal ticking as it cooled, the heat from the engine enveloping her cold vessel. She stroked the hood as she walked past, admiring the strange machinery.

She once again probed the twins' minds. *The man lives alone. The woman is unfamiliar. Perfect. It seems the prey has come to us. Lewis will have to wait.*

Reaching the door of the man's home, she pressed her ear to the wood. The clinking of glass and more inebriated laughter seeped through the door, moving deeper within the house. She listened for a few minutes, biding her time. The faint sounds of music—strange to her ears—filtered through the door.

She gripped the doorknob and twisted. Her smile stretched further, threatening to split the child's face in half as the unlocked handle rotated with her hand. *They make it so easy,* she thought.

She opened the door wide and turned to the twins, performing a comic sweeping gesture with her arm, inviting them in. She followed the boys in and shut the door, turning the lock. They moved like expected guests through the dimly lit house, strolling along, defiling the beige carpet with grimy shoes, skirting crumpled islands of clothing as they made their way toward the music. Like breadcrumbs in the forest, they followed the trail of discarded clothes until they found their treasure.

The man sat on a sofa, completely naked except for a pair of short black socks on his feet. His eyes were shut, his head tilted back, soft breathy sighs floating from his open mouth. One outstretched hand held a cocktail glass half-full with a translucent amber liquid, resting on the back of the couch. His other hand rested on top of the woman's head, bobbing up and down with the beat of the music as she orally pleasured him, her back to the three uninvited guests. Nude as well, she knelt between the man's legs, accepting his length into her mouth with greedy, wet, smacking moans.

The couple continued their foreplay, oblivious to the audience of reanimated dead positioned in the deepest shadows of the room, watching them.

The corpse that used to be Jason Reed strolled up behind the woman. Her hands caressed the hair on the man's thighs as she quickened her pace, the bumps of her spine standing out in relief. Jason casually reached into the crusting cavity of his belly and unfurled a length of glistening large intestine, the squelching of his innards lost amongst the music and the slurping of the woman's mouth. The woman, either sensing someone behind her, or smelling the putrid stench of three dead bodies, lifted her head with a wet *pop*, the man's guiding hand falling away from her scalp. Jason looped the foul entrails over her head and around her throat. He tightened the meaty lariat and dragged her backward.

The man shrieked, lifting his head as the woman's nails dug deep into his thighs leaving parallel furrows of welling red behind. Her strangled gasps caught his attention. His stunned mind had only an instant to register the pain and the insane nightmare unfolding in front of him before Andy's blade penetrated his neck. The man squeezed the cocktail, shattering the glass, and grabbed for the knife. His hands fluttered like butterflies, slapping at Andy's wrist as the boy twisted the blade. The man screamed in pain, but a soft wet gurgle was all he could produce, choking as his lungs filled with blood. Andy removed the knife and watched with amusement as the man's hands explored the gushing wound, and then flopped to the cushions on either side of his spread thighs, a fleeting look of complete confusion meeting Andy's evil gaze. Urine arced onto the dying man's belly from his deflating penis, mixing with the spouting blood from his throat. His head eased back to its original position, surprised eyes staring at the ceiling.

The woman's screams were hoarse croaks as she watched the man die before her. She kicked, her heels thumping into the carpet. She clawed at the strange soft repulsive rope around her neck as her eyes swam with squiggling black shapes and darting explosions of light. A small boy entered her field of failing vision, holding what appeared to be a mason jar filled with a white substance. The boy unscrewed the lid and sprinkled some of the jar's contents into the gaping mouth of her murdered lover.

The last thing the woman saw before her consciousness and life left her, was the man's head lift up. *He's alive,* she thought, even though she knew it couldn't be true, not with his throat looking the way it did, not with all that blood. *It's just a prank, a sick practical joke.*

She tried in vain to scream as his eyes locked on hers.

Inhuman eyes that made her thankful for the rushing darkness.

21

For the second time in a week, police cars cluttered Lewis's street.

Three cruisers were parked several doors down at Maggie Burton's house, the lights on their roofs extinguished, lending an air of somber foreboding for the lone resident. Lewis could see his mother among the throng of onlookers, still in her bathrobe and slippers, talking with Chief Richards on the sidewalk in front of the girl's house, her hands twitching nervously as she spoke. Mrs. Taggart, Lewis's next-door neighbor, stood alongside his mother, holding Doris, her little white poodle. Mrs. Taggart's liver-spotted hand hovered over her lips, and her expression, much like the looks of the gathered crowd, gave Lewis the impression something much worse than spousal abuse was the issue this time.

Clinton joined Lewis on the front porch, rubbing his eyes. "What now?" he asked in a defeated voice.

"Don't know, but it doesn't look good," Lewis said as

he surveyed the scene, his knowledge of recent events filling him with guilt. Lewis had the urge to shout the truth to the mob despite the consequences, but he held his tongue. He had been awake, his nightmare still fresh in his mind, when he heard cars roll down his street, and the thump of the front door as his mother stepped outside. When he didn't hear her return, he got up to investigate. The sight of police cars did not excite or surprise him this time.

Clinton spied Justin across the street, gawking at the crowd and talking to Mike Simmons, the college student that rented the house next door to Clinton. He waved his arms, catching his little brother's attention.

Justin jogged over to the porch. "Have you guys heard?"

Clinton shook his head. "No. What's going on?"

"Mike says that Maggie lady is missing and there's blood and stuff all over her house, splattered all over the walls," Justin said, a little too excited.

Lewis looked at Clinton and whispered, "Shit."

"Yeah," Justin continued, "her friend came over to check on her and found the place that way. They think her asshole ex-husband had something to do with it."

"Okay, well, go hang out with your buddies, all right," Clinton said. "Oh, and be home before dark and stay out of the woods. Better yet, have Mike walk you home, okay."

"What? Why?" Justin asked.

"Duh, stupid," Clinton said, poking his brother in the forehead. "That's four people in a week that's gone missing. Do you wanna be next?"

"Oh, yeah," Justin said, a tinge of fear creeping into his eyes. "Hey, do you think the asshole ex-husband killed all of them?"

"Yeah. Maybe." Clinton shrugged, wishing it were the truth. "Now go, butt-face."

Lewis watched Justin saunter off, then turned his gaze to the milling crowd. He almost envied them. They were oblivious to the danger they all faced, free of the heavy weight of responsibility Lewis felt. He turned to Clinton. "This is going to keep happening if we don't do something, man."

Clinton was also staring at his clueless neighbors. "Yeah. I know. But can *you* kill anybody? Because I don't think I can." He turned to Lewis. "Maybe we should just go down there and tell the cops right now."

"No way. Think about what you'd say. Then think about what *they'd* say. And no, I'm not ready to kill anyone either," Lewis admitted. "Let's just go talk to Mr. Boyd and see if we can find them first, then we'll worry about the rest."

The boys slipped across the street, managing to reach Mr. Boyd's front door without being noticed. Lewis knocked once and the door flew open.

"Get in," the old man hissed.

The boys shuffled through the doorway, Mr. Boyd urging them in with a spastic wave of his hand. He eased the door shut.

Once in the gloomy space, Lewis asked, "What's wrong?"

"All those damn cops, that's what's wrong," the old man whispered. "They see us gallivanting around the woods with guns they're gonna want to stop and ask a few questions."

"Guns?" the boys chorused.

"Yeah. How do ya think we're gonna blow their heads off. With slingshots?"

The boys didn't answer the question. They looked at each other and then at the floor, both of them realizing this was the real deal, not something from a comic book or a horror movie. This was life or death.

Clinton spoke up. "We have to find them first."

"True son, true. But if we do, you're gonna want to be ready." Mr. Boyd made a pistol shape with his thumb and index finger and mimed shooting Clinton in the forehead.

"You really think they're at this tree?" Lewis asked.

Unease flashed across the old man's features before he answered, "If they ain't, then I don't know where the hell they could be. So let's hope they are."

Mr. Boyd waved away the thought with his hand. "We'll worry about that if it comes down to it. For now, wait until all those cops are gone before you come back. And don't talk to any of 'em. They won't believe a word and they'd just get in our way, ruin our chance of stopping her."

As the boys turned to leave, Mr. Boyd asked. "Hey, either of you boys believe in time travel?"

Lewis and Clinton turned and exchanged a confused look. Lewis shrugged as he looked into Mr. Boyd's pleading glare. "I don't know, I guess so. Why'd you ask that?"

"Never mind," Mr. Boyd said, waving the boys away. "Forget about it. Just come back when you can."

The boys agreed and slipped back across the street unnoticed, back to the porch to wait out the police. Clyde Boyd also crept out, sitting on his porch swing, lighting a black pipe. He opened the journal on his lap and scribbled frantically.

❧

FROM A NEARBY STORM drain she watched the crowd with greedy, hungry eyes. The mess leftover from her first meal had been discovered. She reveled in the stunned looks of fear pasted on the faces of the human cattle.

Searching the memories of her group of dead minions, she collected information on several of the onlookers. She knew names, where they lived, how many they lived with —valuable intelligence for the coming night. Her hive-mind link detected fear and respect for one of the men in the crowd, one that seemed to be a leader of some sort.

Cops, was the word that kept coming to her from the twins. *Cops, stay away from cops.* She laughed; a person of power would make a fine addition to her soldiers. His mind, full of information, would be an asset.

Beyond the milling herd of meat, sat an old man on a porch, thick smoke from his pipe circling his head like a halo. It seemed he too did not approve of the cops, his stern glare following the uniformed men. She probed for information on this man and received an immediate response.

Old Man Boyd.
He lives alone.

❦

THE POLICE PRESENCE DWINDLED, but two officers still lingered at the home of Maggie Burton as the sun caressed the treetops on its descent toward the horizon. The officers went in and out of the house, lifting and ducking the yellow police tape strung across the door, conversing with the diminishing crowd and keeping the late-arriving news hounds at bay.

Lewis anxiously wandered about the house as Clinton, still seated on the front porch, busied himself with more drawings. Lewis would steal glances of the pages as he passed. Clinton was finishing a detailed depiction of an Indian jumping from a tree. An arm holding an old-timey pistol entered the frame from the bottom of the page, pointed up to the falling man, smoke and fire exploding from the long barrel. The detail in the ruined head of the flying Indian as the imaginary bullet passed through his brain, and the hollow, dead stare from his eyes made Lewis shudder.

Lewis sat down in the scratchy lawn chair for the umpteenth time and waited for the scene to dissipate and the police to vacate. His impatience gave way to hunger as his stomach growled in protest. *Time to feed the worm,* he thought.

Clinton must have heard the sound. He dropped his pencil and closed the sketchpad. "Dinner should be ready, I better head home."

"Okay. Ask your folks if you can stay over again. As soon as those cops leave we need to go over to his house." Lewis tilted his head to the house across the street. "It'll be dark soon and I don't think we should go into the woods again at night, but at least we can talk to him some more about this thing we're supposed to … you know."

Clinton stood and slid the pencil into the spiral binding of the sketchpad. "All right, I'll see you later." He held the sketchpad out to Lewis. "Keep this here, I'll finish this drawing when I get back." Lewis took the pad, handling it with obvious respect, as Clinton hopped on his bike and rolled away, his shoulders stooped as if carrying a heavy load.

Lewis called out, "And get back here before it gets dark."

Without turning, Clinton raised a hand in acknowledgment.

Lewis, feeling the same weight as his friend, stood and made his way inside to help his mother with dinner, unaware of the watchful eyes following him from two separate storm drains at opposite ends of his street.

AFTER SUPPER, Lewis received a phone call from Clinton with the bad news.

"They won't let me leave the house, dude. They say I have to stay inside at night until the cops find that exhusband guy," Clinton said, then whispered, "like that's gonna change anything."

"Shit," Lewis whispered back, making sure his mother couldn't hear. "Well, I can go over there and talk to Mr. Boyd alone. I'll tell him what's going on and maybe we can try again tomorrow."

"Okay, Lewis, I'll see you tomorrow."

"All right, later."

Lewis placed the phone back in its cradle with a sinking feeling of despair.

Yeah, he thought, *see you tomorrow.*

H is mother—for the same reason as Clinton's parents—would not let Lewis leave the house either. She believed the woman's ex-husband had something to do with her disappearance, and quite possibly the missing boys as well. When she said the word "disappearance" Lewis could tell what she really meant was "death", and until the police caught the suspect, Lewis remained stuck inside—day *and* night. When Lewis protested, she reminded him that Jerry had gone missing during broad daylight.

Foreseeing his mother's reaction, Lewis had already made up his mind to sneak out of the house again. He'd done it plenty of times before with a high rate of success, and what his mother didn't know wouldn't hurt her. Unlike the other night, with his wild goose chase to find Jerry, Lewis had a clear destination. He needed to talk to Mr. Boyd, and phoning him was not an option—his mother could overhear.

Lewis pleaded with her some more, putting on a convincing show: whining, pouting, and pitching a fit. He moped off to bed early, his head down, letting her believe she had won the argument. The sooner he went to bed, the sooner she would too, and then he could get across the street and satisfy his need for information. He figured sleeping wasn't an option anyway, not after what Justin had said about Maggie's house … *The walls were covered in blood.*

Lewis brushed his teeth, turned out the light, and jumped into bed, the horrors of his real life overshadowing any desire to perform the ritual of the hedges. His mother peeked into his room thirty minutes later to check on him.

Years of practice have made Lewis a pro at feigning sleep. The key was not to look too comfortable: kick the sheet off a little, sprawl the limbs out a bit, and breathe slow and heavy through the mouth. Basically, make it look like you just fell off a two-story roof, rendering yourself unconscious. This night, Lewis even mustered some drool, letting it leak out the corner of his mouth onto his pillow.

She closed his door, convinced he was sound asleep, and moved through the house. Lewis could hear her checking all the doors, making sure they were secure, taking more time with the nightly routine than usual. Then the television fell silent and the door to her bedroom clicked shut.

He waited another fifteen minutes before slinking from his bed. The digital clock on the nightstand glowed *9:47* in deep red. Lewis wondered if it might be too late to visit the old man but changed his mind when he peered out his bedroom window; light burned behind the curtained windows of Mr. Boyd's house. He was sure the old man was awake. In fact, Lewis thought the old guy was probably sleeping just as well as himself—not at all.

Wasting little time, Lewis slipped into shorts and sneakers and began his well-practiced route to the front door without making a peep. Once outside, he ventured to the right, past the garage, and peeked around the corner of the house to check his parents' bedroom window. The window remained dark—another successful prison break.

Grinning, he turned to face his destination and his good mood instantly deflated. The light that had been on just moments ago was now extinguished—oddly enough, even the light on the porch was off—wiping the mischievous smirk from his face. *Crap,* he thought, *I'm too late.*

Lewis stood there in his driveway, next to his mother's Oldsmobile, pondering his options, when a *snap* to his left caught his attention. It came from the direction of his bedroom window, a twig breaking under foot.

Probably just Stretch prowling the bushes for something to murder, he convinced himself, and smiled with relief when the gray cat shot from the thickets, sprinting past Lewis with his tail puffed up as if electrified. Just then, the porch light across the street turned on again.

Cool, I can catch him before he goes to bed.

Lewis jogged on tiptoes across the street to the front door, stretching his hand out as far as he could like a sprinter crossing the finish line, his index finger landing on the doorbell. The classic "ding-dong" chimed deep within the house.

He heard the squeak of a floorboard from inside the

house and prepared himself, expecting the door to fly open, a furious Mr. Boyd scowling down at him, his blood-shot eyes burning behind the thick lenses of his glasses.

Nothing happened.

"Mr. Boyd?" Lewis whispered into the door seam. "Clyde? It's Lewis. Clinton couldn't make it. Sorry I couldn't come sooner. Open the door."

A muffled thud sounded from behind the door, deep within the house, like something soft hitting a wall.

"Mr. Boyd?" Lewis whispered louder, scanning his street, hopping nervously. "Someone might see me out here."

The sound did not repeat itself, the house remained dark, the door did not open.

Without thinking, Lewis gripped the doorknob and turned it. The door was unlocked. Startled, Lewis let go of the handle as if it had scorched his hand. The door swung open several inches on hinges that sang out with lack of oil.

Standing frozen on the doorstep, Lewis peered into the dark gap. When he reached out to push the door further he saw that his hand shook.

He opened the door until it hit the doorstop, and whispered into the blackness, "Clyde?"

Still no answer. Lewis stepped into the house and swung the door closed, shutting out the light from the porch, thankful to be out from under its revealing glare. The soft click of the latch as the door closed made him jump. *It's okay. He's probably just in the bathroom.* He fumbled along the wall for a light switch, unsuccessful in his search. He moved further into the house, feeling his way along the wall, inching his way into the room he and Clinton had sat just yesterday, forming a mental image of the room from memory. As he moved deeper into the shadows, Lewis had the sensation of being watched, that he was not alone. Every step he took, he expected his fingers to brush against the soft flesh of the person standing there, quietly waiting for him. His leg bumped a stack of books, knocking them to the floor, the sound like an explosion in the silent room.

"Mr. Boyd? It's just Lewis. Don't shoot," he announced to the dark room, his eyes squeezed shut. *The old man must be deaf if he didn't hear that.*

Lewis opened his eyes. He needed to find a light before he caused an avalanche and broke his neck. The curtains were still closed, but some light from the street-lights filtered through the murky fabric, chasing away some of the shadows. Shapes slowly materialized as his eyes grew accustomed to the darkness, but not enough to allow him safe passage through the gauntlet of books. Lewis cursed himself for forgetting his flashlight—again.

He could make out the black shape of a lamp in front of him. Reaching out, he fumbled for the switch and sighed with relief when he felt the familiar tiny node. He was about to push it in and froze, *what if the walls are covered in blood? What if he didn't answer because he's dead?* Lewis forced the thoughts from his mind and pushed the switch in with a satisfying click. Bright welcoming light filled the room for half a second before the bulb burned out with a crisp *pop.*

In that half a second, Lewis saw the man on the other side of the room in perfect detail.

It was not Clyde Boyd.

A FEW STREETS OVER, Clinton lie in bed chasing sleep with little success.

He'd spent most of the night sketching various scenes from Mr. Boyd's story, his fresh sketchpad quickly becoming a gory scrapbook of Titus and Chitto's battle against the witch. He'd finished that part of the tale and was in the middle of a detailed portrait of Jerry as described by Lewis, the boy's sinister grin the centerpiece of the drawing, when his eyes began to droop. Clinton dropped the pencil and closed the pad. He stumbled to his bed and flopped down onto the soft mattress. Even though his eyes were tired, Clinton tossed and turned for what seemed an eternity, the images he'd put down on paper still lingering in his mind.

He finally tossed the covers off with a loud sigh. *Screw this,* he thought, and heaved himself out of bed. He crept to his bedroom door, opening it just enough for one eye to peek through. His parents were still up watching television. They were out of view, but he could see the telltale dance of colored lights reflected on the living room wall, and the faint sound of canned laughter followed by his parents' muted giggles. He could picture his mother stretched out on the sofa and his father in his recliner, sipping beer and enjoying the peacefulness of the childfree room.

Without a sound, Clinton shut the door and turned to look at his bedroom window. He loved his parents and his little brother. He would die if anything happened to them. He had to help Lewis and Mr. Boyd stop this evil witch if he could. He wasn't doing them any good stuck in the house, he needed to do something about the problem and he might as well start now.

Clinton took a deep breath and made his decision—he was getting out of this room. The threat of being punished by his parents was nothing compared to the threat lurking in the woods. He chose some dirty shorts from the floor and slipped into them. He put on his sneakers, without socks, and a t-shirt he also liberated from the litter of clothing strewn across his room. He opened his window further, pushed out the loose screen, turned and looked at the closed door of his bedroom, then climbed out into the night.

It felt good to be doing something, the anxiety he'd felt while lying in bed fading away the instant his shoes hit the ground; but what to do next? Clinton stood outside his window and realized he hadn't thought past this moment. He hadn't thought about anything except getting the heck out of his room; he had no idea what to do next. One thing was certain: he couldn't lie in bed for another second while the witch stalked his neighborhood. Clinton knew his mother would be sneaking out back to enjoy her nightly cigarette very soon, so he had to get a move on. Out of habit, he started off in the direction of Lewis's house.

At least his friend would have some news from his visit with Mr. Boyd.

23

L ewis stood paralyzed, the image of the man emblazoned in his mind like a photograph, a ghost image seared on his retinas. The man must have been standing there the entire time while Lewis fumbled about the room. Then Lewis realized something else as he quickly studied the image before it could fade away. The man was stark naked, grinning above a scarlet mess where his Adam's apple should be.

Lewis, his hand like a vice on the neck of the lamp, could hear books sliding and tumbling to the floor as the man made his way across the darkened room. He detected the glint of eyes, the nocturnal glowing eyes of a cat, moving through the darkness like fireflies.

Lewis yanked the lamp toward him, freeing the plug from the wall socket with a fizzle of sparks, lifting the stout fixture above his head with both hands.

"Where's Mr. Boyd?" Lewis shouted, his voice sounding like a comedian imitating a frightened child.

The question was answered with a gurgling cackle, turning Lewis's bowels to hot jelly. He launched the lamp at the disturbing sound as hard as he could, aiming for the glowing, bouncing orbs, and heard a gratifying hollow crash. A second later, the twin fireflies vanished, a heavy thump reverberated from the floor.

Lewis mentally screamed at his legs to move; they obeyed at half-speed. He turned in the direction he believed the door should be and stumbled his way over the fallen volumes, his shoes slipping, tearing pages. He moved as fast as he could, his hands stretched out like a blind man, the tinkling of broken glass from behind motivating him to quicken his pace.

Lewis could now make out a thin line of light leaking beneath the front door and lunged toward it, his hands slapping the wood. He searched for the knob, his panicked brain shrieking in his skull, *the knob is gone, they took the knob, THEY STOLE THE DAMN DOORKNOB!* Sounds of movement continued behind him, interspersed with a wet growling that brought back the image of the man's shredded throat.

The cool brass of the doorknob kissed his palm, quieting his ridiculous thoughts. Lewis turned it, thanking himself for not locking it, and swung the door inward with a loud crash; stealth no longer concerned him, freeing himself from this nightmare dungeon did.

Lewis barreled onto the bright porch and pulled the door shut behind him just as the man crashed into the other side, shaking the door in its frame. Lewis let go of the handle and spun around to run, looked up, and froze.

Across the street on the front steps of his own home,

illuminated with perfect clarity from the porch light, stood little Jerry Harris. His face glistened with fresh blood. The bright red blood streamed down his arm to the giant butcher's blade in his small hand, dripping from the sharp tip onto the welcome mat under his sneakers.

Behind Jerry, in the open doorway, stood Lewis's mother. Her nightgown—once white, now soaked a deep dark red—clung to her body.

His mother and Jerry both raised their faces to Lewis, their identical eyes glared into his as their twin smiles taunted him.

NO NO NO NO, This can't be real, this is another nightmare! Lewis stood there shaking his head, refusing to believe the horrors blocking the entrance to his home. The doorknob behind him rattled and the wood thumped like a heartbeat as the naked man struggled to open the door, but Lewis couldn't hear it. The bloody pair on the porch across the street held him transfixed. Lewis's paralysis broke as the door wrenched open behind him and a hand grabbed his shirt, jolting his shocked mind back to the immediate reality. He pulled away from the grip, his shirt tearing, and ran. He ran from the nightmares as fast as his rubbery legs would carry him.

He ran straight for the woods.

24

The street stretched before him, quiet and deserted. Clinton kept to the sidewalk anyway, the many shrubs lining the walk would come in handy if he had to hide from a passing car of someone coming home from a night shift or a night out.

Or worse, Jerry and the twins.

He neared the end of his street—nerves tingling, on alert, but elated to be doing something pro-active—when the bushes just ahead stirred as if from a light breeze. Clinton slowed, his gaze locked on the bushes. The night air was silent and still, the full moon hung bright in a crystal clear sky, no wind at all.

He halted several yards from the tall hedge as he detected movement behind it, a shadow within the shadows. "Who's there?" he asked the bush, feeling like a complete idiot as the words fluttered from his lips. Tense seconds passed as Clinton waited for a response. He started forward again when none came.

That's when the woman stepped from behind the bush and out onto the sidewalk, blocking his path. The streetlight cast its glow on the woman from above, presenting Clinton with a full view. She awaited him, naked from head to toe. Clinton stopped, dumbfounded, his chin dropping to his chest as the naked woman—something he'd only seen in a magazine before—stood there without saying a word. Her skin appeared pale blue in the light, except at her throat, where a dark collar of bruises ringed her slender neck. Other than this minor flaw, she was beautiful.

Clinton's gaze shifted from her neck to her dark nipples, then to the black patch of down between her legs, his gaping mouth clamping shut with a click of teeth. The skin on his face flushed with heat as he felt uncomfortable embarrassment wash over him. That is until he gazed into the woman's glowing venomous eyes, and the wicked smile stretched across her face. His childish discomfort melted away, morphing into icy terror.

Clinton's inner voice spoke up, surprisingly calm.

Run. Just turn and run.

He backed away from the succubus, keeping a wary eye on her, knowing once he turned his back she would attack. She stood still, like a sculpture of a Greek goddess, a mythical deity of death.

Clinton kept back-pedaling until he felt he had a safe distance, and then turned to run—his plan was to put as much space between himself and this fantasy-gone-wrong as he could. He took half a step and collided with something big.

He bounced backward and looked up, staring into the

rotting features of Andy Reed. Before Clinton could react, the dead boy lashed out with cold hands, grasping his face.

25

She relished the reaction of the child called Lewis. The look on his face when he saw his murdered mother filled her with delight.

Her vessel had knowledge of the boy's home, guiding her, informing her of the location of his sleeping quarters. She had been furious after crawling through the boy's window only to find his bed empty, still warm from his resting body, taunting her. A quick search of the house turned up the woman—the boy's mother—and her spirits lifted. Sleeping alone, the woman had been easy prey, another meat puppet to serve her devilish needs. Then the boy appeared. From the eyes of her new soldier, she saw him enter the home of the old man across the street. She finished her ritual, bringing his slain mother back to greet her son with a smile.

What fun she was having.

Her plan had been simple: enter the homes of the easiest prey, extinguish the strange lights—she could see well enough in the dark—and slay the inhabitants, reanimating most, feasting on the rest.

The ranks of her hive-mind band of undead soldiers were filling fast, but not fast enough. She gave up the chase as Lewis fled toward the woods. Let the boy run, she would get him soon enough. Her work was here among the homes of her sleeping cattle. She planned on reigning over these weak humans for a long time, and a silly puny boy would not stop her.

Nothing would stop her this time.

26

L ewis ran. He never looked back to see if the man still followed, he just ran as fast as he could, leaving the hellish scene far behind. He never slowed, even as he reached the ominous dark wall of the woods, he plunged through and sped into the forest of shadows, the sharp sting of fear's spurs driving him forward.

Before he knew it, Lewis stood next to his hidden fort, the brilliant moon casting dark shadows surrounding him like a hungry pack of stalking wolves, where anything could be hiding. Panting from his wild flight, he stooped, lifted the secret door, and crawled into the cave of vines.

Much like Chitto's hideout, Lewis and Clinton had removed several of the fallen tree's smaller branches, allowing enough room for the boys to fit comfortably. He sat down on one of the stumps he and Clinton had rolled in to use as chairs, and lowered his head, swallowing the humid night air. Lewis covered his face with his hands and wept, hot tears rolling down his arms, mixing with his sweat.

The image of his mother replayed in his head, covered in blood, her once loving eyes projecting the fire of the witch's hate, the hag's smile stretching across his mother's pretty face.

She's dead. No … worse … Undead. This thought caused his tears to pump out harder, blurring his vision.

I should have told someone. Now my mom is gone. It's my fault.

My fault … My fault … My fault …

In his mind, Lewis chanted this self-defeating mantra, rocking to and fro on the stump like a mental patient, snot and tears flowing from his face. He wobbled for several minutes, lost in sorrow, when approaching footfalls snapped him back to the reality of his surroundings. Lewis covered his mouth to dampen his sobs and panicked breaths.

They found me!

The footsteps advanced down the trail, heading straight for the hidden fort where Lewis sat. He held his breath as the crunching steps slowed a few feet from where he hunkered beneath the camouflage.

Lewis wiped his tears away but still couldn't see through the thick vines and foliage of the fort, couldn't make out the owner of the noises. The movement stopped next to Lewis for several nerve-fraying seconds, then receded, moving along the connecting trail that led deeper into the woods and circled back toward the homes. The same trail he and Clinton had used to cut through Old Man Boyd's backyard. As the footfalls waned, Lewis breathed again. He caught a faint whiff of a familiar odor.

Cologne?

The pleasant scent evaporated before Lewis could remember where he'd smelled it before.

After several tense moments, Lewis wiped his nose with his arm, cleared the tears away, and gathered his courage. He emerged from the fort, the brightness of the moon in the star-studded sky surprising him after the confined darkness. He waited, listening to the woods for any sounds of pursuit. When none came, Lewis decided to wade further into the dark forest, toward the bike trails, maybe even going as far as the train tracks, leaving his house and the nightmare unfolding there as far behind as possible. He even considered fulfilling his train-hopping fantasy, leaving all his problems behind for someone else to deal with.

He scurried down the path to the main trail and turned in the direction of his deliverance. However, after only a few steps toward freedom, he stopped.

I have to go back. I have to do something.

Lewis stood on the trail, debating the quandary of which direction to go, when more sounds of movement approached his new position. He plunged into the thick bushes bordering the trail just in time, as a lone figure came into view, trudging along with mindless determination. *The woods sure are popular tonight,* he thought, and shook his head, surprised at the calmness of his inner voice. Lewis froze, holding his breath once again.

The shock—that Lewis confused for calm—turned to alarm as he recognized Jason Reed's oafish gait. Moonlight gleamed off something cradled in Jason's left arm—glass of some sort. The boy's right arm covered his mid-section, pressing a lumpy mass to his body. Lewis gagged as Jason's scent assaulted him like a punch to the nose, his eyes filling with tears of a different kind now.

The odor emanating from Jason Reed prompted the memory of Hurricane David and the three-day power-outage it had left in its wake as it blasted through town a few years ago. The miasma of rotting food in Lewis's dead refrigerator had smelled a lot like this: the putrid combination of decay and the sulfurous smog of rotten eggs.

As Jason marched past Lewis and out of sight, the smell dissipated. Lewis inhaled deeply, swallowing the fresh air.

Where was Jason going in such a hurry? ... The tree, maybe?

Lewis knew what he had to do. He couldn't just run and leave his friends and neighbors. He had to follow the shambling, decaying corpse of his sworn enemy deep into the woods at night, to find the tree of an ancient evil witch he apparently had no hope of destroying.

And from the looks of things, he had to do it alone.

III

THE LEFT HAND PATH

A short time earlier, Dolores Norton, unable to sleep, left her snoring husband in bed and waddled her way to the kitchen to clean up the mess left over from supper. Whenever insomnia struck her, no matter the time, this is what she did—clean the house.

She leaned over the sink, humming an off-key tune as she scrubbed the dishes, staring through her reflection in the kitchen window and out into the quiet night, when she saw the most peculiar thing. She bent toward the window for a better look. The boy from across the way, little Lewis Frazier, was running like a lunatic past her house as if fleeing from a fire. That seemed odd enough for this late hour, but the truly strange thing came next. Pursuing the young boy was a man she thought she recognized; however, she couldn't be sure since she had never seen this man naked before. She did a double take, her eyes in danger of popping from their sockets and splashing into the soapy water. She dropped the dish from her grip to the floor with a loud crash.

A stark naked man was chasing a boy down her street.

She shook the suds from her hands and dried them on her apron before snatching the phone from the wall. The rotary dial spun into action as she called the police.

When she got the operator, she blurted, "Chief Richards please, it's Dolores Norton. And hurry up."

CHIEF RICHARDS YAWNED WEARILY. He was starting to get a little tired of this neighborhood. This was the third time he'd been called out here this week, probably more times than all of last year. The hours spent in the mucky woods searching for those kids had exhausted him. He wondered again as he passed the ornate sign at the entrance, *why the hell is it called Poisonwood Estates? There isn't a poisonwood tree within a hundred miles of here.*

The call had come in as he'd been getting ready to head home for some much needed rest. Good ole Dolores Norton: *The Queen of Hyperbole.* That's what they'd called her on the debate team back in high school. She sure could spin a story, which had been great for debate, but a pain in the ass when you're a cop.

He'd been sure things would quiet down and get back to normal when the welcome news of his deputy arresting Dave Burton had reached the station. The suspect was there now, passed out in a cell, recovering from a night out drinking and brawling.

Chief Richards wasn't convinced of the man's alibi;

Dave Burton swore he'd been out of town visiting friends for the last week, but so far nobody could corroborate his claims. The chief was well aware of the man's history of violence and felt him more than capable of murdering his ex-wife. Whether or not the drunkard had the smarts to pull off the kidnapping of three kids, in broad daylight no less, and on his own, was another story. He had to wait until morning for the idiot to sober up, then he hoped to get some answers.

As far as this call was concerned, he felt certain it was just some punks messing around, excited from recent events. Mooning and streaking has become an epidemic among the local teens. And Dolores Norton had a well-known penchant for melodrama and misinformation, so calling in the cavalry on her account would be a gross misappropriation of manpower—at least that's what the Mayor would call it. This seemed like something he could probably take care of on his own, quick-like, and be done for the night.

Dolores stood on her porch, her ample form wrapped in a bathrobe, as the chief swung his car into her driveway. Beside her, slouching and yawning, stood her husband. The scowl on the tired old man's face led the chief to believe that *this* man could definitely be capable of murdering his wife.

She shuffled over to the car when the chief climbed out. "Chief, thank the lord."

"Hello, Dolores, tell me again what happened."

When she concluded her vividly detailed and long-winded story the chief paused writing in his notepad and gave her a skeptical glare, one eyebrow arched.

"Completely naked?" he asked.

"Naked as a newborn. And bloody like one too," she said, then added, "he may have been wearing socks now that I think about it."

"Bloody? You didn't mention that earlier," the chief said, perturbed.

Mrs. Norton shook her head. "I guess I just realized it. Sorry."

"Okay, Dolores. You and your husband go back to bed. I'll handle it."

"Thank you chief, we will, but I don't think I'll be sleeping for a while. This whole darn neighborhood has gone plum crazy." She shooed her half-conscious husband into the house and followed, waving a hand to the chief before closing the door.

Dolores's last words stuck and played over in the chief's mind like a skipping record. He heard the deadbolt of her front door catch—a period at the end of the looping sentence. *This place has been unpredictable as of late,* he thought. He returned to his vehicle and used the radio to call his deputy—backup might be a good idea after all. Knowing it would take at least fifteen to twenty minutes for his deputy to arrive, Chief Richards decided to take a look around on his own. He considered bringing the shotgun, then figured he wouldn't need it against one naked man, and left it locked in the cab; his revolver should be protection enough.

Stepping from his cruiser, he noticed the quiet shrouding the neighborhood. It was late, sure, and most sensible folks were already in bed, but absent was the constant drone of night insects commonplace in summer.

He'd heard people say, "the silence was deafening" before, but never thought he would have use for the phrase. He did now. Despite the heat, a shiver ran up his spine.

He gathered his wits and decided to visit the Frazier house first. If Dolores was correct about the kid's identity then he needed to inform the parents. He crossed the street and strolled up the path to the shadows of their front porch. He instantly noticed how dark the home appeared. The porch light was off as well. The shudder danced up his back again. It wasn't just the absence of lights, but something else.

The house seemed … dead.

Shaking his head, he stepped up to the front door and knocked.

"Talk about a rude awakening," he mumbled, his shoes squishing on the welcome mat.

The house remained dark. He knocked again, louder this time, then rang the doorbell. The chime resonated throughout the home—a hollow, somber tune.

Still nothing. No sounds from within. The notion of the house being dead returned.

Chief Richards knew something was wrong here. Somebody should have answered the door. Maybe the shotgun wasn't overkill after all. He turned, headed back down the path, mentally cursing himself for not taking this call more seriously. If it had come from anyone else other than Dolores Norton he most likely would have. Hell, if the drunk in the cell had been telling the truth, then there might still be some crazy on the loose. He was pondering this misjudgment when he sensed movement somewhere in front of him.

He glanced up to the house directly across the street and noticed a black vertical rectangle where the door should be. *Why the hell is that door open?* He stopped and freed the oversized flashlight from his belt, pressing the switch. The distance proved too far, the beam couldn't penetrate the darkness beyond the doorframe, so the chief, with trepidation, crossed the street and inched closer to the black entrance.

As he approached the doorway he saw fleeting movement within the house, a slight shift of shadows in the gloom. Chief Richards reached the porch of Clyde Boyd, his shoes crinkling on the fake grass doormat, and stopped when he heard a peculiar sound. He moved his feet on the artificial turf again, trying to recreate the noise; he must have mistaken the crackle of his shoes on the mat for the sound of hushed laughter—the breathy sound of a child's giggle to be exact, riddling his scalp tight with gooseflesh.

He directed the light through the open doorway and regarded the room in full detail. Books littered the area, along with furniture, disarrayed and flipped over. Then, with a dropping sensation in his bowels, he saw the blood. The red splashes stood out in the light, brilliant against the white pages of several open books.

With his light, the chief traced the trail of blood from the middle of the room to his shoes. Turning, he illuminated the dark red trail from the porch, across the drive, and to the grass of the front lawn—a perfect line pointing to the Frazier house.

"What the hell?"

Behind him, shuffling came from somewhere inside the dark house.

He spun, shining the beam through the doorway again, sliding his pistol from its leather holster. "This is the Chief of Police. Come out with your hands in the air."

The house remained quiet. Chief Richards mentally counted to three, and entered Clyde Boyd's home, following the blood trail on the carpet through the maze of overturned furniture and books, all the while thinking, *where the hell is my goddamn deputy?*

"This is Police Chief Richards. Show yourself."

The thrumming pulse in his ears was his only answer.

The blood trail led him to the left, to a closed door. Crimson handprints stood out on the white wood of the door like a child's finger paintings stuck to the fridge of a proud parent. The brass doorknob also displayed glistening red. The chief stopped in front of the door, blood welling up around his shoes from the saturated rug. He wedged the flashlight in his left armpit, turned the tacky knob with his left hand as his right fist clenched the revolver next to his ear. In a single motion, he pushed the door open, retrieved the light, pointing it, and the gun, into the dark room.

A woman lie on the floor in the middle of the room, on her back, her slender arms spread out as if making snow angels in the carpet. Stacks of books surrounded her, filling the room with the pleasant musty odor of an old library. Then a second smell hit him in the face like a slap from a jilted lover—the unmistakable stench of blood and spoiled meat.

Shielding his nose and mouth with the back of his gun hand, Chief Richards examined the woman in the cone of light. The copious blood soaking her nightgown appeared fresh, the malodorous scent of the room led him to believe otherwise.

He searched the wall for a light switch, found one, and flipped it several times with no result. A quick check of the ceiling revealed the overhead light, its bulb missing.

Holstering his pistol, Chief Richards crouched to perform the obligatory pulse check on the obviously deceased woman, his hand trembling as it touched her cold throat. She was stone dead, nothing shocking there. He directed the beam of light to her face and shook his head, downcast, as he recognized the woman from earlier that morning. He had questioned her about the Burton woman, and remembered with sadness how kind and pretty she'd been.

He had to call this in, and his desire to leave this tomb of a room overwhelmed him, but still he remained crouched above the woman, her pale delicate face and the events of the day draining his spirit. That's when the sound from earlier came again—the low giggling of a mischievous child. He raised the light to the stacks of books behind the dead woman's head and sucked in a terrified breath at the image glaring back at him: a pale, leering face of a young boy, a grin stretched below demonic blood-red eyes. He recognized Jerry Harris from the many photos provided by his mother.

The chief reached for his gun again, instinct shouting that this was not some innocent child. But before he could grab the weapon, cold hands covered his ears, grasping his head, pain lancing his scalp where his hair ripped free. Strong hands forced his gaze down to the woman lying at his knees. His empty gun hand latched onto one of the woman's frigid wrist while his other hand trained the light on her face; he cried out, an incoherent tremulous babble of panic. The woman on the floor smiled, her powerful hands pulling him in for a lover's kiss.

She's dead. I checked her. No pulse. She's dead!

These were the only thoughts his horror-stricken brain could assemble, overloaded with fear, as the dead woman forced his head to her grinning mouth. Her face lunged forward, and she bit into the soft flesh of his throat. The searing pain snapped the chief back into motion. With a bubbling shriek, he jerked his neck free from her clamped jaws, leaving behind a large morsel of himself that she swallowed whole with a sigh of gluttonous pleasure.

The chief watched as someone's blood splashed across the white flesh of the woman's face, causing her to convulse in rapturous bliss. He fell backward on the seat of his pants, thinking, *That's a lot of blood. That can't be my blood. I'm not hurt that bad. It doesn't hurt that bad.* He probed the bite with his gun hand, feeling the hot blood pumping over his fingers from his torn jugular. His essence spilled down his chest, under his shirt, and pooled in his lap. The blood-covered woman writhed and moaned before him in the glare of the flashlight, like a Gothic beauty from a movie; a scene from an old Hammer horror film.

He heard a soft *click*, and light filled the room, revealing the hellish tableau in vibrant hues of red. The small child—momentarily forgotten—stood by a lamp, the cruel smile still on his face. The child examined the lamp with a look of wonder as if he'd never seen one before, the smile never wavering.

Chief Richards fumbled for the revolver still on his hip with numbing, blood-slick fingers. Somehow he managed to free the weapon and lift the quaking revolver, aiming for the boy's smirking face. His weakened muscles ignored his pleas as he strained to squeeze the trigger.

The boy set the lamp down delicately and focused on the trembling gun, a bored expression replacing the smile. He sauntered over to the dying cop, reached out and seized the weapon. He regarded the cold, black instrument with disdain for a brief moment, then slammed the grip of the gun on the crown of the chief's head.

Bone crunched, and lights flashed when the child whipped him with his own pistol. The chief's blurred vision cleared just enough to see the woman launch onto him, forcing him onto his back, wet growls filling his ears as she lapped and gnawed at his draining throat.

Warmth crept into his cold limbs, and the slurping sounds of the feeding woman faded into the distance. The terrible ache that had filled his head dissipated, the burning at his throat a memory. *Glad I'm out of there. Now I can finally head home,* he thought, as his lids slid down over unseeing eyes.

L ewis followed Jason Reed, the moonlight guiding him along the intimate trail. He pursued at a safe distance, his eyes watering from the rank air left in the dead boy's wake. The deeper they went into the woods the more Lewis became convinced he was being led to the tree. Jason marched on with blind resolve. Lewis had the feeling he trailed an automaton hell-bent on destruction; however, unlike the robot from one of his favorite films, *The Day the Earth Stood Still*, he doubted "klaatu barada nikto" would have any effect on the thing that had once been Jason Reed.

The pair approached the fork in the trail and to Lewis's astonishment, Jason chose the left hand side without slowing, vanishing into the thick vegetation like a ghost. Lewis and his friends never used the path, they never even dared one another to use it, never questioning why either, it just naturally seemed like the wrong way to go.

Even now, as the mouth of the trail swallowed Jason, Lewis hesitated to follow. Then it dawned on him, making perfect sense. The spell from Mr. Boyd's story. The one cast by the old shaman all those years ago, weakened now, but still working its protective magic.

Lewis inched forward on leaden feet until he stood at the mouth of the forbidden trail. He could hear the diminishing sounds of Jason plowing through the brush. Lewis inhaled as if to jump into the deep end of a pool, and for the first time in his short life, entered the dense tunnel of vegetation. The caress of the leaves made his skin crawl, and Lewis exhaled the stale air from his lungs. He struggled to pull in another breath as his fear level increased a notch.

He took a single step and his fear lessened.

His panic subsided in increments with every step, vanishing altogether after just a few yards. Despite Jason's lead, Lewis could still hear the boy's movement further down the trail, sparking him into chase mode once again. Lewis tracked the dead boy, thankful for the commotion the lumbering beast made, using it to cover the racket he caused himself as he parted the wild vegetation of the under-used path. Lewis moved deeper into strange territory, the sounds and smell of his quarry the only indications he still followed the possessed bully.

The trail meandered through the woods, a twisting tunnel carved through the overgrowth. Lewis had the sensation of traveling through the bowels of a giant snake. Suddenly, the trail opened up, widening, the moonlit sky visible overhead. He turned another corner and saw the dark form of Jason squirming through a wall of tangled vines. Lewis halted, much closer to the creature than he had realized. If Jason decided to turn, Lewis would be exposed in the moonlight as plain as day. Luckily, Jason didn't turn; he vanished behind the dark wall blocking the path.

Lewis crouched and slithered his way to the barrier. Peeping through the vines, he could discern the dark shape of Jason against the moonlit glow of white sand. The large boy knelt, filling a glass jar with the sparkling substance.

This must be the clearing, Lewis thought, and glanced beyond the silhouette of Jason. A tree stood like a sentinel, protecting the genuflecting shape at its base.

Lewis instinctively tried to step back, but his feet ignored his pleas. He knew without a doubt that this was *the* tree. He had found it, here in his woods all this time. He could feel its malevolent power drape over him, like a hovering storm cloud swollen to capacity, the pressure a tangible force on his small body.

The surface of the tree, blacker than the night, absorbed the moon's rays. It appeared to be a tree-shaped hole against the backdrop of the woods and sky, a doorway to another world. Lewis would have thought the tree dead if not for several healthy leaves suspended from its skeletal branches, the moon glinting off their smooth surfaces. As Lewis studied the wicked tree, another leaf sprouted from the dark wood, like a time-lapse scene from a nature film.

Finished with his task, Jason stood. Lewis, still captivated by the leaf, saw the movement from the corner of his eye. He wheeled around to find a place to hide, the flap of his torn shirt snagging on a vine. Before he could stop, the dry vine snapped like a firecracker in the quiet woods.

Jason's head whipped around; he locked eyes with Lewis, the diseased yellow irises shining in the darkness. The jar thumped to the sand of the clearing as Jason lunged for Lewis with a bestial howl of pure loathing, vines splintering as he clawed his way through the barrier.

Once again Lewis fled for his life. He ran back down the trail, the overgrowth drawing blood from his hands and face, the predatory sounds of pursuit close behind.

Deputy Jack Dixon arrived at the Norton residence and parked his cruiser in the driveway behind the chief's car. He sprang from his vehicle and started up the drive to get filled in on the situation, still buzzing from collaring Dave Burton. The arrest had proved easy enough —the man was soused—but hauling in a possible murder suspect had been a first for the young officer. This was a feeling he could get accustomed to.

He stepped onto the Norton front porch and stopped with his finger inches from the doorbell when a light to his left caught his eye. A figure on the porch of the house next door signaled him, turning a flashlight on and off, begging for his attention. The porch light above the figure blazed; the deputy recognized the chief straightaway, even though the man wore his favorite aviator sunglasses, which seemed a little strange. He also noticed the leather jacket the chief wore, zipped all the way to his chin, and thought to himself how hot the man must be. He shrugged and greeted the chief with a friendly wave.

Chief Richards waved the flashlight in a come-hither-motion, then disappeared into the open door, swallowed whole by the house. Deputy Dixon shrugged again, trotted across the manicured grass, and stood on the front stoop, staring into the dark doorway of Clyde Boyd's home.

"Chief?" he asked the empty doorway; a flicker of light from within answered him. He wiped his shoes on the mat and entered the dark house, stopping at the sharp edge of light spilling in from the porch.

"Chief? What happened to the lights?"

The front door slammed shut behind the deputy like the jaws of a crocodile, shutting out the meager light, leaving him blind in the pitch-black belly of the house. As he jumped and spun around to face the closed door, an odd tingling burn traced the curvature of his neck. The thick sound of liquid splashing on the wall and carpet confused the deputy. He reached up to his throat, the tingling burn building into a searing white hot fire, and felt hot, sticky liquid coat his hands, spewing from a wide opening in his flesh. Moaning in the dark, the deputy cupped his draining blood in his hands, trying his best to save the vital fluid.

Deputy Jack Dixon dropped to his knees in the black room, tilting forward, plunging into an even deeper darkness.

30

L ewis ran as fast as he could through the tangled brush. His leg muscles burned, threatening to seize up as sweat ran down his face, stinging his eyes. Panting, he pressed his hand to the stabbing pain in his ribcage, using his other to push the slicing sawgrass away from his face. Despite his pain and tiring muscles, Lewis managed to outpace his pursuer. Jason's lunatic growls faded further behind.

Lewis needed a place to hide while out of sight of the beast, but this section of the woods was too dark and unfamiliar. He had to make it to his part of the woods, the woods he knew like the back of his hand. It seemed to Lewis he should have reached the fork and the mouth of the trail by now, causing panic to take root in his mind. Had he somehow gone the wrong direction and gotten lost?

As if in answer to his query, he burst into the open air of the fork, his panic subsiding at the sight of the familiar surroundings. Now he had to make a quick decision: go toward home, or run deeper into the woods down the trail he knew well, the intimate forest providing him with coverage.

The thought of home brought a string of emotions. First, sorrow for his mother and Mr. Boyd. Second, rage at the creatures, or creature, that had taken them away from him. Then fear, hopelessness and guilt needled their way in as well.

Thrashing and snarling grunts from behind Lewis forced a decision. He veered left and continued running, deeper into the woods, racking his brain for a possible hiding place that would extend his life a little longer. His newfound anger rose up above the sadness and fear, clearing his mind.

He knew of the perfect place to hide

31

Q uicker than he expected, Lewis found himself balanced on the edge of Horse Crap Lake, the foul humid vapors rising from the boggy lake attacking his nostrils as he bent over, struggling to catch his breath.

He stared up at the full moon and said a heartfelt thanks; falling into the lake would have been the end to his plans. It would have also been the end of Lewis. The heavy rain had filled only the deepest part of the lake. Lewis stood above the shallow edge, the moon's light glistening from the saturated loam and pools of disgusting water pocking the surface, revealing the dark bog before he could fall into its sucking clutches. Lewis looked down again, twelve feet above the crusty quagmire that stagnated at the bottom, and released a huge sigh. A fall into that morass would've pulled him down like quicksand and never let go.

His plan had been to hide in the old oak tree residing on the rim of the lake, wait for Jason to come near the edge, and jump down, shoving the beast into the swampy soup. That plan was shot when the approaching din of the ravenous boy filled Lewis's ears.

"Shit," Lewis spat, realizing his hopes of climbing the tree unseen were dashed. Lewis did the only thing he could think of—he dropped to his hands and knees, crawled to the lake's edge, and latched onto the oak's exposed roots protruding from the lip of the lake wall.

Lewis sucked in a deep breath, gripped the roots, and swung his legs out into space above the lake. He held the breath, willing himself to be light as a feather, and prayed the roots wouldn't snap as his feet dangled above the gaseous bog. When he stopped swinging, he reeled himself in until his back slapped the cool, moist soil of the lake wall, partially hiding him under the ancient roots. He dug his heels in for purchase, tightened his grip, and waited.

The animal grunts of his pursuer drew closer until they were directly above Lewis. His heart pounded so hard against his chest he was certain Jason would hear it. Lewis prayed again, he prayed the Jason-thing lacked the intelligence to look over the edge.

Soil cascaded into Lewis's hair. Looking up, he knew his simple request had not been granted. Jason stood above him, one hand held onto a limb of the tree, the other pressed to his mid-section, as if the creature was about to do a Latin dance to flaunt his victory.

Jason leaned out, as Lewis pressed himself deeper into the soft wall until he could go no further. The dead boy locked eyes with Lewis again, and whispered a single word through the fragments of his front teeth. A word that turned the trapped boy's blood frigid.

"Leewwiisss."

The voice—the same one from Lewis's nightmares— sifted down, sounding like pebbles stirred in a rusty tin can, yet the malice behind those two syllables were unmistakable, clear as day. Lewis wondered how much of the real Jason remained in the animated husk of his archenemy.

With his left hand anchored to the tree, Jason squatted and reached out for Lewis, once again releasing the innards from his decaying abdominal cavity.

Lewis clung to the roots, revolted, as Jason's intestines showered down on his face and shoulders, bouncing off, falling through the roots and hitting the lake's surface with a soft slap. Anger and disgust rushed through Lewis as cool, viscous fluids drizzled into his hair and ran off his face, the putrid juices smelling of road kill simmering in the summer sun. Lewis shook his head like a dog after a bath, released a growl, and latched onto the dangling guts with both hands. Freeing his heels from the wall, Lewis hung onto the soft intestines with all of his weight. A limb cracked above, and he felt the tightness of the guts slacken. He released the repulsive rope and grasped the tree roots once again.

Jason Reed's body plummeted past Lewis without a sound, headfirst, one hand grasping a broken branch. The bully hit the lake bottom like an Olympic high-diver, no splash, sinking in up to his belt, legs kicking the air.

Lewis hung above the lake and watched as Jason continued to struggle, causing him to settle deeper into the muck until all that showed were a pair of combat boots twitching above the surface. Between the moving boots, the boy's entrails were stretched taut like a deep-sea diver's lifeline, snared in the roots next to Lewis.

Gathering his strength, Lewis hauled himself up over the edge. He collapsed onto his back in the grass below the tree, gulping in the night air, grateful for the awful smell of the lake. Anything beat the smell of Jason's decomposing innards. He dragged himself to the rim and glanced down at his handiwork. Jason's boots still wiggled like a child throwing a tantrum.

Lewis barked laughter. His plan had worked.

Basically.

The laugh quickly changed to choking sobs as his nerves settled and the rush of adrenaline wore off. He stared at the kicking boots, thinking of his mother and Jerry standing on the porch, anger welling inside him

"FUCK YOU!" Lewis cried, tossing a rock at the boots. He'd thought of this phrase many times before, but it was the first time he'd used it out loud. It invigorated him, filling him with courage. He'd bested Jason. He knew now that he wasn't powerless against them. There actually might be a chance of defeating them. He also knew where to find the tree; down the left hand path. Maybe there was hope after all. He stood, brushing the vile sludge from his hair and wiping the tears from his cheeks.

Mr. Boyd insisted the tree couldn't be destroyed by fire, but Lewis was keen on testing this theory out for himself. The image of the gas can, nestled next to the lawn mower in his garage, flashed in his head.

He shot one last glance at the twitching boots, and then started toward home.

He had another plan.

C autious, expecting to run into Andy around every turn, Lewis made his way back to the edge of the woods without incident. The open field of grass loomed before him, seeming much larger than usual, like a football field void of all players. He stopped and scanned his street. The quiet disturbed him. Lewis thought that if Mr. Boyd was correct about "her being them", and "they being her", then the witch knew what had transpired at the lake.

Why hadn't they come after me?

Lewis could see his mother's car in the distance, parked in the drive. The house seemed miles away and every dark window he had to pass to reach his home appeared to be watching him. Disabling fear crept into his mind, rooting his shoes to the ground.

I can still run …

No. I can't. I have to do something.

The welcome sight of two police cruisers across from

his house lifted some of his fear. Lewis coaxed his feet into moving in the direction of his destination.

He sprinted across the open field, reaching the first home on his street. He leaned against the brick wall until his breathing slowed, listening for signs of trouble, then started toward his home once again. He kept to the bushes, slinking from house to house, avoiding any windows when possible, the feeling of being watched threatening to push him into panic mode. He passed Maggie Burton's house, the yellow police-tape strung across her front door glowing in the moonlight. Lewis kept his cool and continued on, past the cop cars parked in the Norton's driveway on the opposite side of the street.

It was too quiet.

Where were the cops to go along with these cars? Every house remained dark and still, nobody in sight.

The light on Mr. Boyd's porch still burned, giving Lewis a fleeting glimmer of hope. Maybe the old man was home, he thought. He recalled the image of the naked maniac and decided he wouldn't like what he would find if he went back into the old man's house.

Lewis reached the side of his own house and concealed himself in the bushes lining the wall of the garage. He hid in the dark for a minute, letting his pulse slow, catching his breath again as sweat crawled through his hair and ran down his face, the lingering scent of Jason's insides returning in force. Lewis reached out in the shadows, grasping the outdoor spigot. He turned the handle, cold water spewing forth. He splashed water onto his face and hair, and drank directly from the spigot. Refreshed, he turned the valve off and waited several more seconds before continuing his journey.

In a crouch, Lewis skulked from the bushes, around the corner, to the big garage door. He grabbed the handle and tried lifting it. Locked, just as he had expected. He checked his street for signs of movement again, and crept to the front door. The porch light was off now. Lewis began to wonder if the witch doused the lights to mark the houses she'd already visited. He looked up his street, and noticed most of the homes had their porch lights extinguished—he hoped he was wrong.

His shoes squished on the welcome mat. Lewis knew what he stood in, but refused to look down, realizing that doing so would probably send him running for the woods, never to return.

Lewis tested the handle, it moved freely in his grasp, unlocked.

He paused, straining his ears for any movement within the house, listening for sounds of danger. He eased the door open and entered the structure he'd called home his entire life. The once welcoming front room now felt long abandoned, like an ancient mausoleum. Lewis stepped further into the shadows, and froze when something brushed the back of his calf, forcing a yelp from his throat. Lewis spun, expecting an attack. He released a shaky breath at the sight of his cat.

Stretch purred softly, rubbing against his leg again, twirling around his feet.

Lewis nudged him with his foot. "Shoo, Stretch. Go hide, buddy."

The cat obeyed, darting out the open front door. Lewis

closed the door behind Stretch and thought how pissed his father would be if he knew the cat had gotten into the house.

His father!

What would he tell his father? Would he believe him? … Blame him?

Maybe this is *all my fault.* Lewis felt tears roll down his cheeks again at the thought of his mother. *If I had just told someone instead of trying to handle this myself she would still be alive. I guess I should have listened to Clinton.*

Clinton!

He'll help me. I'll get the gasoline, go get Clinton, and we'll torch that ugly tree to ashes.

Lewis wiped his eyes and made his way through the gloomy interior of the house to the open door of his parents' bedroom. The darkness made his progress painfully slow, but turning on a light could attract unwanted attention. He entered the bedroom, thankful for the deep shadows now; he did not want to see the bed where his mother must have been murdered. Shuffling his way past the dark shape of the bed, he came to the garage entrance. A wreath of fake flowers adorned the door to the garage—his mother's attempt to make the plain entrance more appealing. It was another sad reminder of her, but it propelled him forward. He had to destroy that tree; his mother's death would be avenged. He opened the door and entered the garage

The darkness inside the room was impenetrable. He desperately needed a light in here, but feared it would leak from the base of the garage door. He would just have to creep through the clutter and try not to make any noise—

or break his neck. The image of the naked man flashed in his head. *There could be someone in here with me. That same man could be in here, hiding, just like at Mr. Boyd's house.* Lewis fought the urge to turn on the light, waited for his fear to subside, and began the slow process of navigating the minefield that was the Frazier garage.

Arms outstretched as if playing Pin the Tail on the Donkey, Lewis blindly felt his way, forming a map of the cluttered space in his mind, the intimate aroma of exhaust, oil, and old cardboard boxes soothing his frayed nerves. Familiar objects brushed his stretching fingers: bicycles, punching bag, his father's massive toolbox on wheels, and at last—the lawnmower. Kneeling, he reached for the spot he knew the gas can should be; cool metal kissed his fingertips. With a smile, he lifted the can, the joyous sound of sloshing liquid music to his ears.

With his excitement mounting, Lewis stood and turned, for a brief instant forgetting his need for stealth, bumping the bicycle in front of him. The bike toppled with a resounding crash as it knocked the other bikes over like dominoes. In the silence of the dark room, the crashing of the three bicycles sounded more like a hundred. He cringed, helpless, as the noise seemed to last forever.

Silence returned. Lewis stood frozen, still cringing, his eyes shut, the air around him buzzing. He remained still for several more seconds, waiting to hear the grunts and growls of the enemy. The garage and house remained quiet. Relieved, Lewis exhaled, and threaded his way among the wreckage, tracing his path back to the door.

Just before entering the house, Lewis heard the heavy

garage door rattle in its tracks—someone trying to lift it from the outside.

They heard me!

His mind in a panic, Lewis tried to remember if he had locked the front door of the house.

He hurried into the front room just as a shadow passed over the window next to the closed front door. He moved as fast as he could in the dark, reaching the door and turning the bolt as quickly and quietly as possible. The handle rattled less than a second later as someone turned it from the outside.

The doorknob jiggled several times then stopped. Lewis sighed and rested his forehead on the rough wood. From inches away, on the other side of the door, he heard his name whispered for the second time tonight.

Impossible! There's no way he could have gotten out of the lake.

"Screw this," Lewis whispered. *Go to the kitchen, grab a lighter, head out the back door, get Clinton, and get to the tree.*

Lewis turned, headed for the kitchen, when the five familiar knocks came from the other side of the door.

'Shave and a haircut'

Lewis stopped and spun, ran back to the front door, knocked twice and flipped the switch on the wall, turning on the porch light. Beaming with excitement, he spun the deadbolt and flung the door open to greet his friend.

Clinton stood on the front porch smiling back.

The joyful expression melted from Lewis's face when he saw his friend.

It wasn't Clinton.

The malignant grin and nauseating angle of Clinton's swollen neck was proof enough for Lewis. On top of that, Clinton's usually tan skin glowed a chalky pallor, his blue eyes now burned with the evil red and yellow of Jerry's. Several holes in his t-shirt leaked blood, running the length of his bare legs, into his sneakers.

Through clenched teeth, still grinning, Clinton whispered, "Leeewwwiissss."

About the same time Lewis entered his house, Dolores Norton sat up in bed. Like she had expected, sleep was not on tonight's agenda. Unable to erase the image of the nude, crazed-looking man from her thoughts, she decided to continue her late-night housekeeping. She left her snoring husband and went back to the kitchen. There had to be something else to clean— there always was.

She looked at the empty sink (she had finished the dishes), then glanced out the kitchen window again. The chief's car still sat in her drive. Another cruiser was tucked in behind it; both cars appeared empty. She tied her robe shut and strolled to the front door, cracked it open a couple inches, and peered outside.

"Officers?" she asked the quiet driveway.

She swung the door open further and ventured out onto her front stoop. Wrapping her arms around her chest as if it were the dead of winter instead of the heart of summer, she scanned the drive and street. Nobody there. Dead quiet.

"Chief?"

A gray cat darted from under the rear police car, vanishing into her hibiscus bushes with an angry hiss.

Dolores shuffled further out toward the parked vehicles, her slippers scraping on the concrete driveway. Squinting, she looked through the windshield of the chief's car. The reflection from the full moon made it difficult to see inside, but a glance through the driver's window showed the emptiness of the vehicle, just as she'd suspected. She scooted down the drive to the second car and repeated the process with similar results.

Shaking her head, Mrs. Norton scraped her way back up the drive and stopped when she saw the chief casually striding toward her across Clyde Boyd's immaculate lawn.

She put a hand over her heart. "Oh thank heavens, there you are. I was starting to think something bad had happened to you."

When the chief didn't reply and continued moving toward her, she backed up, her ample behind pressing into the front fender of the chief's car. "Is everything all right, chief?"

That's when Mrs. Norton spied the small crowd following the chief. Another officer led the pack; his neck, covered with a white substance, seemed to grin at her as he walked. Behind him strolled her neighbor from across the way, Mrs. Frazier, her face and nightgown glistening, the moon's glow reflecting from the dark fluid covering her from head to toe. Holding the hand of the woman was a small child Dolores recognized on the spot as one of the missing boys. Several more figures spilled out of Clyde Boyd's house. She recognized all of them—her neighbors.

"I demand to know what's going on here," Mrs. Norton stated in a terrified tone masquerading as a voice of authority.

The chief answered the woman's request. He raised his nightstick to the sky like a General signaling his troops to charge, and brought it down on her head with a hollow crunch.

Dolores Norton's eyes crossed as she followed the path of the nightstick to her skull, offering an inquisitive groan to the chief when her blood sprayed the windshield of the car behind her. She fell backward, collapsing the hood of the car.

The baton whistled through the air as the chief swung it repeatedly onto her ruined skull like a child attacking a piñata, releasing the delicious contents of her head to the night air. The onlookers waded in with hungry lust in their matching eyes.

Mr. Norton snored away in his cozy bed as the pack feasted on his wife's plentiful, soft flesh

L ewis slammed the door on Clinton's smirking face, twisting the deadbolt. He could hear his name whispered over and over on the other side of the wood, threatening to send him over the mental brink he so precariously teetered. The beast inside Clinton's body taunted Lewis, knocking on the door between each hiss of his name.

Tears blurred Lewis's vision as he spoke to the door, "Go away, Clinton. You can't come in. Just go away … please."

As if in answer to his pleas, the knocking ceased, along with the mocking whispers.

Lewis wiped his eyes and leaned his back to the door, waiting for his name to come again.

A clatter arose from the direction of his bedroom. From the sound, Lewis guessed Clinton had moved from the front door and was attempting to climb through the bedroom window. He used this opportunity to find the lighter.

Running into the kitchen, he flipped on the light and slid drawers out at random, dumping the contents onto the tile floor. Defiling his mother's kitchen filled Lewis with guilt, but he continued his desperate ransacking as the noises from his bedroom intensified. He glimpsed the shiny chrome Zippo as it bounced amongst the jumble of utensils, and snatched it up. A crash from the bedroom signaled the Clinton-thing's arrival into his home.

Lewis pocketed the lighter on his way to the front door, grabbed the gas can and flung the door open. He ran onto the porch, glancing to his left, toward his bedroom window, and caromed off the naked man.

Gasoline sloshed from the can's nozzle as he bounced off the naked fiend, soaking the creature's bare stomach. Lewis instinctively retrieved the lighter from his pocket, clicked the lid back and thumbed the wheel. Fearing it wouldn't light—like in some bad horror film—Lewis barked a cry of relief when the spark ignited on the first try.

The naked demon stood before Lewis, staring at the shimmering flame with obvious respect and hatred. Then, with a savage roar, the creature charged. The naked man's hands curled into claws as they sped toward Lewis's face. Lewis lunged backward and to the side, dodging the talons, swiping the lighter to the man's midsection. Yellow fire flared with a loud whoosh of air, engulfing the man's torso. The creature stopped and stared down at the blaze, the fire blowing his hair back, the flames lighting the man's amused grin. The skin of his face crackled and popped, blisters formed and burst, hissing on the flames. The distinct odor of burnt hair filled the air as the fire enveloped the man's face, which he raised to Lewis, still grinning. Lewis splashed more of the fuel onto the flames, turning the man into a human torch. The man's grin melted into a sneer; he lunged with a tremendous howl of rage.

Lewis dodged the flaming man's outstretched claws again, the tremendous heat singing the hairs on his arms, and ran toward the cop cars parked across the street. A sudden scream to his right forced his head in that direction. Doris the Poodle zoomed past Lewis with the speed of a greyhound, a white puff of fur flying into the night; Mrs. Taggart followed, a bestial scream rumbling from her throat as she charged toward Lewis. By the firelight of the naked man, now fully ablaze, Lewis could see bleeding cavities where the woman's eyes should have been. Lewis wasn't sure if his neighbor was one of the creatures or not, but it became a moot point as she blindly tackled the blazing man, igniting her bathrobe, and sending them both to the ground. The fiery couple struggled to rise, pulling one another down as the intense heat fused their limbs together. Lewis left them to burn, running for the police cars.

He found the police, but from the look of it, he doubted they were going to serve and protect. He braked, his sneakers sliding on the grass as the heavy gas can carried his momentum closer to the infernal tableau before him. Two cops, his mother, Jerry, and several others reared their heads from the savaged carcass on the hood of the car, their faces painted red.

Lewis didn't scream. He couldn't have screamed if he had wanted to. His tongue dangled useless in his open mouth as he took in the scene. He simply turned and fled toward the woods, the gasoline sloshing in his grip.

The revelers focused once again on their feast. Her siege on the quiet hamlet had begun; the bothersome child could wait. It was time to feed.

Lewis stopped and turned before entering the woods. Nobody pursued him across the field. The conjoined burning figures on his front lawn moved in sluggish slow motion, then fell still.

That answered one question: fire could stop them.

He saw no sign of Clinton, and wondered who else had been turned into a cannibalistic maniac. Was Justin still alive? What about their parents?

He reminded himself to be on the lookout for Andy; the cretin had yet to make an appearance and Lewis hoped it stayed that way. He also hoped Jason was still imprisoned in the lake, and he could make it to the tree without incident.

He looked down at the red and yellow can labeled **GASOLINE**.

This better work.

Nerves tingling, on full alert, Lewis trudged his way along the familiar meandering path, the bright moon his only source of light. Thick advancing clouds obscured the shining disk periodically, slowing his progress to a crawl as the shadows deepened around him. Furthermore, the weight of the gas can and his fear of running into Andy did little to help his forward movement. The breeze pushing the dense clouds brought the scent of rain with it. Lewis looked up to the black clouds and quickened his pace.

After what seemed an eternity, he arrived at the split in the trail without incident.

Eyes adjusting to the darkness, Lewis stared down the constricted throat of the less traveled path. He knew the tree waited at the end of this trail, but still felt the urge to veer right, or turn around, or go any direction but the one he needed to go. He trembled, a cold sweat beading on his flushed face.

Lewis knew he could face the trail and its protective spell. He'd done it earlier. The problem, he realized, was that he felt like the only person on the planet.

Abandoned.

Alone.

His mother was gone. His best friend in the world was gone. The only home he'd ever known was gone as well. Never would he be able to look at his house, his street, or these woods with a feeling of joy. All his fond memories were blighted with horror, like a cancer eating away all that is good, leaving behind an infectious soul-sucking rot.

Lewis squeezed his eyes shut and shook his head. The amplified feelings of despair—spurned on by the barrier spell—deteriorated, fleeing his mind like steam. He opened his eyes and waded in, the trail swallowing him like a snake devouring a mouse. As he moved down the path the spell weakened, allowing Lewis to focus on his plan.

Mr. Boyd had clearly warned the boys that an attempt to torch the tree would start a fire on the perimeter of the clearing, trapping the fire-starter inside a ring of flames. Lewis, however, had thought of a simple but ingenious plan. His source of inspiration had been the childhood memory of *Yosemite Sam,* and his infamous trail of gunpowder leading to the hole of *Bugs Bunny.*

First, dowse the tree with gasoline; then, leave a trail of fuel to a safe distance down the path, outside the clearing; and finally, light the river of gas and sit back at a safe distance. In his head he could envision it with perfect clarity: the flame shooting down the trail, through the wall of vines, and the grand explosion at the end as the witch's tree ignited. He just hoped his plan didn't backfire like poor *Yosemite Sam's*—the fire burning him in the ass.

Lewis plodded on, the image of the burning tree a beacon of hope, a figurative light at the end of this literal dark tunnel.

The humid night air clung to Lewis like a soggy jumpsuit. The leaves and sawgrass crawled over his skin like razor-edged insect wings. Vines and roots snagged his shoes, causing him to stumble. He concentrated on the image of the burning tree, his destination, but the poisoned woods persisted, trying its best to thwart his plans. Just as the heat, slicing grass, and darkness of the trail threatened to send Lewis into a panic, he breached the overgrowth and entered the stretch of trail open to the night sky. He stood in the fresh air for a moment, allowing the breeze to blow away the dampness covering his body, letting his nerves calm. He was close.

With the open air and bright moon lifting his spirits, Lewis followed the path as it approached the final dogleg turn that would take him straight to the wall of vines. He recalled making the turn earlier, nearly being seen by Jason, and reassured himself the boy remained trapped in the boggy lake; there was no way he could've gotten free. So there was no chance of running into him this time. Lewis made the final turn, and halted, paralyzed. His spirits shattered, falling away like a broken mirror.

A figure blocked the path.

Not Jason. But someone even worse.

Andy Reed scowled at Lewis, his face glowing in the full moon's glare, a visage of unadulterated hate. For a moment, Lewis swore he was looking at the everyday normal Andy, one half of the feared Reed twins, the scornful expression on the boy's face no different than usual. Until the moon reflected a dull yellow from Andy's eyes—the wolf-like glow of a predator's stare. An enormous hunting knife protruded from the boy's grip, the tip of the weapon sheared off, glowing in the moonlight like an eldritch blade.

A sudden eerie calm washed over Lewis. His initial shock at seeing his old enemy melted away. Surprisingly, for the first time in his life, Lewis wasn't scared of the bully. The things he'd seen on this night may have scarred him, but they've also made him stronger, like a mended bone.

Lewis let the gas can drop to the forest floor and stood his ground, refusing to run. He was sick of running. Plus, he had nowhere or nobody to run to anymore, and it was all due to the abomination standing in front of him.

Stabbing his index finger toward Andy, Lewis uttered the forbidden phrase once again. "Fuck you. I'm not afraid of you anymore."

Frustration and anger swelled within Lewis. He glanced around the trail, searching for anything to use as a weapon against the brute. He could try and torch Andy, but wanted to save the remaining gasoline for the tree.

Andy advanced, taking his time, a smarmy look of victory on his filthy face. Lewis knew the expression belonged to the witch, but his anger focused on Andy, the bane of his childhood. Lewis spied the familiar vines crawling up the trunk of a tree next to him; he plucked several of the swollen swamp potatoes, cradling the ammo in his torn shirt as his rage boiled over. He faced his longtime tormenter and threw the first potato, striking Andy in the shoulder. The boy stopped and smiled, unharmed as the tuber bounced away, plunking to the ground. Lewis wound up again and threw the next even harder. The second potato hit the thing that used to be Andy Reed in the chest with the same outcome.

Lewis launched a third and a fourth. One sailed over Andy's fat head, the other lodged in the boy's gaping throat wound with a satisfying thump. Andy halted, removed the potato from his neck with all the nonchalance of plucking lint from his navel, flicking it to the ground. He advanced again, unharmed.

Lewis gripped the last potato. It filled his small hand, heavy and hard as a rock. He reared back and focused all the years of torture and suffering from the hands of the Reed twins into his tired muscles, casting the missile with all his might, hurling it at Andy's massive head, now only ten feet away.

The potato struck Andy in the forehead—a perfect bull's-eye.

The dead boy's head exploded with a deafening blast and a brilliant flare of light.

Lewis crashed to the ground, his ears ringing in pain as warm bits of Andy sprinkled down around him. Stunned, Lewis sat on the trail and gawked at the mostly headless body teetering before him, then pumped his fists in the air as the knife fell from Andy's limp hand and the body toppled backward to the ground.

Still seated on the trail, Lewis continued his private celebration, fists punching the air. Until a hand gripped his shoulder.

Lewis jumped to his feet, grabbed a potato from the dirt and spun, ready to take on the next foe with his new incendiary wonder weapon. He blinked rapidly to remove the purple afterimage from the bright explosion of light, and stared at the man on the trail.

Bathed in moonlight, cradling a smoking, double-barreled shotgun, stood his friend and neighbor.

Clyde Boyd.

36

M r. Boyd snapped the shotgun open, discarded the empty shells, pulled two from his shirt pocket and reloaded the weapon.

"You okay, son?"

The question was muffled to Lewis, as if hearing it underwater, but he understood it well enough. He responded with a slow nod, his mouth and eyes stuck wide open, and pushed his index finger into his left ear, jiggling it back and forth.

Mr. Boyd nudged the gas can with his boot. "I told ya, you can't burn the damn thing. And using gas would turn these woods into Hiroshima, son. We have to kill the first one infected."

The old man nodded to the headless corpse on the ground. "Hope I just did."

Lewis let the potato roll from his fingers, and then jumped on Mr. Boyd, hugging the man around the waist, smashing his face against his chest. He could smell the old man's cologne: *Old Spice,* just like his grandfather wore.

"I thought you were dead. One of those things was in your house," Lewis said, his muffled voice a thin vibrato of emotion.

Mr. Boyd shook his head and pushed Lewis back, looking into the boy's watery eyes. "Nope. Still kickin'."

"Where were you?" Lewis asked.

"Got tired of twiddlin' my thumbs, waiting for those damn cops to skedaddle, so when it got good and dark, I grabbed my guns and hopped the wall behind my house. Went straight to the tree and hid there for a while but nobody showed, so I've been walkin' these trails all night."

Lewis recalled the footsteps that had come within inches of where he crouched in his hidden fort, and the lingering scent of cologne; he smiled. "Did you find anything?"

"Yeah. I followed a butt-naked lady for a bit. She went down into a ditch and crawled into the big run-off pipe that flows into the lake. I'd just worked up the nerve to go in after her when you came stomping along. Couldn't tell if you were one of them or not, so I followed you instead. Glad I did." He patted Lewis on the head.

Lewis nodded. "Me too. You saw one go into the drainpipe?"

"Yep. I bet that's where they've been hiding out and sneakin' around."

"I saw a bunch on our street," Lewis said. "They were in Mrs. Norton's driveway … eating her … at least, I think it was her. Jerry was there. So was my mom."

Lewis grabbed the man's shirt. "She's one of them, Mr.

Boyd … her and Clinton too. What are we gonna do?"
The tears flowed freely again.

Mr. Boyd pulled Lewis in and hugged him with his
free arm. "I'm sorry, son. I'm truly sorry." After a moment,
when Lewis's hitching sobs weakened, he pushed the boy
back again and stared into his moist eyes. "We have to kill
the Harris boy. And anyone else that gets in our way."

He patted Lewis on the head again, and then moved
the hand around to the small of his back; it returned with
a blue-black snub-nosed revolver resting in the open palm.
He handed it to Lewis.

His hands sluggish, Lewis accepted the offering with
apprehension and respect. He held the small gun in both
hands, the weight surprising him. It looked like a gun
from an old crime movie, one the detectives always carried
and shot from the hip. Lewis looked from the small
weapon, to the large shotgun in Mr. Boyd's grip.

"Don't worry, I shortened that barrel myself. She
shoots straight and packs a wallop. Your daddy ever teach
you how to use one of these?"

Lewis gripped the .38 in his right hand, shaking his
head. "No."

"Well, time for a crash-course: Just point it at what
you want to kill and squeeze the trigger. That easy. You got
six shots. Make 'em count."

He slapped Lewis on the shoulder and pulled a flashlight from his belt. "Let's go."

Clyde Boyd turned and marched back down the trail,
away from the clearing, following the beam of his flashlight, the shotgun resting on his shoulder.

Lewis followed, leaving the gas can and headless bully

behind, hoping Andy *was* the first one infected, and that this nightmare was over. He gripped the cool pistol as a distant scream of anguish reached his ears, dashing his hopes.

Maybe the nightmare had just begun.

37

Lewis followed his neighbor along the dark trail, the faraway scream echoing in his mind. He hadn't heard another sound since, causing the seed of hope to flower again. *Maybe the scream came from someone discovering the bodies on my street. Maybe Andy was the first infected, and this is all over.*

Mr. Boyd burst from the dense vegetation of the trail and stopped in the fork. "I'm an idiot," he whispered and turned back to look down the trail they'd just left.

"What's wrong?" Lewis whispered back.

Mr. Boyd sighed. "I could've just checked the damn tree. If the leaves were all gone then we would know if that boy had been the first infected."

Another shriek of terror wailed in the distance. Mr. Boyd turned his head toward the sound. "Never mind. I think that answers that question."

Standing in the relative brightness of the main trail, Mr. Boyd clicked the flashlight off and secured it back onto his belt. He turned to Lewis and whispered, "I think we can see good enough by the moon the rest of the way back. I don't want 'em to know we're coming."

"Good idea," agreed Lewis, the flower of hope wilting. "But if she controlled Andy then she knows we're out here."

He faced away from Lewis, looking down the trail. "Yeah, you're probably right. Let's move quietly, and be ready to—"

Before he could finish, a naked woman sprang from the bushes with a feral screech, landing on the old man's back, sending the pair sprawling to the dirt in front of Lewis.

The shotgun flew from Clyde's grasp and tumbled away into the bushes lining the trail. The old man wrestled with the wild woman, freeing her from his back with a well-placed elbow to her temple. She quickly regained her composure and pounced onto his chest as he rolled over. The old man threw punches from the bottom, connecting with the woman's jaw, but was unable to dislodge her again.

Lewis raised the revolver and aimed the short barrel at the struggling couple on the ground. His aim wavered as the woman's nakedness finally registered, hypnotizing him. The gun sank toward his feet.

"SHOOOOT!" screamed Mr. Boyd as the woman bit into the flesh of his forearm, the word trailing off into a howl of pain.

Lewis raised the weapon again but hesitated once more, this time in fear of shooting his friend.

"SHOOT HER!" he cried again, driving her head back with his arm still in her jaws.

Point at what you want to kill and squeeze the trigger. Point at what you want to kill and squeeze the trigger.

Lewis aimed at her head and fired the revolver, the report and recoil of the small gun surprising him. Nothing happened. He had missed her completely from just a few feet away. He aimed the pistol again, steadying the gun with his other hand, and squeezed the trigger once more.

The second shot surprised Lewis as well, making him jump, but this time the woman's nose vanished, the divot of flesh flying off into the brush. Dark blood oozed from the triangular cavity in her face. She calmly opened her jaws, freeing the mangled arm, and turned her seeping face to Lewis. Her glowing eyes met his. Releasing a ferocious animal squeal, the woman sprayed Lewis with thick blood as it dribbled into her mouth. He shut his eyes, the cool liquid spattering his face.

Lewis didn't hesitate this time. Knowing what to expect, he opened his eyes, aimed, stepped closer to the yowling beast, and fired point-blank into her face.

The bullet entered her left eye and exited the back of her head, her dark hair lifting as if from a sudden breeze. Lewis could hear a soft patter on the bushes behind the woman—the contents of her skull decorating the woods. This soft tapping sound, not the sight of the woman's destroyed face, is what caused Lewis to fall to his knees and relinquish the meager cargo of his stomach to the forest floor. The woman's limp body toppled backward off the old man.

Panting, Mr. Boyd managed to get to his feet. He

stumbled toward the retching Lewis and placed a hand on the boy's thin shoulder. "Good job, son. Couldn't have done it better myself."

Lewis used the front of his shirt to clear the vomit from his shaking lips, and the woman's blood from his face. He pointed to the leaking bite on the old man's arm. "You all right?"

"I'll be fine," he replied, pulling a bandana from his pocket, wrapping the wound tight. "Been bit by worse before. Remind me later and I'll tell ya about the time I tussled with a gator."

He helped Lewis up. "Well Lewis, at least we know for sure that boy I shot back there wasn't the first infected. And you were right, they knew exactly where to find us. Better get moving before more show up."

They stared at the dead woman, her one eye stared back, now a normal human eye. Lewis looked away from the accusing glare, his knees threatening to buckle. She was just a woman now, not a monster. Maybe someone's wife, or sister, or mother. And he had killed her.

Mr. Boyd shook his head. "Damn shame, she was quite a looker."

He retrieved the shotgun from the bushes and turned back to Lewis. "That's all the bullets I could find for that gun. You got three more shots, son. Don't waste 'em. Who knows how many of these things there are now."

Lewis didn't respond, so Mr. Boyd asked, "You say you saw a bunch of 'em at the Norton house?"

Lewis nodded as Mr. Boyd patted him on the shoulder again. "Come on then. Let's go home."

Lewis inhaled a deep breath and released it slowly,

regaining his composure. Stealing one last glance at the dead woman, he said a silent apology, and followed his friend.

38

T he loss of the other twin angered her. Regardless, she kept feeding, gorging on the delicate bone marrow of the obese woman. Then three more gunshots, and another one of her creatures were taken. Maybe she underestimated the little child; she has lost five valuable servants because of him and that old man. It was time to tend to the nuisance.

She sent the two cops to take care of the pesky brat and his aging cohort, and decided to hide in the safety of the underground lair while her other servants continued to build her ever-growing army.

Several pops of gunfire erupted from a street over as she lifted the manhole cover—her marauding servants were struck but not harmed. Stupid cattle and their silly weapons. Delightful screams of pain followed the shots, filling her with joy. She watched, her eyes their eyes, as her minions sprinkled the magical sand down the dead throats of their victims. She would need to replenish the substance from the clearing soon, after she took care of the pests in the woods.

Sated for the moment, she conceded, realizing this particular vessel was too small and vulnerable to be out in the open. Once the troublesome child and his old friend were either killed or turned, she would emerge and seize her land once again. She dropped through the dark hole into the storm drain.

This time she would be more careful.

This time her reign would last.

Forever.

39

J ustin sat up in bed.
Firecrackers? Why are there firecrackers going off? What time is it?

He rubbed his sleep-crusted eyes and listened for more of the celebratory pops. He glanced around the dark bedroom, confused. It wasn't even close to the 4th of July.

A sudden sound from inside the house awoke him fully: the unmistakable hollow liquid crash of a bottle hitting a tile floor. Justin formed a perfect image in his mind of his father dropping a beer, and waited for the obligatory inebriated curses that usually followed such a mishap—none came. The only response was a single loud bark from Chewy, followed by the soft thumping *tick-tock* of the dog door swinging on its hinge.

Chewy rarely barked, and when he did, it was usually a happy yap of greeting when the boys came home from school. This bark, however, had a completely different aura. This bark had a tone of fear, and warning.

Tossing the sheet away, Justin swung his bare feet to the floor. He stood slow and silent, the need to be quiet overwhelming him, the reason for this necessity unknown, instinctual. He crept to the bedroom door, his footsteps muted by the thick carpet, and cracked the door just enough to peek through. The hall was dark. Strange shadows danced on the living room wall at the end of the hallway. He could hear the T.V. now, and realized something was moving in front of the light from the television, casting shadows into the next room. The volume was low, but he could make out the tinny sounds of actors voices and the occasional laugh track.

Justin inhaled, about to call out for his mom to see if everything was okay, when Chewy spoke up again, another single bark, this time from the backyard. Justin could swear he sensed an urgent plea for caution in the dog's bark. He released the breath, the need for stealth staying his tongue. He opened the door further and squeezed through into the shadows of the hallway.

He made his way to Clinton's room across the hall. The door remained closed, a sign reading **KEEP OUT** with a perfectly rendered drawing of Justin's dripping, severed head adorning the entrance. Normally, Justin would knock and ask for permission before entering, the wrath of his older brother nothing to toy with; this time, however, being quiet felt imperative, outweighing his fear of Clinton's fury.

He turned the knob and pushed on the door. Justin knew—even before he saw the open window and the pushed-out screen—the room was empty. He could somehow sense the absence of his brother, the energy of the room rendered inert.

"Clinton?" he whispered anyway, and cringed at the loudness of his voice.

A crash came from the direction of the family room. Justin whirled, his quickened pulse humming in his ears. After a few seconds, he inched his way along the corridor toward the noise, approaching the pulsating shadows on the wall. The closer he got, the more sounds he could discern: a low intermittent squeak; quiet laughter and voices from the television; and above that, a strange slurping and smacking, like Chewy devouring his bowl of foul smelling canned dog food.

The shadows stopped moving just as Justin reached the end of the hall, then after a couple of seconds, resumed their strange dance; he cautiously peered around the corner. He could see the back of his father's favorite chair —the beat up old recliner his dad refused to replace despite the complaints from his mother. The chair sat in its usual spot, silhouetted in front of the glowing television. Justin could see it rocking slightly, and could hear the old springs squeaking in protest. The wet smacking sounds also came from the vicinity of the chair.

Sure enough, Justin could see a broken bottle on the floor below a dangling hand, and smell the sweet tang of beer. His father's silver wristwatch gleamed on the wrist above the suspended hand as it swayed in rhythm with the movements of the chair.

Justin turned the corner and approached the recliner. Outlined against the bright television, he could now discern the familiar shape of his mother's head above the back of the chair, facing him. She was sitting on his father's lap, straddling him. Her head dipped up and down, and moved side to side. She didn't notice her son creeping into the room.

With disgust, Justin realized what was happening on the other side of the chair.

Oh, gross! They're making out!

Justin scrunched his face into a melodramatic pucker of repulsion and turned around to head back to bed, relieved, but also regretting the picture burned into his retinas forever, an image that would surely haunt his dreams for the rest of the night. He inched his way back toward his room.

From behind, the slurping and squeaks halted.

Knowing he'd been caught, Justin stopped. Taking his time, he turned to accept his fate.

He spoke up before his parents could say anything: the preemptive-strike-method of innocence Clinton had taught him. "I'm sorry. I heard weird noises so I got up to … Mom? Are you okay?"

The sound that spewed from his mother's blood-smeared face turned Justin's flesh to ice. With her hands propped on the top of the chair she barked an evil laugh— a hyena celebrating a fresh kill. Justin could feel the strength leave his body like a flock of frightened birds, then the jarring impact of his tailbone against the tile floor as it hit him from behind like a rogue wave. Justin lay on the floor, staring at the ceiling, completely confused.

His mother's mocking laugh caught his attention. The laugh morphed into a low growl, and Justin could only watch as his mother crawled over the high back of the recliner, tipping it, and his father to the floor with her. Justin stared into his father's open eyes, then into the gaping cavity that had replaced his nose, and finally into the skeletal smile formed from his missing lips.

Justin's mother landed on all fours, snarling like a wolf, blocking the sight of his dead father's ruined face. Justin regained some muscle control and scooted back, away from the wild animal wearing his mother's face, the thick pain of his bruised coccyx breaking his mental paralysis.

His mother stood, casual and calm. She sauntered to her youngest son, teeth bared, her hands at her sides shaped into claws, dripping with his father's blood. Justin could sense her muscles coiling under her pale flesh, like a snake on the verge of striking, but could still not find the strength to rise. He propped himself on one elbow and raised his other hand to his mother.

"Mom ... Stop ... Please," he begged, his voice quaking along with his outstretched hand.

She laughed at his pathetic pleas. A hearty laugh that brought her head back, her face to the ceiling. Justin knew nothing of the witch's tale, but he knew the chuckling monster standing above him was not his mother.

The beast stopped laughing and dropped her eyes back down to meet Justin's. She whipped her head to the left as something caught her attention. That's when the growling, brown blur flew over Justin, knocking the crazed woman to the floor.

Chewy attacked his owner with the ferociousness of a badger, latching onto her shoulder and shaking with savage, tendon-snapping force.

Justin stared at the attack with awe. Chewy—the lazy family pet—had gone wild.

With his execution pardoned, Justin's energy returned. He pounced to his feet, ignoring the hot flare of pain in his tailbone. Chewy sensed the recovery and released the woman. The dog barked once at Justin and ran to the back door, disappearing through the flap of the dog door. Justin received the message loud and clear and followed his savior. As he reached the door another crash and hissing growl came from behind; he glanced over his shoulder to see his mother rising, pulling furniture over to right herself, her left arm hanging limp at her side.

With tears blurring his vision, Justin opened the back door and ran into the night, following Chewy's commanding bark—a beacon in the darkness.

Away from one nightmare.

Straight into another.

40

L ewis watched the back of Mr. Boyd as the old man led the way down the moonlit path, stopping now and then to listen to the woods, slowing when the advancing clouds obscured the moon's glow. Old Man Boyd didn't seem quite so old anymore, and Lewis was grateful for his reassuring presence. Lewis shuddered when he thought of what would have happened if he hadn't come along with his shotgun.

As he followed his neighbor along the path, Lewis thought of his father, returning tomorrow from his business trip. How would he explain to his father the insane string of events that have unfolded since he left for California? Lewis had overheard his mother's phone conversation with her husband yesterday, so his father was informed of the disappearances, but that was all.

Lost in thought, Lewis ran headfirst into Mr. Boyd's back.

Mr. Boyd turned, finger pressed to pursed lips, and

motioned for Lewis to duck down. He obeyed without question, crouching along with Mr. Boyd, peeking over the man's shoulder. He saw nothing but dark woods and an even darker slash in the earth just a few feet away— Horse Crap River. Then he heard it, the sounds of hurried footfalls approaching, swelling in volume with every passing second, more than one set of feet.

Stooped over, Mr. Boyd shuffled his way to the edge of the ditch. He peered down into the dark trench, turned back, and motioned for Lewis to join him. Lewis sidled up beside the old man.

"Hide in the ditch?" Lewis whispered.

Clyde Boyd shook his head and pointed into the darkness. Lewis followed his finger and felt his flesh pimple and his stomach churn; the finger pointed to the black mouth of the drainpipe.

Clyde slid his way down the rocky slope to the base of the ditch, surprising Lewis with his nimbleness. Lewis hesitated for a heartbeat, then followed, joining him at the bottom. They hunched over and made their way along the rocky ditch bottom to the black tunnel as the disembodied footsteps drew closer.

His terror increasing as the pipe's opening widened, Lewis followed Mr. Boyd on shaking legs. Andy and Jason were the only people he knew of that ever ventured into the pipe. Their tales of gators, snakes, and rats living in the drainage system kept everyone else away; not to mention the urban legend of the ill-fated little boy that had chased his football to his doom, and his vengeful spirit haunting the underground labyrinth. Lewis was sure the twins told the stories just to keep other kids from using their hang out, but he never had the desire to test the validity of their tales.

Lewis stopped as Mr. Boyd bent over further, and without hesitating, disappeared into the black hole. Lewis stood just outside the opening, frozen with indecision.

A faint whisper called out to him, "Come on."

Lewis bent at the waist and poked his head into the cool opening.

Strong hands sprung from the darkness, grasping Lewis's arm, pulling him into the shadows just as two policeman materialized at the edge of the ditch.

From inside the dark tunnel, Lewis and Mr. Boyd could plainly see the policemen in the distance, bathed in the full moon's light. Chief Richards—his face drenched with glimmering blood, a nightstick dangling from his wrist—started down the side of the ditch, causing a miniature landslide. His deputy followed close behind, also covered in gleaming blood; the blood appeared black as oil in the moon's monochrome glare. When the pair reached the bottom, they paused—close enough that Lewis could smell the gamey scent wafting from the obviously dead policemen—and looked up the opposite slope of the ditch. Lewis noticed the deputy's neck spread open in a toothless grin as he tilted his head back.

Lewis could feel Mr. Boyd twitch behind him, sensing the man's desire to jump out and kill the cops. He braced his hands against the curved walls of the pipe, blocking the old man's way, the revolver in his hand scraping the concrete in the process.

The chief turned his head toward the sound, his faint glowing eyes burning twin holes into Lewis's own.

Lewis held his breath for what seemed an eternity, and didn't release it until the chief turned his gaze and the pair moved up the other side of the ditch, vanishing over the lip.

"Come on, let's kill those bastards," Mr. Boyd whispered from behind with disturbing enthusiasm.

"Shouldn't we find Jerry?" Lewis whispered back to the darkness.

Mr. Boyd sighed. "Yeah. You're right. Just got a little excited at the thought of getting me a cop."

Before Lewis could ask his neighbor why he hated the police so much, a hollow clang echoed deep within the tunnel, freezing the question on his tongue. Instead, he asked, "What the heck was that?"

"Dunno. Sounded kinda like a manhole cover moving. I bet this pipe connects to all the other storm drains in the neighborhood."

The noise came again. A metallic scraping followed by a hollow toll like a death knell.

"You said they were probably using the drains to hide out, right?" Lewis asked.

"Yep."

"Then maybe we should get out of here."

Instead of a response, Lewis heard a click, and the beam from Mr. Boyd's flashlight shot down the gradually descending tunnel. Where the light ended, a circular wall of total darkness stared back, like a drop-off into an abyss. Graffiti surrounded them—profanity and logos of heavy metal bands adorning the curved walls. Lewis glanced to the right and observed a giant penis and hairy testicles spray-painted on the wall next to the old man's head, with the phrase **SUK ME HARD** scrawled below it—definitely the work of the Reed brothers.

"They don't know we're down here. Maybe we can sneak up on 'em," Mr. Boyd said.

"What if we get lost?"

"If they can figure it out, then I know we can. Come on, let's go."

As the old man inched forward, the light revealed more pipe, chasing the chasm's edge further down the tunnel. Lewis could hear the stock of the shotgun scraping the floor as the old man used it like a cane.

"Smells bad down here," Lewis commented, hunched over, scooting forward in the confining space. "Like something died."

"Something did ... Let's go get 'em."

Lewis followed, his left hand on the old man's stooped back, his right clutching the pistol. Slimy sweat coated his skin, and he fought to breathe in the stagnant, stifling space. The graffiti dwindled as they ventured deeper, until the walls were eventually free from the moronic scrawls. Unease swept over Lewis as he realized he must have gone further than the twins ever have, followed by a strange sense of pride as well.

The tunnel connected to a slightly smaller one, forcing them to bend over further. Lewis had the sudden image of the small pipe that hung out over the lake; it was too small for a person to fit through unless they were crawling on their belly. Soon, he realized, this tunnel would be that size, causing the first hints of claustrophobia to creep into his head. Just as this thought came to Lewis, Mr. Boyd's light revealed a hole to the right.

"Look," he whispered, stabbing the light into the new tunnel. "I bet this pipe links up to the storm drains from our streets."

Lewis looked at the small opening, "Can you fit through there?"

"It'll be tight but I think I'll manage."

"Look," Lewis said, pointing to the edge of the opening. A single dirty handprint stood out on the cement above the pipe, urging them to stop. The handprint of a small child.

"Well, at least we know which way to go," Mr. Boyd said. Lewis couldn't see the old man's face, but his voice sounded like it was filtered through a smile.

Hunching over even more, Mr. Boyd entered the side shaft, Lewis close behind. The confining space and slight incline slowed the pair down. This was probably for the best since the slickness under their shoes threatened to send them back the way they'd came. The walls of the tunnel were oily as well, making it difficult to grasp. At one point Mr. Boyd slipped, dropping the shotgun. Luckily, Lewis had a free hand to save it from sliding back down the shaft; he didn't want to run into any of those creatures with just the snub-nose.

After a thankfully short climb, the slanting shaft terminated at a junction with a larger intersecting pipe, leading off in opposite directions. They stood to nearly their full height, their eyes following the light's glare to the left, then to the right. Identical paths stared back at them.

"Which way?" asked Lewis, instantly breathing better in the larger space. He was amazed there was this unexplored world below his neighborhood this whole time. He wished he could share it with Clinton. The thought of his friend deflated his brief excitement.

Mr. Boyd paused, gathering his bearings. "If we go right I think that'll take us toward our street. That's where you last saw the boy, so that's the way we'll go. And if he's down here, it makes sense he would be that way too."

"You really think they're hiding out down here, Mr. Boyd?"

"Sure as Shinola, son. That handprint back there proves it. It's perfect if you think about it. They can come and go unseen. And that sounded like a manhole cover moving, so somebody's down here.

"And call me Clyde, dammit," he added.

Clyde headed off to the right with Lewis close on his heels, their soaked shoes splashing in a thin layer of murky water. Fat cockroaches scurried from the light, making Lewis's skin crawl with imaginary bugs.

Despite their attempt at stealth, their movements and whispers reverberated throughout the tunnels.

They did not go unheard.

41

Mike Simmons—Clinton and Justin's next-door neighbor—hung the phone back on its cradle and stared at the corpse on his kitchen floor: his roommate he had just moments earlier bludgeoned to death with a marble rolling pin. He'd never used the pin before and wondered why he even still had it.

Guess I finally found a use for it, he thought, and squeezed the dishtowel harder to the bite wound on his forearm—one of many bites, but definitely the worst. He shuffled backward as the widening pool of blood on the kitchen floor reached his toes.

The emergency dispatcher had asked him several times if he'd been drinking, or doing drugs. He didn't blame the woman for asking, his story sounded crazy, even though he could still hear screams from outside, and the occasional report of gunfire, reassuring him he was sane. Maybe the only sane person left.

Mike had awakened to the ruckus just a few moments

earlier. When he had realized the shouts and gunshots were real and not a part of his dream, he had risen from bed to investigate. He'd then knocked on his roommate's bedroom door. "Tim? You home? Some weird shit's going down outside, man."

There was no answer so Mike opened the door, to an empty room. Not really a shock; Tim slept at his girl-friend's house more than he slept here.

Mike then went to the living room and looked out the front window. Tim's car was parked at the curb—again not very odd, since he could easily walk to his girl's house. What was odd, especially for this late hour, were the people outside on his street, casually walking around as if nothing was wrong, all of them wearing a peculiar grin. Then, while surveying the strange nightwalkers, Mike spied his next-door neighbor, Justin, barefoot and in paja-mas, chasing his shaggy dog across the front lawn. No, not chasing, Mike realized, but following, running from some-thing. The kid dodged the outstretched hands of a man at the edge of Mike's yard and kept going full tilt down the street.

Mike recognized the man. *Tim? Why the hell did Tim try to grab Justin? What the fuck is going on?*

Mike, anger now taking over his confusion, swung the front door open, stood on the threshold, and repeated his thoughts out loud. "Tim? What the fuck is going on?"

Tim looked up, and Mike knew right away that situa-tion-normal had left the building. Tim's eyes shined in the darkness and his face glistened with blood. The most disturbing thing, however, was Tim's smile. The hungry smile of a starving man in front of a juicy steak.

Tim lurched toward Mike, who in his shock, backed away from the door without closing it.

"Tim, what's wrong, man? It's me, your bro," he pleaded as Tim entered the house, the smile stretching wider.

The attack was ferocious. Tim scratched and bit the larger man several times before Mike could free himself and run toward the kitchen. The image of the marble rolling pin flashed in his mind, a gift from his parents when he'd moved away from home. It had belonged to his grandmother who apparently had been quite the baker; Mike always thought it was an odd parting gift, but never said so to his parents. The pin had never strayed from its spot on the kitchen counter since he first moved into the rental; he had a sinking feeling it wouldn't be there.

Thankfully, the pin waited exactly where it should be. Mike grabbed it by one handle and whirled around, already swinging the heavy utensil. It struck Tim in the forehead with a loud cracking smack. The blood-soaked man backed away two steps, paused, and charged again, roaring like an angry bull. Mike swung the pin again, this time connecting with the side of his friend's skull with a dull crunch. Blood splattered Mike's face, and Tim crumpled to the linoleum at his feet.

Panting, adrenaline causing his muscles to quiver, Mike white-knuckled the rolling pin and watched in disbelief as Tim started to rise. He stopped his friend's ascent with three powerful swings of the unforgiving marble pin, opening the man's skull. He dropped the weapon to the floor, his shoulder throbbing from swinging the hefty object.

That's when Mike Simmons—after locking the front door and waiting a minute to regain speech—called the operator with his incredible story. She informed him the police were on their way.

It was the first of many strange calls she would receive that night.

42

Lewis followed Mr. Boyd along the pipe for some distance, the feeling they were lost worming its way into his brain. His sneakers and socks were soaked from the tepid water standing in the pipe, not helping his dour mood. He needed to talk, to say anything to keep his mind off the tight space and scurrying roaches.

"Mr. Boyd? Clyde, I mean. You said something yesterday that I've been thinking about."

"What's that, son?"

Lewis flicked a roach off his forearm, the disgusting touch of the bug's sticky legs lingering like tiny phantom limbs. "You mentioned something about a Viking folk tale or something. What did you mean?"

Mr. Boyd continued inching forward along the pipe, took a deep breath and said, "Well, I found a couple stories of an old legend, from a couple different books. I pieced them together best I could. Story goes that a widow and her daughter—the stories differ, but suggest the daughter was in her early to mid-teens—story goes they were both powerful healers that lived in a small fishing village. They cured the villagers' ailments with herbs and spells and stuff like that, in exchange for goods. Some of my books refer to healers like them as *Hedge Witches*. And let me tell ya, them witches can use nature in ways you wouldn't believe."

"So they were good witches?" Lewis asked.

"Yeah … so it would seem. But when a plague fell on the village, the mother and her daughter did everything in their power to cure the infected folk, but a bunch of 'em died anyways, most of them little kids. It sounded to me like some sort of influenza. Anyways, the parents of these dead kids blamed the witches for them dying."

"Why?"

Mr. Boyd paused and turned, the flashlight illuminating his sad face. Shrugging, he said, "I don't know, Lewis. Sometimes people just do that. Usually out of fear. Sometimes they just have to have something or someone to blame. Especially if it's something they don't understand. Somethin' different. *Someone* different."

Mr. Boyd turned and continued along the pipe. "Anyways, the villagers came for the woman and the girl. They showed up at their house with revenge on their minds. Luckily, the girl was out collecting herbs and berries and whatever else a Hedge Witch uses in her spells. The mom weren't so lucky. The girl came home to a burned down house and her dead mother, tied to a stake, charred extra crispy."

"Jeez," Lewis whispered.

"Yeah. Not a nice thing to come home to. Well as you

can imagine, the girl was none too happy with the villagers. The very people that her and her mother had tried to help."

"What did she do?"

Once again Mr. Boyd turned to face Lewis, this time with a slight smile. "She got revenge on *them*, that's what she did. She cursed the whole village. Crops withered. Livestock croaked. People came down with every sickness you could think of. And from the descriptions it weren't too pretty. Well, the few men in the village that were still able to do so, hunted her down. And eventually caught her."

"And?"

"And—this is where the stories agree—the men tied her to a tree, a special tree used in pagan ceremonies that stood all by itself on a small rocky island, in the middle of a big lake near the village. They tied her up and burned her just like her mother."

"Man. That sucks."

"Yeah, it does. But, here's where it gets really weird. You see, they were afraid her spirit would haunt the village, so before they set flame to her, they carved a symbol into the bark, something to keep her spirit trapped in that tree, forever, out there on its tiny little island in the middle of the lake, away from the village. One of my books even had a drawing of the symbol."

Mr. Boyd shined the light to the tunnel wall and used his finger to draw the symbol in the muck coating the cement. He stepped back, admiring his work. "That's it. Simple, huh?"

Lewis stared at the circular symbol. "Yeah. It looks like a maze. An *easy* maze. What's it mean?"

"I dunno what it means, it's just supposed to keep her spirit trapped. In fact, that's what it's called—a spirit trap. But it didn't do 'em any good. Because not too long after they burnt her up, guess what happened when folks ate fish from that lake, or drank the water."

Lewis shrugged and took a guess. "They got sick?"

"Yeah, they got sick. Got sick and died." A sinister grin split his wrinkled face. "Then they came back to life, started attacking everybody."

"Holy crap," Lewis said. "That sounds like your story of Chitto and Titus. Like what our tree does."

"Yeah. It sure does. My guess is that the tree poisons anything its roots touch, just like the sand from the poor old shaman's sacred burial ground, letting her spirit possess the living … or in this case, the dead. But there's just one problem. That tree in the lake was on the other side of the Atlantic Ocean, somewhere in Scandinavia I think, thousands of miles away. And I checked the tree here in our woods. No symbols are carved in the bark."

"Well, does your book say what happened to the tree in the lake?" Lewis asked. "What happened to the village?"

"Yeah … sort of. After a long battle, the last of the infected villagers were put down. The killing finally stopped. The lake was off limits, guarded to keep folks away, kind of like what I've been doing here with our tree. Then, out of nowhere, some strange men showed up in the village. From the descriptions of their white robes it sounds to me like they were Druids. Actually, I'm positive that's who they were. Don't know why, but the villagers allowed these men—whom, according to my book, never spoke a word to any of the townsfolk—to row out to the tiny island. Later, after it was dark, chanting could be heard, and a bright flash of light came from the direction of the tree, as bright as a hundred bolts of lightning, followed by a clap of earthshaking thunder. In the morning the villagers awoke to find the Druids gone, along with the tree. Even the small rocky island it grew from was gone. Everything had vanished." Mr. Boyd paused, shaking his head, his eyes staring through Lewis. "Anyways, it's just a legend, Lewis. I seriously doubt it's the same tree. I mean, not unless it traveled back in time, here, to our woods."

"Traveled *back* in time?" Lewis asked.

"Yep. That's what I said. *Back in time*. Sounds nuts, huh?"

Mr. Boyd chuckled at his last remark, but Lewis sensed a hint of unease in the old man's laugh, like he was trying too hard to convince himself of the ridiculousness of the statement. When he stopped laughing, he sighed, shaking his head again. Then, when he continued talking, his voice was lower. "I didn't want to believe something so crazy, Lewis. But a couple weeks ago I read an article on those Windover Bog People. You remember, the ancient remains we talked about, the ones that backhoe operator uncovered, the ones that were dated back seven or eight thousand years?"

Lewis nodded.

"Well, some egghead scientists claim some of the skulls appear to be European in shape. I assume they can tell that sort of thing, I don't know."

After shaking his head again for several seconds, Mr. Boyd continued. "Now, I'm no historian, but I'm pretty damn sure no Europeans discovered this land seven to eight thousand years ago." Mr. Boyd pointed toward his feet as he said *this land*.

Lewis absorbed the man's information for a few seconds, and then realized what he was hinting at. "So you *do* think it's the same tree, and that some of those Windover bones are the Druids that disappeared with it?"

Mr. Boyd waved his hands, attempting to quell Lewis's excitement, the flashlight dancing along the damp tunnel. "I don't know … I honestly don't know. I've been reading everything I can find on Druids, and supposedly there were these high-level ones, called Ovates, that could travel through time. I've been thinking that maybe, and it's a big maybe, that they sent the tree—along with themselves to safeguard it—as far back as they could to be rid of the damn thing. I even think I might've figured out their incantation. But, even if such a thing were possible—which I'm not saying it is, mind you—it just don't make no damn sense. If it is the same tree, and if it was sent back in time, then how did the girl ever get burned to it in the first place?"

Lewis mulled over this question for a few seconds before asking, "But if it is the same witch, the Hedge Witch, why do you think she's so evil now? I mean, I can see why she hated the villagers, but why would she want to kill us?"

The old man shrugged again. "Most likely it's because she's been a vengeful ghost for so long she can't control her blood lust. She's literally gone insane with vengeance.

That's what happens when a spirit stays in this realm too long, looking to get back at those that wronged them. And eight thousand years is a long time to be pissed off."

"How do you know all this stuff, Mr. Boyd?"

"Oh, I've seen things that'll make your toenails curl, son. And I'm sure you noticed, I read quite a bit. But those are stories for another time. We know what we gotta do right now. We gotta kill her vessel. We'll worry about the tree after that. Come on, son, enough jabber-jawing, we need to move. All this talk is making my head hurt."

At that, Mr. Boyd turned and followed the beam of his flashlight down the tunnel, done with his story. Lewis glanced at the strange spiral symbol before the darkness swallowed it, then followed him in silence, pondering the tale. It might have been just a silly legend, but the similarities had his mind buzzing with questions: if it was the same tree why had it ended up here? How could you stop her for good? Did the symbol have something to do with it? Could they actually send the tree back in time like the Druids had supposedly done?

Lewis was toiling over these and other questions when Mr. Boyd halted. Lewis looked past the old man and saw an opening up ahead on their left where a faint glow seeped through into the tunnel. Mr. Boyd motioned for Lewis to hang back, but he refused to listen, never letting his shaking hand leave the old man's back, actually pushing him forward toward the faint light, eager to be out of the damp, bug-ridden tunnel, regardless of what awaited them above.

They reached the source of light and faced an arched opening, the flashlight revealing a small brick chamber beyond. The sodden bricks inside the chamber were coated with hanging green algae that reminded Lewis of seaweed from an old B-movie. Rusted metal rungs protruded from the bricks straight ahead, leading up to a circular manhole cover and a storm drain. Light from a streetlamp shone in through the wide slot of the drain, casting a pale blue glow into the small room.

"I wonder where we are?" Mr. Boyd asked, his voice echoing as he swept the light around the green bricks and then to the small puddle of dark water at the bottom of the room.

Lewis's eyes followed the circle of light as it flashed over a dark object floating in the still water.

A football! He'll drag you down into his watery tomb!

Lewis wrenched the light from Clyde's grasp and illuminated the object, the beam vibrating. The innocent chunk of wood stared back.

"You okay, Lewis?"

"Yeah. Sorry. I'm fine. Thought I saw something is all," Lewis said, embarrassed, handing the flashlight back.

"Hey. Can you look through the drain and see where we are?" asked Mr. Boyd.

"No problem." Lewis secured the pistol in the waistband at the small of his back, waded through the shallow puddle, and crawled up the short ladder, the metal of the rungs slimy in his grip. He reached the top and peeked through the drain. A street sign was visible in the shadows of the world above.

Lewis turned. "I see a street sign but it's too dark, I can't read it."

Mr. Boyd sloshed his way to the base of the ladder and

held the light up to Lewis. "Here, use this, but do it fast. I don't want anyone to know we're down here."

Lewis reached down, grabbed the light, and turned it off. Mr. Boyd disappeared into the shadows below. He pointed the bulb through the drain, toward the dark street sign, and thumbed the switch on and off as if taking a photo.

Lewis smiled at the familiar street names that appeared in the flash and whispered, "Hey, we're only three streets over from ours."

He hooked his arm through a rung, clicked the light back on, and turned. "Here's the—"

Gasping in surprise, Lewis almost fell as the light's beam splashed over the old man at the base of the ladder.

Jerry stood behind Mr. Boyd, a large kitchen knife raised in both hands, a look of demonic glee spread across his filthy face.

"LOOK OUT!" Lewis yelled, and watched helpless as Jerry plunged the giant knife between the old man's shoulder blades. Mr. Boyd's shocked face let loose a strangled cry. The shotgun fell from his grasp, landing upright against the brick wall as he pitched forward into the filthy puddle, the knife jutting from his back. Jerry placed his small foot on the old man's back and yanked the blade free. A garbled scream in an unknown language swelled within the chamber. Lewis clamped his mouth shut, stunned the horrible voice was his own.

Lewis switched the light to his left hand, slid the revolver free with his right, and fired two quick shots, the blasts deafening in the small space. One bullet sparked off the bricks, the other tore into the flesh of Jerry's shoulder as he turned and fled through the opening and down the pipe.

Lewis released the rung and splashed to the floor to help his injured friend. Through the ringing in his ears, he could hear scuffling and splashing diminishing down the tunnel—Jerry running away.

He hefted the wounded man to his side. "Mr. Boyd? Clyde?"

"Go, Lewis. Get out of here," he croaked, his face pale in the bright light.

"I can't leave you," Lewis said, his voice trembled as tears filled his vision.

Sounds from both directions floated down the pipe: rasping animal grunts, and splashing, echoing through the tunnel.

"Go," Clyde repeated. "I can't feel my damn legs. Go, climb out the drain."

When Lewis didn't move, the old man shoved him, harder than Lewis would have thought possible. "GO," he shouted this time, red spittle spraying from his lips.

The grunts and growls in the tunnel were much louder now. Lewis tucked the gun back into his shorts, rose on shaking legs, and scaled the ladder. He reached the top rung and turned to look at his friend one last time in the glare of the flashlight.

Propped up on one hand, his useless legs submerged in the dark puddle, Mr. Boyd was using a small rock to scratch the circular maze symbol into the algae-covered brick wall. He finished, tossed the rock aside and reached out, retrieving the shotgun. He looked into the light and showed Lewis a weak smile.

"What're you doing?" Lewis asked.

Go, Mr. Boyd mouthed. He turned the gun and his still smiling face to the arched entrance, the big barrels of the shotgun waiting for something to peek into the room.

Lewis turned, tossed the light through the opening onto the dark street, grabbed the edges of the drain and pushed off with his feet. His sneaker squeaked as it slipped off the metal rung, and Lewis kicked the air trying to find the ladder again, holding on with his fingertips. Finally, he found his footing and pushed, squeezing his head and shoulders out into the fresh air like a newborn child.

Lewis felt the pistol in his waistband scrape and snag on the underside of the drain's lip, pressing into the base of his spine, then the pressure subsided as the gun came free. He heard the metal *clang* and wet *plop* as the .38 bounced off the ladder and hit the pool at the bottom of the drain.

Before Lewis could mourn the loss of the weapon, the shotgun thundered with a blaze of fire from below, lighting the chamber with a quick flash of hot white light. Lewis pulled his feet from the drain, dragging himself out on his belly. A crescendo bellow followed the blast: a fierce war cry. Splashes, shouts, and growls echoed up to Lewis, culminating with a scream of tortured agony. Then a second flash lit the drain as the shotgun roared again, amplified by the brick walls, drowning out all sounds of struggle.

Lewis grabbed the flashlight and spun on his belly, the macadam rubbing his flesh raw through his shirt. He stabbed the beam into the black maw of the storm drain.

"Mr. Boyd?" he called out, his voice bouncing around the now silent chamber.

Strong hands shot out of the darkness, clamping onto Lewis's wrist, causing the flashlight to follow the gun down the drain. Lewis sat up, braced his feet on the concrete edge above the drain, and pulled with all his might. The crazed, jaundiced eyes of Chief Richards appeared between his planted feet, glinting a pestilent yellow in the light cast from the streetlamp, like twin egg yolks floating in pools of blood. Lewis pulled free, his wrist sliding from the slippery grip. The blood-slicked hands and deranged eyes disappeared down the drain, followed by a splash.

Lewis pushed away from the opening, putting himself out of reach as the manhole cover flew into the air and crashed down next to the hole with a deep gong. The leering face of the deputy appeared through the aperture, sporting matching grins on face and throat.

Lewis stood, took two long strides, and like an NFL place-kicker, kicked the cop square in the face. The head dropped back through the opening and another splash floated up to the street followed by howls of anger.

What now? Where do I go? Lewis asked himself as he backed away from the hole, gasping for air.

He had no weapon, no light, and he was alone once again. He could hear distant screams and gunfire floating on the cool breeze—his neighborhood under siege, just like Mr. Boyd had warned.

The image of the gas can popped into his head again, this time sitting on the trail next to the corpse of Andy

Reed instead of by the lawnmower. *I can still try my Yosemite Sam plan.*

What other choice do I have?

Lewis knew what he had to do. He would have to go into those god-forsaken woods yet again and try to destroy the tree.

He tapped his pocket and felt the hard lump of the Zippo. "Screw it," he said as the deputy's head reappeared from the manhole, dripping foul water and blood, the slash along his neck wider now, like the red mouth of a sock-puppet. A lunatic's sock-puppet.

Once again, Lewis ran.

Into the woods.

L ewis.
The name had filled the memories of the twins with such contempt. Now, fingering the bullet hole in her vessel's shoulder, she too experienced the hatred the boys must have felt while still alive. The child was like an annoying bug you couldn't kill—a gnat or mosquito buzzing in your ear, and just when you thought you had him, he slipped from your grasp. At least the gnat's old friend had been dealt with.

She blocked the image of the troublesome youth and concentrated on more important matters. She spread her thoughts to all of her undead slaves, her mind-link programming their simple carnal instincts to take over, like an autopilot. Her instructions were simple—kill everybody. Kill every living being, feed on some to keep her vessel healthy, but leave most of them to be turned later. She had minions already returning from the clearing with a supply of sand.

She would handle the boy herself. She knew exactly where he was going. Through the deputy's eyes she could see the child run through a yard and scale a wall, entering the woods.

She already had a surprise waiting for him when he reached his destination.

Her wicked laugh echoed through the dark tunnels.

E xhausted, his ribs stinging and chest burning, Lewis slowed. Monsters or no monsters, he had to walk, the endless running had finally taken its toll.

He looked at his empty hands and yearned for the pistol. Even though there'd been only one bullet remaining, the small but surprisingly hefty weapon had given him much needed comfort. *No matter,* he thought, convincing himself that the chances of getting another shot at Jerry was slim anyhow, and by the sound of it, he had the entire neighborhood to contend with. He just hoped Mr. Boyd was wrong about the tree; that it *would* burn, because that was all he had left—hope. Without that hope he was utterly alone. Lewis clung to the vision of the burning tree. He would have to do this on his own, or die trying.

He marched on, too tired to care about what might be waiting for him on the dark path. The sky flashed like God taking his photo—heat lighting from an approaching storm. Lewis groaned; if the rain beat him to the tree his plan would definitely fail. He picked up his pace, but still did not have the energy to run. He tapped the bump in his pocket, checking every few seconds to make sure the lighter still resided there.

The shadows of the dark forest pulsed as the stampeding clouds passed in front of the moon and distant lightning lit the blanket of advancing thunderheads. Lewis headed toward the forbidden trail, the fitful lights illuminating the way.

More distant screams reached him, along with a sound that could only be a car crashing. Lewis could picture the chaos unfolding in his once quaint community and hoped Justin was okay. He wondered how many of his schoolmates and their families were already turned into flesh-eating fiends, or how many had become a meal for them. The thought was surreal. Then Lewis thought of something even more terrifying: the sound of the car crashing. What if they got downtown? Or further? Where would it end?

He had to stop her. This had to work.

Lewis entered the over-grown path, breaching the barrier spell without hesitating this time. He expected resistance around every bend, but none came. The distant sound of approaching sirens lifted his spirits; *I hope they don't end up like the other cops.* He walked on with stubborn determination, his skinny twelve-year-old frame feeling stronger now with every step that brought him closer to the clearing.

He knew it would work.

The first responders fared slightly better than the chief and his deputy, but not much. The two cruisers—half of the remaining force of the Hopkinsville Police Department—slowed to a crawl as they entered the neighborhood, quieting their wailing sirens.

Their headlights washed over the denizens of Poisonwood Estates. The once normal, hard working folk now resembled escapees from an insane asylum, standing still as statues on porches and front lawns, watching the vehicles as they passed. One home had the back end of a giant yellow station wagon protruding from its living room windows, one blinker still flashing. Both officers had to repeat themselves many times as they described the scenario to the station.

Some of the frozen onlookers wore pajamas, others were half-naked, and a few were totally nude. One thing they all had in common was the varying amounts of blood covering their skin, usually their face. And the other thing they shared were their eyes—crazed, and glowing.

Both cars had their windows down on this muggy night, and that proved to be their undoing. The officers drove past the odd assemblage, describing the onlookers as your stereotypical junkie, a hungry look in their awful eyes. The sheer number of people made the officers want to turn around and drive out of the neighborhood at high speed, regroup and wait for reinforcements, but the dispatcher reminded them there was a citizen in need. Not to mention the fact that the chief and Deputy Dixon had responded to a call in Poisonwood earlier, and had yet to check in, neither one of the officers answering the dispatcher's calls.

They stopped their vehicles in front of the residence of Mike Simmons. The windows of the house were dark, no sign of anyone home.

Mike *was* home. He had turned off all the lights shortly after hanging up the phone, grabbing the flashlight from the kitchen drawer. He peeked through the small window at the top of the front door, his stunned face illuminated by the colored police lights. He could only watch, helpless, as the static mob suddenly converged on the cars with deceptive speed, moving as one creature as they attacked the vehicles, reaching through the open windows to get to the officers. Several gunshots rang out from the cars, the interiors flashing with every report. A few of the attackers fell to the ground and didn't get back up, but their numbers were too much for the cops.

A scream reached Mike over the grunts and snarls of the attackers, a shrill scream of tormented pain that shook

Mike with despair and guilt. The terrified shriek died, and Mike could see the lead car rocking as it filled with the blood-hungry ghouls.

The other cruiser sped off, tires screeching, several of the beasts falling from the car, and Mike was filled with hope that the officer would get away. That hope was dashed, along with the officer's life, as the car lost control and plowed into a light pole with a deafening crunch. The driver flew through the windshield, his limp body bouncing off the hood and smacking face first in the street as sparkles of glass twinkled around him. A woman Mike instantly recognized crawled from the front seat and perched on the hood, admiring the crumpled body on display in the one surviving headlight. She jumped from the car, joining the hungry horde that waded in to feast on the dead man.

Hey Tim, Mike thought, and trained the flashlight on his dead friend, his grip on sanity slipping a little further, *it's your girlfriend. I think she's pissed. You better stay inside with me, buddy.* Mike turned, leaned against the door and slid to the floor. His blank expression matched the one of his friend staring back at him from the kitchen.

The doorknob next to his head rattled, and the door shook against his back. Mike put his head down, and for the first time since he was a little kid, he prayed.

T he strobe of lightning revealed a familiar shape on the trail ahead—the gas can.

Lewis smiled and jogged to the can, lifting it, the sloshing sound of gasoline boosting his spirits. However, his smile wavered as the far off sounds of gunshots, followed by another crash, reached him. The sirens had stopped and the silence left after the crash was disheartening. The smile returned, however, as more lightning revealed the headless corpse of Andy Reed sprawled along the trail, the bushes still gleaming with gore.

Lewis shuddered. He must have walked right past the carcass of the naked woman, the darkness and his eagerness to reach the tree concealing her. The memory of her brains sprinkling the trail once again turned his stomach, wiping the grin completely from his face this time.

He still couldn't believe he had shot her like that. Lewis thought of his mother and hoped he wouldn't have to do the same to her. He spat on the remains of his old nemesis and ventured on, moving faster now, his anger building. Lewis tramped down the trail, his mind focused on the tree, not caring about the witch and her growing army. The tree is the key to victory.

Another blaze of lightning revealed the barrier of vines just up ahead. Distant thunder followed the flash this time, rumbling across the sky like approaching cannon fire.

Lewis approached the wall with caution and peered through the vines; the glow of the white sand exposed the emptiness of the clearing. He barged his way through the dry tendrils, unscrewing the cap of the gas can as he went. Luck seemed to be on his side and Lewis was eager to take advantage of it.

He advanced on the tree, its dark limbs reaching for him like bony fingers, their tips covered with healthy leaves. The shiny leaves undulated as a cool breeze swept across the clearing, reminding Lewis of the scurrying roaches in the sewers. He could feel the air around him change, growing heavier the closer he got to the tree. He knew the feeling wasn't the shaman's old spell, this was the tree itself, projecting an atmosphere of evil that made his skin flutter and his breath catch in his chest.

Lewis splashed the trunk of the tree with the gasoline, the pleasant scent burning his nostrils, dispelling his feelings of dread.

Please let this work.

Lewis soaked the tree again with two more swings of the can.

This has to work.

On his fourth dowsing, a dark shape lurched out from behind the tree. A staccato burst of lightning scattered the shadows like startled bugs, revealing the figure.

Clinton.

"Mike. It's Justin, let me in."

The muffled voice came through the door, followed by a sharp bark that vibrated down his spine. Mike stood and peered through the small window. It was Justin all right, and his dog too. The creatures on the street were still occupied with the fresh meat of the cops, the bark thankfully not drawing their attention over the din of their feast.

Mike opened the door and Chewy barged in, growling, and barked once more. "Shhh. It's all right, Chewy," Justin said, following the dog into the dim house. He closed and bolted the door behind him.

"What the hell is happening?" Mike asked, calming Chewy by rubbing the dog's furry head.

"Don't know," Justin said, his voice shaking, tears welling in his eyes. "Everyone's gone crazy. My mom killed my dad and tried to kill me. The whole neighborhood is killing each other."

"Tell me about it. My roommate tried to eat me." Mike pointed the light to the corpse on the kitchen floor.

Justin averted his eyes and stabbed a thumb back to the door. "We were hiding in the bushes across the street. I saw the cops pull up so I thought it was safe to come out. That's when I saw your face in the window. Then, when everyone was busy … you know … with the cops, we snuck over. I'm glad you answered."

The front door shuddered in its frame as something slammed against the other side. Justin jumped and spun in mid-air. "Crap they know we're here," he whispered. Chewy growled at the spinning doorknob.

"It's all right. They can't get through that door, it's solid oak," Mike boasted.

Glass shattered into the house as Tim's girlfriend jumped through the front windows of the living room, landing on the shabby sofa that her and Tim had used for other activities besides lounging.

"HOLY SHIT!" Mike cried out. "This way, quick."

Justin followed Mike down the hall and into a dark room. Mike slammed the door and turned on the light. He pointed to a heavy chest-of-drawers. "Come on, help me move this in front of the door."

Justin glanced around the small room. "Wait. Where's Chewy?"

Before Mike could answer, Justin flung the door wide and ran out into the hall.

Thunder shook the sand beneath Lewis's feet as his best friend staggered toward him. Clinton's body jerked and swayed, fighting for balance as if the ground actually trembled from the thunder. Lewis realized why the creature was stumbling—Clinton's broken neck. Controlling his body must be difficult with a shattered spine.

The stab wounds across Clinton's chest made Lewis moan with sadness as he began to understand what must have happened to his friend. The witch had broken Clinton's neck, and then stabbed him repeatedly, the cracked spine not doing the job quick enough. Then another thought hit him, *if she got Clinton then she most likely got Justin too.*

Bitch!

"I'm sorry, buddy," Lewis said, choking back tears. "I hope it didn't hurt too much."

Lewis splashed gasoline onto Clinton's twitching,

shambling corpse, the head leaning awkwardly on the broken neck in an inquisitive gesture, as if asking Lewis to repeat the last sentence. The dead boy continued forward, his sneakers dragging in the white sand, his arms raised, begging for a hug from his old chum.

Lewis backed away, tossed the almost empty can to the side. *So much for my plan.* He freed the lighter from his pocket, flipping the lid back, the *click* summoning tears to his eyes. "I'm sorry," he repeated.

Lewis thumbed the wheel of the Zippo. Sparks jumped from the lighter, but no flame.

"Shit," he hissed, flicking the lighter three more times.

On the fifth try, fire erupted from the beautiful chrome invention, just as Clinton's outstretched hands came within reach.

Lewis tossed the lighter at Clinton's chest, the fuel-soaked t-shirt igniting with a rushing gasp of hot wind. Lewis fell to his ass and scooted away from the shuffling inferno that had once been his best friend in the whole world, a friend that had once saved his life—at least that's how he liked to tell the story.

Clinton continued forward. Lewis raised his hand to shield his eyes, the few remaining hairs on his arm smoldering, the intense heat from the flames roasting the skin of his face. Lewis scurried further away from the flaming boy, until his back pushed against the palmettos and dense vines lining the perimeter of the clearing. The scent of cooking meat and burning hair made him gag as he turned, looking for an exit. The perimeter wall was too tall and thick, he wouldn't get very far before the flames toasted him.

Above the crackle of flames and the popping of Clinton's searing flesh, Lewis heard the distinct and familiar laughter. Turning his face toward the entrance, Lewis could see Jerry—or rather the vile thing that has stolen Jerry's flesh—illuminated by the fire, lurking on the other side of the entrance. The spindly vines cast shadows like ancient runes across the boy's cackling face. Behind Jerry, stood Lewis's mother, bathed in flickering yellow and orange. She laughed as well, her teeth and face stained red.

This is it then, Lewis thought, exhausted, his mind no longer able to except the horrors of this long night as reality. *This is how it ends. Burned to death by the flaming reanimated corpse of my best friend while my possessed, dead mother watches and laughs. I guess it's better than being eaten alive.*

Lewis gave in to his fate, cowering against the wall of the clearing, the heat of the nearing flames burning into his arm as he shielded his face. He glanced again toward his mother and Jerry. They were both watching the scene from the entrance, their widening smiles threatening to split their heads in half. Then, their expressions changed, the giant grins fading slightly into a look of confusion.

Lewis felt the scorching heat diminish.

Confused himself, Lewis lowered his arm to see Clinton walking away from him.

Walking toward the tree.

"Justin," Mike called out too late. Justin had already vanished around the corner. Canine and human growls reverberated down the long hallway, and Mike could hear Justin's voice screaming for Chewy to come back.

He's just a little kid. I gotta help him, Mike thought, and went after Justin. The house was still dark so Mike flipped the hallway switch on his way. Light flared, revealing the action to go along with the commotion. Chewy was on top of Tim's girlfriend, his jaws latched to her throat. Mike watched in awe as the mutt whipped its head back and forth, and heard the snap of the woman's spine clearly over the dog's deep growls. Just as the body went limp in the dog's death grip, two more people came through the window. Mike knew the couple well: Mr. and Mrs. Chung, the nice elderly Asian couple from two doors down.

The old couple attacked Chewy with a ferociousness

that shocked Mike. The dog squealed as the woman tackled it, biting into the furry flesh on its back. Mike started forward to help Chewy when a cry from his right stopped him. Justin flew from the kitchen, past Mike, screaming at the top of his lungs, the stained marble rolling pin held above his head like a battle-ax.

Mrs. Chung jerked her face up just in time to see the rolling pin crash down on her head, splitting the scalp wide open. A clump of soggy brown fur rolled from her mouth as she tumbled backward, her face a mask of red. Her husband—the once quiet, always smiling Mr. Chung —rose to his feet, faced Justin, and released a bestial screech so fierce that Justin's knees gave out, sending him crashing to the floor. Mike swung into action and drop-kicked the old man in the chest, sending him flying back out the broken window.

"COME ON!" Mike screamed.

Justin and Chewy both sprung upright at Mike's scream; together, they ran down the hall and into the bedroom. Mike followed. When he reached the bedroom door he glanced back; the old couple were back on their feet, and they had plenty of friends.

Mike entered the room and slammed the door, the sense he was closing the lid on his own coffin squirming into his brain.

"Lock it," Justin said, panting. He sat on the bed, hugging the injured dog. The dog's snout was coated with blood, but Mike was sure most of it belonged to Tim's girlfriend. *Ex-girlfriend.*

"It doesn't lock. Quick, help me with this thing." Mike motioned once again to the bulky dresser.

Justin stood and helped Mike slide the heavy piece of furniture in front of the door. A second later the door flew open, smashing into the barrier. Hissing snarls came through the thin opening. Bloody fingers appeared in the gap and Justin promptly smashed them to pulp with the rolling pin.

"We need more stuff to put in front of this," Mike yelled over the animal screams on the other side of the door. "Help me with the bed."

Chewy was up and off the bed before they could tell him to move, and they flipped the mattress and box spring over, blocking the door.

"That won't hold them for long. They can bust right through that door," Mike panted, leaning against the box spring, his eyes wide.

"What about the window?" Justin asked.

Mike shook his head, catching his breath, and motioned toward the window. A brand new air conditioner filled the space. "That beast is screwed into the frame. Works great, though." As if to prove this point, the unit clicked on and hummed, blowing cool air into the room.

"Great. What do we do?" Justin asked, his voice quaking, the night's events taking their toll on the young boy.

"Give me the rolling pin. There's a baseball bat in the closet. We're gonna have to fight them when they come through," Mike said as the barricade shuddered against his back.

"*When* they come through?"

Seeing the terror in their eyes, Mike shrugged and gave boy and dog his best smile. Ever since Justin had nearly drowned in the public swimming pool a couple years ago, where Mike had been working as a Lifeguard, he'd felt a need to protect the little guy from harm. If Mike hadn't performed CPR on Justin, he most likely would have died. Now, he felt a deep responsibility for the boy's safety. "*If,*" he vowed. "*If* they come through."

It was the best he could do under the circumstances.

Dresser and bed shuddered again.

When *they come through,* thought Mike.

50

C linton stumbled toward the tree, bits of burning cloth and flesh dropping to the sand. Lewis watched his friend, grasping the situation with disheartening clarity: the evil witch was planning to light the tree, trap Lewis within the circle, letting him die slowly and painfully. Payback for being such a nuisance. Then Lewis recalled the perplexed gaze on Jerry's face. *Or maybe there's some of Clinton left in there that she can't control,* he thought. He hoped. But either way the outcome would be the same. The perimeter was going to burst into flames.

Lewis decided to take advantage of the reprieve and charge the entrance, take his chances with Jerry and his mother. He stopped before he could even start, his opportunity slipping away as the chief and his deputy waltzed up next to Jerry, fresh blood gleaming on their faces. Lewis remained seated, accepting his fate again. He noticed the gaping wound across the chief's chest. Mr. Boyd's last shots had done some damage at least. He turned his attention back to Clinton.

Clinton reached the gasoline soaked trunk of the tree and without pausing, hugged it like a long lost pal. Lewis scampered away from the edge of the clearing as the tree ignited, the rushing wind from the explosion of flames like the enormous sigh of a sad giant. Lewis ducked his head between his knees to protect his face from the flames. The boiling air rolled over his back like winged razor blades, slicing through the thin fabric of his mutilated shirt and into his flesh, sucking the air from his lungs.

He looked up, squinting at the bright flaming pyre. Through the shimmering heat, Lewis could see Clinton still clinging to the trunk like a condemned heretic. He glanced around the clearing, thinking his plan had worked after all. The perimeter wasn't burning, only the tree was ablaze, now fully engulfed in beautiful fire, all the way to its highest branches.

Fully ablaze, but not burning.

The fire covered the tree, but Lewis could see that the leaves were unmarred by the flames, the black wood unchanged. He had the distinct feeling the tree was laughing at him.

That's when the noise started. Not laughter, but something much more troubling. It was the sound of the initial explosion, only played in reverse, like a record spinning backward. The sad giant was now inhaling. The flames on the tree began to follow the sound, the film being rewound as well. Starting slow and gaining speed, the flames were absorbed by the dark skin of the tree. Even the few curling flames still burning on Clinton—now fused to the tree—were being drawn into the bark.

Gasping for air, Lewis could only watch as the fire vanished into the tree and the rushing noise condensed to a high-pitched hiss. The woods were dark once again, lit only by the full moon's glare and a few chunks of Clinton's flesh that still burned in the sand. Laughter rose above the hissing sound now. Jerry—hands on his hips, cackling at the sky in a stereotypical villain's pose—stood a safe distance from the clearing, his undead minions waiting obediently behind him. Jerry lowered his gaze, a smug grin of victory on his moonlit face.

On his knees, Lewis met the glowing eyes that once belonged to his frail companion, and showed them his middle finger. Lewis closed his eyes, his finger still raised, as the hissing abruptly ceased.

51

The box spring and mattress tipped over, smothering Justin as he fell to the floor. Mike dropped the rolling pin and tossed the cumbersome bed from the child. That's when the first one came through the widening crack in the door. Chewy sailed past Mike's face, landing on the dresser, and tore into the first attacker, forcing it back through the gap. Mike pushed, managing to close the door again, Justin once again there to help. Chewy—his snout covered with fresh blood, and teeth dangling pink flesh—jumped from the dresser and went back to Justin's side.

"They're gonna get through," Justin whimpered over the din of snarls on the other side of the thin door.

"Let 'em. I'll bash their brains in," Mike shouted to the shuddering door as he pushed on the dresser.

The door pounded into the barrier and splinters flew into Mike's face, stinging the flesh of his forehead. He looked up to see a hole forming in the door just inches from his eyes. He ducked his head down as another blow showered him with fines pieces of the cheap wood. Two more crashes and the hole in the door grew to the size of a basketball.

Mike looked up again, straight into the bleeding yellow eyes of Mrs. Chung. Her face disappeared for a second and then returned as she crashed her head against the door. This time her head breached the barrier, pushing through the hole with a rasping scrape. Her scalp hung to either side of her head like fresh slices of corned-beef, exposing white skull underneath. She bit at the air, her teeth clicking together like deadly castanets, trying to reach Mike's face. The wooden baseball bat came down on the woman's head with a hollow clunk, and she disappeared back through the ragged hole in the door.

The already weak door was now a loss. Mike stood up and flashed Justin a nervous, apologetic grin as the wood cracked under the stress of the onslaught.

"Get ready, Justin. Here they come."

Man and boy stood ready with their weapons raised. The dog bared his lethal teeth, also ready, as the top half of the door tore to kindling.

52

Another second ticked by. Still nothing happened. The woods were silent.

Anticipating a maelstrom of fire, Lewis opened one eye. He saw the expression of joy evaporate from Jerry's face, replaced with another look of confusion. Lewis lowered his middle finger and let his hand drop to the sand. He opened the other eye as a faint cracking reached his ears, like heavy footfalls crashing through the woods in the distance, approaching from every direction. Lewis could feel the air change, a static charge tickled his follicles, the same sensation he felt before an intense thunderstorm, only tenfold. On hands and knees, he inched closer to the center of the clearing, closer to the tree, as far away from the edge of the circle as possible, sensing the coalescent threat surging around him.

Clinton's roasted husk separated from the tree with a wet crackling sound, thumping into the sand just in front of Lewis.

The distant snapping intensified, drawing nearer from all sides, accelerating until it resembled the tearing of fabric. The sound surrounded Lewis, spinning around the clearing now, gaining speed with each revolution until it became one droning whir. Lewis covered his ears as the ripping increased to a deafening volume.

Just when the sound threatened to drive Lewis insane, it stopped. It did not fade out. It just stopped.

Lewis, realizing what must be coming next, flopped onto his stomach, his hands protecting the back of his head.

The silence ended with a colossal explosion, the giant roaring in anger. Sand from the base of the tree blasted Lewis's scorched flesh. The perimeter wall burst into flames, rocketing upward and shooting outward. A ripple of blazing destruction spreading through the woods, away from the clearing.

The top half of the door bounced off the dresser with a spray of splinters.

Mike and Justin, backed by Chewy, took action as the horde pushed through the remains of the door. Mike swung the rolling pin, cracking the skull of the lead attacker with a hollow moist *pop*, vaguely recognizing the man but not caring at the moment. Two more ravenous beasts replaced the first, with the hallway behind packed with snarling, gore-caked people, queued up for their next meal.

Justin swung the wooden baseball bat with all his might, but to little effect. The creatures poured through the hole, tumbling over the dresser, falling into the room. Chewy attacked them as they hit the carpet, and Mike continued swinging the rolling pin. Streamers of blood filled the air.

Despite their brave efforts, it was a losing battle. One that would end soon.

Just when Justin was on the verge of collapse, his muscles seizing from swinging the heavy bat, the house began to shake.

Mike could feel it come up from the floor and crawl up his legs. He could hear the walls rattle above the hungry cries of the attackers. The rumbling built, moving the entire house around him, increasing in intensity.

More of the crazed demons fell into the room, overwhelming the trio, backing them across the vibrating floor until man, boy, and dog were stopped by the far wall. That's when Justin raised the bat above his head, and screamed.

The small boy let loose an immense wail overflowing with all the night's terrors and frustrations. After all he had been through, he was going to die anyway. This thought angered Justin and he refused to go down without a fight, even if he could barely raise his weapon.

The mob of ravenous intruders froze at the sound of the boy's emotional cry. They stopped in unison, inches from the three defenders, their arms dropping to their sides, their hands swaying like crooks from a gallows pole. They too started to scream. The screams mirrored Justin's cry perfectly: angry, frustrated, refusing defeat.

Mike assumed the monsters were mocking the boy, a cruel joke before they slaughtered him and his companions. Then he heard the screams transform.

They changed into a cry of pain.

And fear.

The anguished scream could be heard above the roar of flames. Still on his belly, surrounded by a wall of fire, Lewis searched for the source, squinting against the heat as it singed his exposed flesh.

The shimmering bodies of Jerry and his minions could be seen through the towering flames, shadows stumbling against the solid wall of fire, toward the flame-free clearing. The violent release of fire from the perimeter had launched them down the trail like burning rag dolls, disintegrating their clothes and hair instantly.

Lewis watched the figures wade through the inferno, the calamitous howl rising into a screech of suffering that brought a smile to Lewis's face. One by one the bodies dropped, succumbing to the flames, until only one was left. Swaying left and right, Jerry danced with the fire, fighting his way back to the clearing, his thin arms fanning the flames as if they were a swarm of annoying insects.

Jerry stumbled as flesh from his legs cooked away, regained his balance, and plodded on.

Lewis breathed in, the biting heat pricking his lungs, and screamed through a throat lined with sandpaper, "DIE! JUST DIE!"

The flaming child fell to his knees just short of where the barrier of vines once stood, now a solid wall of flames; the muscles in his legs, burned to leathery strips, could no longer support his meager weight. He fell forward onto his face, his roasted hands breaching the wall of fire and puffing down into the white sand. The black hands grasped fistfuls of the chalky sand and pulled, dragging the charred remains across the threshold.

Jerry's bald, blackened head broke through the flames and released another scream, a defeated bellow of pain. He lifted his face toward Lewis and stared at him through melting eyes. Thick viscous blood burst from the dripping eye sockets, bubbling away into steam as it flowed down his shrieking, charred face.

The chin of the creature that used to be little Jerry Harris stabbed into the white sand, shutting off the pathetic wailing. Dark liquid gurgled from the boy's empty sockets; his black, skeletal hands relaxed, resting on the pale sand like two withered spiders.

55

The roomful of paralyzed attackers crumpled to the carpet. The house still shuddered slightly as the rumbling faded away.

Justin, his rasping breaths loud in the quiet room, stared at Mike. Mike looked back and shrugged, his eyes in danger of popping from their sockets, his breathing also labored. Mike poked the nearest body with his bare foot and raised the pin, ready for an attack.

"I guess you scared them to death," Mike joked, and jumped when Chewy released a victory bark.

Justin laughed. A tired, weak laugh laced with sobs. He dropped the bat, knelt down, and hugged the shaggy dog; Chewy cleaned Justin's grimy face thoroughly with his long tongue.

"Come on," Mike said, still panting, his face freckled with blood. "Let's check out the street."

Justin retrieved the bat and followed Mike out of the room, threading his way through the bodies littering the floor, trying his best not to touch them. The dog followed the same path, sniffing the corpses as he went.

The trio worked their way down the hall, into the living room and through the front door—now missing from its hinges. They stepped onto the front lawn, chins dropping as they took in the sight of their street. Under the glow of the streetlights, bodies dotted the pavement and lawns, folded in various positions. Children and adults alike littered the street.

Mike grabbed Justin's shoulder and shook the boy gently. Justin looked up, saw Mike staring off, and followed his gaze. Smoke and clouds above the woods glowed a bright orange and red like a beautiful sunset. Lightning flashed through the clouds, and thunder rumbled under their feet.

"The woods are on fire," Mike said. "The lightning` must've caused it.

"Justin?"

Mike turned to see Justin staring at a body on the sidewalk, Chewy at his side. Justin stared into the open eyes of his dead mother, once again their normal shade of brown, and fell to his knees next to the body. Chewy sniffed the corpse and whimpered, nudging the lifeless hand with his snout. Justin sniffled, wiped tears from his eyes with his shirt, and stood up. He began checking the other bodies strewn about. He paused briefly at several he recognized, then moved on, continuing his search.

"Justin? What are you doing, buddy?"

"Looking for Clinton," Justin said, choking back his tears. "He wasn't in his room earlier. Do you think he's still alive?"

Mike looked around at the assembled corpses and stared up at the blazing sky. "I'm sure he's around here somewhere."

Another clap of thunder rolled across the glowing clouds.

56

Lewis stared into the empty eye sockets, a feeling of relief washing over him. He closed his eyes and rested his forehead in the sand. He opened them again and lifted his head at the sensation of something soft touching the back of his outstretched hand. A beautiful leaf rested there, shining in the firelight. He watched as the leaf withered and crumbled away to nothing, the memory of its delicate touch on his scorched skin the only proof of its existence.

Lewis rolled onto his back and looked up into the tree. Countless dark shapes floated down around him, silhouetted against the burning woods, turning to ash and vanishing when they hit the sand. Sadness filled his heart as he grasped the meaning of the downpour of leaves. He cried for the souls raining down around him, and rubbed the back of his hand, the feel of his mother's loving caress undeniably there.

It was done.

The thing that had stolen Jerry's life and body was dead, or at least imprisoned in the tree once again. Despite his predicament, despite his loss, and the tears that welled in his eyes, Lewis laughed. Surrounded by flames, he looked up to the glowing clouds.

I did it, Mr. Boyd! I sent her back!

His laughter soon turned into hacking coughs as the thick smoke from the raging forest began to settle on the clearing. Lewis got to his knees, scanning the circle for any chance of escape.

He was trapped.

The blaze surrounded him, the smoke thickening, making it harder to see and breathe. Lewis choked and gagged as the acrid smoke filled his lungs. He recalled the silly films his teachers had made him watch in school: the safety films in which the narrator instructed the boy with the funny haircut to drop to the floor during a fire, where the air remained clear of smoke. Lewis pitched forward to his stomach again.

The smoke actually was thinner close to the sand, giving Lewis some air to breathe, but it did nothing to fix his problem with the ring of fire. Lewis realized his only option was to wait for the rain to come and save him from the flames. *If* the rain came.

Lewis lay on his stomach for several minutes, his forehead resting on the back of his hands, coughing into the snowy sand. The smoke and fumes grew worse, burning his lungs with every struggling breath. He felt sleepy, his tired muscles warm and relaxed. *I'll just hang out here with Clinton until the rain comes, then we'll head home for supper when mom calls me.*

Lewis lifted his face, searching for Clinton. The thick smoke, glowing a beautiful orange, now caressed the sand. His eyes burned and leaked as he searched for his friend. Reaching out he felt the hot, crispy flesh of Clinton's arm. *There you are, buddy. I thought you'd left me.* Lewis clasped onto Clinton's arm and smiled weakly as his faced dropped back into the sand.

Lewis and Clinton relaxed on the tree stumps in their secret hideout, the warm sun and blue sky peeking through the woven roof. The boys giggled, tears rolling down their cheeks. Lewis hadn't a clue as to what was so funny, and it didn't matter. He was with his friend.

With his eyes closed, Lewis hacked a rasping cough as the radiant smoke engulfed his still form.

A lilting voice drifted on the pine-scented breeze, catching Lewis's attention.

His mother's voice.

Calling him home.

With his face buried in the cool white sand, Lewis sucked in one last breath that never left his lungs. His hand relaxed, resting delicately on Clinton's arm.

A clap of thunder split the heavens.

The sky wept.

EPILOGUE

The storm brought enough rain to aid the firefighters, keeping the flames from engulfing most of the neighborhood.

With the fire defeated, and with the rising of the sun, the search and investigation began. What was found startled and confused everyone. The few survivors all told similar tales of being attacked by their friends, families, and neighbors; stories of crazed people eating the flesh of others, like a pack of wild animals, then without reason, falling dead to the ground. Mutilated bodies were recovered from the streets and homes, half-eaten and torn to shreds, validating their insane claims. Men, women, and children were all affected by whatever blight had struck the peaceful hamlet.

Several bodies were also recovered from the burned-out woods. Two of the three missing boys from a week earlier were among the dead, identified later through dental records. The third, Andy Reed, was never identified, but a headless, burned body was found and assumed to be him; the boy's teeth were too destroyed for proper identification.

Sadly, one child from the neighborhood was never found. A body never recovered.

Trees were toppled as if a massive explosion had occurred in the woods. The story of a possible explosion prompted some folks to spread rumors of a chemical attack, most likely from Iran or the Russians. Others claimed it was tainted water that caused the people to go insane, or a military experiment gone wrong, but no evidence could be found to corroborate any of these conspiracy theories. Officially, nobody, not even the proper authorities, could explain the events that had taken place at Poisonwood Estates. Tall tales and theories abounded among the townsfolk.

But by far the most intriguing tale, had to be that of the tree.

৯৯

ON THE MORNING following the explosion, after the fire is in check, a fireman discovers the remains of little Jerry Harris. He also finds one other body—a child as well—in a strange circular clearing, at the base of a peculiar tree, the apparent epicenter of the destruction. The man calls for his fellow firefighters, shouting for them to come see the find. When they arrive and gather around the man, they see the charred corpses: one at the edge of a perfect, burn-free circle of white sand, another resting in the sand at the firefighter's feet. Then, they notice the man staring up into the strange tree.

The tree stands in a shallow crater, as if it has fallen from a great height. At the base of the trunk, just above the line of sand, an unusual spiral symbol with broken lines is carved into the wood, inches from the burned foot of the small corpse—a circular, maze-like pattern.

Unlike everything around it—even the corpse at its base—the tree is not smoldering, not a single tendril of smoke rises from its dark form.

The group follows the fireman's gaze up through the black, bony branches of the odd tree, and they see what has captured the man's attention. Miraculously, untouched by the fire that has destroyed everything, a single leaf hangs from the end of a high branch.

A beautiful green leaf, with vibrant crimson striations.

Alive.

A distant train whistle shatters the silence of the blackened woods, wailing the song of a lost child.

ABOUT THE AUTHOR

Craig Wesley Wall is the author of short stories, novellas, and novels, primarily in the horror and thriller genres.

A lifelong horror enthusiast, Craig's work is the culmination of too many hours spent watching scary movies and reading books by such authors as Stephen King, Robert R. McCammon, Brian Keene, and many others.

Craig resides in the wilds of the Pacific Northwest with his wife and a bevy of dogs and cats. He's constantly in search of the elusive Bigfoot, all the while convincing his neighbors that he's not one.

The best way to keep up with his new releases is to subscribe to his newsletter, or follow him on Facebook and Twitter.

www.craigwesleywall.com

 facebook.com/craigwesleywall

 twitter.com/CraigWesleyWall

 instagram.com/craigwesleywall

Made in the USA
San Bernardino, CA
21 August 2018